Praise for

The Alehouse Murders

"I loved *The Alehouse Murders*. Combining marvelous period detail with characters whose emotions and personalities would ring true in any era, Maureen Ash has launched a terrific new historical mystery series. I'll be standing in line for the next Templar Knight Mystery."

——Jayne Ann Krentz, *New York Times* bestselling author

"A deft re-creation of a time and place, with characters you'll want to meet again."

——Margaret Frazer, national bestselling author

"An excellent mystery, very suspenseful and clever, with a sympathetic sleuth sure to captivate readers."

——Sharon Kay Penman, *New York Times* bestselling author

"A delightful addition to the medieval mystery list. It is well researched and, even better, well written, with distinct, interesting characters and plot twists that I didn't expect . . . I look forward to more books in the series."

——Sharan Newman, author of *The Witch in the Well*

"Fans of quality historical mysteries will be delighted with this debut . . . the first in what will hopefully be a long-running series of Templar Knights whodunits."

——*Publishers Weekly*

"[Ash's] complex hero, Sir Bascot de Marins, immediately engages the reader as he tracks a ruthless killer in a mystery that will keep the reader guessing until the very end."

——Victoria Thompson, national bestselling author

continued . . .

A Deadly Penance

A Templar Knight Mystery

✠

Maureen Ash

BERKLEY PRIME CRIME, NEW YORK

THE BERKLEY PUBLISHING GROUP
Published by the Penguin Group
Penguin Group (USA) Inc.
375 Hudson Street, New York, New York 10014, USA
Penguin Group (Canada), 90 Eglinton Avenue East, Suite 700, Toronto, Ontario M4P 2Y3, Canada
(a division of Pearson Penguin Canada Inc.)
Penguin Books Ltd., 80 Strand, London WC2R 0RL, England
Penguin Group Ireland, 25 St. Stephen's Green, Dublin 2, Ireland (a division of Penguin Books Ltd.)
Penguin Group (Australia), 250 Camberwell Road, Camberwell, Victoria 3124, Australia
(a division of Pearson Australia Group Pty. Ltd.)
Penguin Books India Pvt. Ltd., 11 Community Centre, Panchsheel Park, New Delhi—110 017, India
Penguin Group (NZ), 67 Apollo Drive, Rosedale, Auckland 0632, New Zealand
(a division of Pearson New Zealand Ltd.)
Penguin Books (South Africa) (Pty.) Ltd., 24 Sturdee Avenue, Rosebank, Johannesburg 2196,
South Africa

Penguin Books Ltd., Registered Offices: 80 Strand, London WC2R 0RL, England

This book is an original publication of The Berkley Publishing Group.

PRINTING HISTORY
Berkley Prime Crime trade paperback edition / November 2011

Library of Congress Cataloging-in-Publication Data

Ash, Maureen, 1939–
     A deadly penance / Maureen Ash. — 1st ed.
          p. cm.—(A Templar knight mystery)
     ISBN 978-0-425-24336-7
     1. Templars—Fiction. 2. Murder—Investigation—Fiction. 3. Middle Ages—Fiction. I. Title.
     PR9199.4.A885D43 2011
     813'.6—dc22   2010054200

PRINTED IN THE UNITED STATES OF AMERICA

10 9 8 7 6 5 4 3 2 1

List of Characters

PRINCIPAL CHARACTERS
Bascot de Marins—a Templar Knight
Gianni—a mute Italian boy, former servant to Bascot
Nicolaa de la Haye—hereditary castellan of Lincoln castle
Richard Camville—Nicolaa's son
Petronille de la Haye—Nicolaa's sister
Richard de Humez (Dickon)—Petronille's husband
Alinor de Humez—Petronille's daughter
Ernulf—serjeant of Lincoln garrison

KNIGHTS AND SERVANTS FROM STAMFORD
Stephen Wharton—knight
Hugh Bruet—knight
Aubrey Tercel—cofferer
Margaret—sempstress
Elise—maidservant

MERCHANTS AND TRADESMEN IN LINCOLN TOWN

Guild Leaders and Their Families
Gildas—barber-surgeon
Simon Adgate—furrier
Clarice Adgate—Simon's wife
Thomas Wickson—Chandler
Edith Wickson—Thomas' wife
Merisel Wickson—Thomas' daughter
John Sealsmith—seal maker
Imogene Sealsmith—John's wife

Other Merchants and Tradesmen
Hacher—barber-surgeon
Reinbald of Hungate—wine merchant
Harald—Reinbald's nephew

AT RISEHOLME
Stoddard—bailiff
Willi, Mark, Joan, Emma and Annie—foundlings

OTHERS
Pinchbeck—coroner
Everard d'Arderon—Templar preceptor
Lambert—clerk
Nicholas—groom
Hedgset—leech

A Deadly Penance

Prologue

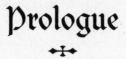

Lincolnshire—January 1177

THE AIR IN THE CONVENT CHAMBER WAS CLOSE, AND REDO-
lent with the scent of purifying herbs. Outside, the stormy
weather of the past few days had calmed, but it was still
cold, and the casements were shuttered against the chill.
The single source of warmth was from the burning embers
of a brazier set in one corner.

Shadows danced and flickered from the light of candles
set in sconces around the walls as the young woman sitting
on the horseshoe-shaped rim of the birthing stool strained
against the pain that had engulfed her for the last fourteen
hours. Her long tangled braid of pale brown hair was darkened with perspiration, as was the thin shift she wore. Behind her stood a young and sturdy nun who provided a
bulwark for the woman to lean against in the throes of her
exertions. In front of the stool, crouching at the woman's
feet, was an older nun, the infirmarian of the convent, who
was massaging the swollen mass of the mother's belly with
sweet oil of lavender and murmuring words of encourage-

ment. The woman could feel her strength coming to an end. The room was beginning to swim in and out of her vision and she knew it for an incipient warning of unconsciousness. Against the incoming tide of darkness, she could hear the infirmarian's soft voice urging her on. "Just one more try," she said gently. "The babe is nearly here." With what she knew would be her last effort, the woman did as she was bid and, to her relief, the child, with an angry howl of protest, slipped from her womb.

With deft hands, the infirmarian cut and tied the natal cord and wrapped the infant in a length of clean linen. Handing the swaddled bundle to the sister who had stood behind the birthing chair, she signalled for her to take the babe from the room. Then she bent to attend to the after-birth.

"It is a boy," she murmured as she helped the exhausted mother up from the stool and eased her onto a nearby pallet, "and he appears healthy. I have instructed that he be placed into the charge of a wet nurse, as arranged."

The woman nodded. She had seen the gender of the child as he emerged and also the fuzzy growth of down that, moistened by birth fluids, lay like a cap of molten gold on his head. She did not make any protest at his removal. As the infirmarian had said, it had been agreed. And she was exhausted. Her bones felt as though they had no substance and were incapable of sustaining even the slightest movement. All that consumed her now was a desire to sink into the oblivion of sleep.

The woman closed her eyes as the nun, with a cloth dipped in warm water, cleansed her body of the detritus left by the birthing. It was imperative that she regain her strength for the trials that lay ahead. Tears trickled down her cheeks as she thought of them, for she had no doubt they would be even more daunting than the long months of her confinement. She would need all her wits about her if she was to survive.

The infirmarian, her task finished, quietly left the room. Outside, the sister who had taken the babe away returned, her arms empty and her hands folded inside the black sleeves of her habit.

"She will sleep now," the senior nun said as she removed the capacious apron she had worn to protect her clothing. "I will leave her in your care while I attend to my duties in the infirmary. Sit with her until she awakens and then give her a bowl of hearty meat broth and a cup of ale. Encourage her to take as much of both as she can. She is very weak and her spirits are low; nourishment will help restore her vitality."

"Is it certain she does not want to see the babe?" the other sister asked, her young face creased into lines of sympathy for the suffering the woman had endured. "Mayhap she will change her mind now that he is born."

The infirmarian shook her head firmly, her countenance regretful. "No, I doubt she will rescind her decision. Soon, the boy will be given into the care of another, one who will see to his future welfare." She gave a little sigh. "We must offer up prayers that the child has not inherited the morals of the man who sired him. If he has, I fear his life will be naught but a travail of sorrow."

One

✦

Lincoln castle—Late February 1203

LINCOLN CASTLE STANDS HIGH UPON A KNOLL OVERLOOKING the rolling Lincolnshire countryside. Within the castle's large bail are two keeps, one a recently built fortress that is the main residence of the hereditary castellan, Nicolaa de la Haye, and her husband, Gerard Camville, and the other an older tower where the bottom floor is used as an armoury and the chambers above for the accommodation of visitors. Now, within the early darkness of a winter evening, the old tower was uninhabited except for a room on the top storey where a man and a woman lay languorously entwined after a brief but passionate session of lovemaking.

The woman, oblivious to the hardness of the floor on which she was lying, snuggled close into the shoulder of her companion, relishing the masculinity of his smell and the silkiness of his short beard. Solicitously, he kissed her tenderly and covered her with the cloak he had discarded so hastily a short time before.

"We will have to leave soon, my sweet," he said, fondling

one of her thick auburn plaits. "Your husband may return at any time."

"If he does, he will go to the guest chamber below. He will not come up here," she replied petulantly. Their tryst had been far too short and she did not want it to end.

"And how will you explain your absence?" her lover asked in amusement.

"I will tell him I went out for a breath of cool air to relieve the headache I am supposed to have."

The man gave a chuckle. "I admit he is gullible, but I doubt that even he would believe such cold weather would serve as a remedy. No, you had best go now, before he decides to retire."

Reluctantly, she rose and started to straighten her clothing. As her lover began to pull up his hose, a slight noise came from the passageway outside. The man quickly doused the small rush light burning in a corner. "Hush," he warned her, and crept stealthily to the door.

He waited in silence for a few moments before deciding there was no cause for alarm. "Hurry," he said to the woman as he pushed the door open. "Go down and get into bed. I will wait at the top of the stairs to ensure you get to your room safely."

Swathing herself in the expensive fur-lined cloak she had been wearing when she entered the room, the woman did as she was bid, pausing only to give him a quick kiss before stepping through the door. The small landing beyond was shrouded in inky blackness and the man grasped her arm to steady her until her foot found the top step of the circular staircase. As she slowly descended, he held his breath and listened until she reached the lower floor and he heard the sound of the guest chamber door opening and then closing behind her.

He stood motionless for a moment, listening. He was certain he had heard a noise earlier but now all was quiet. On the other side of the landing was a small basin with a tap fed by water collected in a tank on the roof. An occasional drip from the faucet was all that broke the silence. Deciding he must have been mistaken, he turned to make his own descent to the lower floor when he heard a voice softly call his name. Startled, he turned in the direction of the sound, which seemed to be coming from an archway a few steps above the landing. He knew that the door within the arch gave access to a wooden catwalk spanning the gap between the top of the tower and the ramparts. Why would someone be standing up there? It led nowhere except out onto the parapet. And why would they have opened the door, which had earlier been closed, to let in the cold night air that was now sweeping around him in icy gusts?

As far as he was aware, no one had known of his intent to meet his lover. Could it be that one of the guards on the palisade had detected their presence and come to investigate? But if that was so, surely any of the men-at-arms would have issued a more forthright challenge. A thrill of dread ran through him as he wondered if it could be the woman's husband, but a moment's reflection dismissed the notion from his mind. He and his paramour had been most discreet in their meetings and he was certain that her spouse had no inkling of their liaison. And if, by some chance, the husband had come to see if his wife was recovering from her supposed illness and found her missing from the chamber where she should have been resting, it was unlikely he would have crept stealthily up two flights of stairs in an effort to locate her. He would surmise that she had returned to the hall and their paths had crossed unnoticed in the darkness of the ward. It was in the main keep that the husband would search for her, not within the top stories of the old tower.

Again the voice came, urging him to come through the arch and out onto the catwalk. The man's hand dropped to his belt and the small eating knife strapped to his side. He had no other weapon on his person, but the little blade was sharp and, if necessary, would provide a modicum of defence. He hesitated and the person spoke again, more command-ingly this time.

Still, he vacillated, reluctant to step away from the security of the tower walls. Should he obey the summons or not? His heart leapt with hope as he wondered if the command came from the person he had recently been pressing for informa-tion. Was he finally about to receive an answer to the ques-tion that had all but taken over his life? The thought of such a lure was almost impossible to resist but, nonetheless, he took a deep breath and cautioned himself to be circumspect. He stood for a moment, indecisive, and then straightened his shoulders and laid a hand on the hilt of his small knife. If he fled, he would never find out.

Stepping through the arch, the frigid air struck his face like a blow. The sky above was a canopy of stars, pinpricks of hard brightness in the blackness of the cold night sky, but except for the distant figures of the guards pacing the crenellated ramparts surrounding the castle bail, there was no sense of any other human presence. Neither of the guards was near; in the dim light of torches placed at inter-vals along the perimeter of the walls, the outline of one man-at-arms could just be seen some hundred yards to the west and another soldier a similar distance to the east. Behind him the solid bulk of the old tower loomed, throwing the length of the narrow wooden bridge into deep shadow. Whoever had called must be hidden within that tunnel of blackness.

He took a step and halted at the edge of the wooden planking. "Who calls?" he said softly into the darkness. "Show yourself if you wish to speak to me."

There was no answer, only a small click and the soft whirr of a crossbow bolt taking flight. The missile ran true to its aim and took the man in the chest. So forceful was its thrust that it penetrated through his rib cage and beyond, severing his spine before exiting through his back. He fell without a sound.

IN THE GUEST CHAMBER ON THE BOTTOM FLOOR OF THE TOWER, the woman disrobed and climbed into bed. The room was moderately warm, heated by the coals of a brazier that a castle servant had lit earlier in the day. She lay in silence for a few moments, listening for her lover's step on the staircase beyond the closed door of the chamber to indicate that he, too, had left the building. After a few moments, she heard what she thought was the sound of his passage, the small noise of footsteps scurrying past the door and fading as they exited the tower.

Sighing, she lay back and snuggled into the warmth of the thick woollen blankets that covered her. Her lover was far too cautious, she thought. Her husband was not a man prone to suspicion; he had been solicitous when she had told him of her aching head and had even offered to keep her company while she rested. It had been easy to persuade him to stay within the hall and enjoy the company of the other guests gathered there. She felt a little sorry for deceiving him, but not much. He was a good husband, but elderly, and his lust had faded with the passage of years. Her involvement with her young lover provided an excitement she had never before experienced. The element of danger was so exhilarating that it overcame thoughts of the repercussions she would suffer if her adultery was discovered.

She closed her eyes and relived the stolen moments she and her paramour had shared in the chamber above. Her lover was a vigorous man and his embraces were all that a woman could ask for. She recalled how tenderly he had caressed her and the words of endearment he had murmured in her ear. As she drifted into slumber, her dreams were full of remembered passion, and she was completely unaware that, from that night on, memories would be all that were left to her.

Two

✝

THE BODY WAS NOT DISCOVERED UNTIL DAWN THE NEXT MORN-
ing. Just before first light, Ernulf, the serjeant of the castle
garrison, went up onto the ramparts, as was his habit, to
oversee the changing of the guards from night patrol to the
shift that manned the walls during the daylight hours. As he
crossed the bail, all was silent. The previous evening Nicolaa
de la Haye had invited a large company of guests to a feast
in celebration of the opening of a new foundling home that
she had spent many months in establishing. Also present
had been Nicolaa's sister, Petronille, who had been on a visit
to Lincoln since the season of Christ's Mass and had brought
her daughter, Alinor, with her, along with a small retinue of
servants. The festivities had gone on until late and not only
the guests but most of the servants were still abed.

Ernulf went up to the ramparts by means of one of the
half-dozen ladders that gave access to the walkway that lined
the inner circumference of the palisade. The ladder Ernulf
was accustomed to use was near the old tower, and set a little

way from the gatehouse that guarded the eastern entrance
into the castle ward. Behind him, the four men-at-arms of
the day shift were assembling for duty and Ernulf gave
them a backward glance as he reached the top of the ladder
to ensure all were present. The serjeant was a grizzled old
campaigner who treated his men with a gruff fairness but
could, nonetheless, mete out a harsh punishment to any
who took advantage of his equable temperament. All of the
men-at-arms under his command appreciated this and, for
the most part, obeyed his orders promptly and without re-
sentment.

The sky was almost fully lightened as he strode along the
walkway to the gatehouse, where the men of the night shift
would have gathered as the time approached for them to
come off duty, his breath rising in steamy puffs on the cold
air as he glanced southwards through the crenellations.
From his high vantage point, the town spilling down the
hillside formed a giant tableau, bisected by the great
thoroughfare of Ermine Street, the high road that started in
London and travelled up the length of England to York. At
the lower perimeter of the town, the Witham River tra-
versed the plain. To the east, and sharing the height with the
environs of the castle, was the Minster, where Lincoln cathedral was located, its spire sparkling brightly in the frosty air.
Ernulf pulled his cloak close around him as he scanned the
panorama below him; the weather was bitterly cold, with a
stiff breeze that brought tears to the eyes, and he was grateful for the fur-lined cap he wore. In the gloom of approaching dawn, the serjeant could see the gleam of frost on the
slated rooftops of the houses. There were no coverings of
thatch; a town ordinance had been instituted some years before forbidding the use of this combustible material in an

effort to prevent the spreading of fire in the event of an accidental conflagration. Most of the houses were built of timber infilled with wattle and daub—only the more affluent of Lincoln's citizens could afford an edifice built completely of stone—and the chequered squares of the walls, usually white, were grimy and showed a sore need of their annual spring coating of lime.

Ermine Street had been renamed Mikelgate within the confines of Lincoln's town walls, and lesser byways branched from the thoroughfare in a haphazard manner, some running parallel to it, others winding around in a crescent, many of them little more than narrow alleys, but most debouching into a street that led to one of the two main entrances into Lincoln; Bailgate in the north, just below the castle precincts at the top of Steep Hill, and Stonebow at the southern end. Suburbs had sprung up in the lee of the walls, giving rise to an impoverished collection of hovels in Butwerk and a straggle of more affluent residences alongside Ermine Street below the river. Lincoln had prospered in the centuries since the Romans had built the first stronghold on the ground where the castle now stood and its good fortune gave no indication of diminishing.

Now, as Ernulf walked along the ramparts, he could see little sign of activity among the populace except for a few wisps of smoke from the ovens of the town bakers. Not only was it very early in the morning, but the cold weather was keeping everyone inside and, with the exception of a couple of stray dogs searching hopefully for scraps in the refuse channel that ran down the middle of Mikelgate, the streets were empty. The serjeant nodded with satisfaction at the tranquility. He was proud of the town in which he lived, and even prouder of the mistress he served. He guarded both of them with the determination of a man of simple character and bluff honesty.

He entered the guard room at the top of the gatehouse and found the men of the night shift sharing cups of mulled ale that had been warmed over a fire burning in the middle of the low-roofed stone chamber, a brief respite they were allowed at the changing of the guard. With them was the gateward, a man-at-arms who was approaching middle age and had been a member of the Lincoln garrison since his youth. His seniority earned him the coveted duty in the gatehouse and he had no need to venture out into the cold, his watch involving only the overseeing of the closing of the gate at night and surveillance over the entrance until the morning when he was relieved by the man-at-arms who performed the same duty during the day. When Ernulf came in, the gateward offered him a mug of warmed ale and the serjeant downed it gratefully.

"The night passed peacefully, serjeant," the gateward said, "but since it's colder than a witch's heart outside, I'm not surprised."

Ernulf agreed and, as the men of the day shift came up to the tower and were handed mugs of warmed ale, he dismissed the men who had been on patrol during the night.

"Don't take all mornin' to drink that ale," he warned the new arrivals. "Staying in here won't make the day any warmer. And Lady Nicolaa doesn't pay you for standin' around being idle."

Most of the men-at-arms smiled behind their ale cups as they nodded their acceptance of his admonishment. Ernulf had been in service in the castle since Lady Nicolaa had been a young girl and he was devoted to her. Anyone found guilty of negligence in their duty to the hereditary castellan of Lin-

coln castle would, at the very least, receive a severe chastisement from the serjeant, if not instant dismissal, but they
accepted this easily; along with Ernulf, all of them held Lady
Nicolaa in high esteem.

After they went outside, Ernulf's routine was to pace the
perimeter of the castle wall, leaving one of the men-at-arms
at the south-eastern corner and one at the south-western,
before stopping at the gate that led out from the western
side of the bail into open countryside and checking with the
gateward there that all was in order. Once that task was
completed, he would continue his perambulation of the
ramparts, leaving another soldier at the north-western corner and the last man at the north-eastern before completing
his circuit back at the gate that led out onto Ermine Street.
Behind him the soldiers would commence their slow pacing
back and forth, keeping vigilance over the section of wall
they had been allotted. The serjeant would repeat this pro-
cedure at dusk, when the guard changed again.

This morning, however, the twice-daily ritual had hardly
begun before it was halted. By the time Ernulf approached
the narrow bridge that connected the ramparts to the old
tower, the sun had risen and dispersed the shadows within
its length, revealing the body that lay stretched upon the
wooden boards. Beyond the corpse, the crossbow quarrel
that had killed him was embedded in one of the posts that
formed the frame of the archway. A layer of frost covered the
bolt and its leather fletching and, as the rime slowly melted
in the early morning rays of the sun, the flecks of gore along
the shaft sparkled a deep pink. As Ernulf came into view of
the gruesome spectacle, he stumbled to a startled halt and
uttered an oath.

"So the night passed peacefully, did it?" he exploded. "I'll

have the flesh off the arses of those two who were guarding
this stretch of the ramparts last night. This body's already
starting to stiffen, they must have passed it a dozen times,
not to say never noticed somebody firin' an arbalest right
under their noses."

The soldiers looked down at the body in horrified amaze-
ment. "But, Sarje," one of them dared to protest, "they
wouldn't have been able to see anything. When it's dark, it's
all in shadow along here, 'specially on the catwalk. . . ."

"Do you think you're just up here to keep watch over
where any fool can see?" Ernulf shouted. "Useless cowsons—
I've told you time and again to keep your eyes peeled and
that means checking every corner. . . ."

Ernulf bit off his words. He knew his anger was not really
directed at the soldiers who had been on night duty; as the
man-at-arms had just said, the narrow bridge was perhaps
twenty feet long with side walls five foot in height and, at
nighttime, its length would have been shrouded in darkness. No, his fury was at the villain who had killed the man
lying at his feet, for the death would cause distress to one
close to Lady Nicolaa. The dead man was well-known to
Ernulf. He was a member of the retinue that the castellan's
sister Petronille had brought with her to Lincoln. His name
was Aubrey Tercel.

LESS THAN AN HOUR LATER NICOLAA'S SON, RICHARD CAMVILLE,
had been apprised of the situation and joined Ernulf up on
the ramparts. Since Richard's father, Gerard Camville, the
sheriff of Lincoln, was at present away in London attending
a convocation of the realm's sheriffs ordered by the chief jus-
ticiar of England, the serjeant had reported the death to his

son, who was deputising for his father in matters concerning the shrievality.

When Ernulf showed Richard the body and drew his attention to the bolt that was lodged in the frame of the archway, the young man's face became grave. He was a handsome well-built knight in his middle twenties, with his mother's flaming red hair and his father's restless manner, but now, as he viewed the corpse, his figure went still with disquietude.

"A nasty death, but a quick one," he said. "The bow must have been fired at close range to have penetrated the body so forcefully. It went straight through his heart and beyond; he would have died in an instant."

"The guards swear they saw no one on their rounds," Ernulf said, "so the killer must have hidden himself here, on the catwalk."

"Yes, that makes sense," Richard replied, crouching down and gauging the distance to the doorway. "It looks as though Tercel came through the archway and the murderer was waiting for him here in the shadows. Once the bow was fired, and Tercel dead, the killer then stepped over the body and returned to the bail by going down the staircase in the tower, never once having been in view of the guards."

"Got Tercel up here on some ruse, I expect," Ernulf opined. "Even if he knew he was meeting an enemy, he wouldn't have thought he was in much danger with the guards so close by."

Richard nodded absently and then, stepping carefully over the body, inspected the crossbow bolt embedded in the frame of the door.

"Have you looked closely at this?" he asked.

"No, lord," Ernulf replied.

"Then do so now," Richard commanded.

Moving carefully around the corpse, the serjeant hunkered down and then gave a gasp of disbelief. "That looks like a quarrel from that old crossbow your grandsire gave to your mother."

"I would swear it is the very same," Richard confirmed. The shaft's metal tip had not wholly penetrated the door and there, at the base, a tiny inscription could be seen—RH to NH.

"But that crossbow was never meant to be used as a weapon," Ernulf exclaimed. "It is only a small replica that your grandsire had made as a gift to commemorate your birth."

"Even so, it is capable of being fired." Richard thought for a moment. "My mother keeps the crossbow in the armoury, does she not?"

"Aye, in a wooden box, along with a few of the bolts that was made to go with it. The castle fletcher has the care of it and sees that the mechanism is kept free of rust and regularly oiled, but other than that, it's never taken out of its case."

"Well, it was taken out last night," Richard said, "for that bolt is too shallow to have been fired from a regular-sized arbalest. Loath as I am to say it, it would appear that whoever murdered Tercel used my mother's crossbow to carry out the deed."

Three

✦

AFTER DIRECTING ONE OF THE MEN-AT-ARMS TO FIND SOME-thing to cover the body, Richard and Ernulf went down to the armoury and to the shelf where the box containing Lady Nicolaa's small crossbow was kept. The wooden case shone with a coating of linseed oil and was fitted with two simple catches to keep it closed. When they opened it, the crossbow lay on a bed of much faded green velvet, nestling in a space indented to take its shape.

Richard lifted it out. "Well, if this is the bow that was used, it has been replaced from whence it came. After the murderer had accomplished his purpose, he must have re-turned here and put it back in the box."

He lifted the arbalest up to the light coming through one of the narrow casements. It was well crafted, the stock made of yew that had been kept as polished as the box in which it rested, the winding mechanism, trigger and release nut all fashioned of steel, as was the curved portion of the bow. The bowstring of glue-soaked hemp looked fairly new, so it was apparent that the castle fletcher, during his maintenance of the implement, had changed it recently. It was small, with a span of no more than eighteen inches, far less than the two to three feet of a full-sized crossbow. On one side of the stock was a small silver plate inscribed with the words—"To Nicolaa from her loving father, Richard de la Haye." In essence, it was a toy but, for all that, a dangerous one.

"I remember the day Sir Richard gave that to your mother," Ernulf said. "It was his gift to her in celebration of your christening and, after they returned from the service at the cathedral, your grandsire presented it to her and ordered a butt set up in the bail so she could test it. Although 'tis difficult for a woman to wind a regular bow, that one was small enough for her to manage, and she did it well. Took aim and hit the center of the target with her first shot." There was pride in Ernulf's voice as he spoke of the incident.

"I recall my father telling me of that day," Richard said. "He said that my grandsire had never been sorry that he had sired only daughters, for my mother, his eldest and principal heir, had the heart and stomach of a man." Richard did not have any certain memories of the man after whom he had been named, for his grandfather had died when he was just a toddler, but he recalled an occasion when a tall man with a thatch of flaming red hair had tossed him high in the air and then, with a booming laugh, caught him to his chest. He had often been told by those old enough to remember that he resembled Richard de la Haye and he supposed that it was true, for he was much taller than his father and had his mother's bright colouring.

Ernulf counted the bolts laid in the box alongside the crossbow. "There are only seven quarrels here," he said. "I remember clearly that your grandfather had eight made, each engraved with his and your mother's initials."

Richard rubbed his hand along the groove in the stock and nodded in confirmation. "The layer of oil has been disturbed, as though it had been recently fired. I think, Ernulf, there can be no doubt that this is the weapon that was used."

He replaced the crossbow and closed the box, and then gave the serjeant an order. "Send a message to Coroner Pinchbeck. Tell him there has been a suspicious death and he needs to come and make an inspection of the body. I don't suppose the lazy bastard will want to come out in this cold weather, but tell him my father is away and cannot, as he usually does, carry out a duty that is rightfully the coroner's. An inquest must be held and, since this death has been inflicted on the servant of a member of our family, I want all the niceties observed. We will leave the corpse in situ until Pinchbeck has been to view it. Tell him there will possibly be a deodand to collect and he will be more likely to get here quickly. If Pinchbeck runs true to his previous behaviour, once he has collected the monies, he will lose all interest in catching the murderer, but that is of no consequence. I am ready to act on my father's behalf in the matter."

Ernulf nodded. A deodand was the name given to any instrument that had caused a person's death, and it was within the province of the coroner to put a valuation on the object and take it, or its value, into custody until a law court decided if it was to be awarded to the family of the victim as a compensation for their loss, or kept for the monarch's purse. Any item could be declared such—an animal that had caused a person's death by a bite or a kick, a cart that had run over some unfortunate in the street and caused a fatality, or simply a weapon, such as a knife or, in this case, Lady Nico-

laa's crossbow. While Coroner Pinchbeck was usually averse
to expending his energies in any direction that involved ac-
tual effort on his part, he did relish collecting fees for the
royal coffers, for he felt that by doing so he enhanced his
prestige in the eyes of the king.

As Ernulf hurried away to Pinchbeck's fine stone house in
Lincoln town, Richard left the armoury and strode across the
bail in the direction of the keep. Even though it was still
early, he would have to rouse his mother and aunt from their
bed and tell them what had happened.

IN THE HUGE CHAMBER THAT FUNCTIONED AS THE HALL OF THE
keep, servants were clearing up the remnants of last night's
feast and placing scraps into baskets to be given as alms for
the poor. The fire in the capacious hearth had been replenished with fresh logs and steaming jugs of mulled wine were
being brought from the kitchen and placed on the trestle
tables, ready to serve with the morning meal. Richard called
to one of the maidservants and told her to go up to his mother's bedchamber and tell her he wished to speak to her.

The young woman returned a few minutes later, informing Richard that his mother was ready to receive him.
Since Petronille was sharing Nicolaa's bedchamber during
her visit, the castellan's son knew he would be able to speak
to both women at the same time.

Nicolaa's bedchamber was a large one, fitted with a good-
sized bed and a few comfortable chairs and stools. After
knocking at the door and bidden to enter, Richard went in
to find his mother and aunt seated at a table awaiting him;
both wore bed robes of soft velvet and close-fitting linen
bed-caps over their loosely braided hair. The resemblance

between the two sisters was slight. Nicolaa had the bright
red hair that Richard had inherited, but now, with the approach of her fiftieth year, was sprinkled with a few threads
of grey. She was a small woman, a little plump, with slightly
protuberant blue eyes that held a discerning look. Petronille,
on the other hand, was dark haired and had an olive com-
plexion, traits inherited from their mother. She was a little
taller than her older sister, and had a softness about her that
was not evident in Nicolaa. Consistently kind and caring,
she regarded Richard with a slightly anxious look in her
dark brown eyes, concerned at the reason for such an early
arousal.

Richard studied his aunt for a moment before he spoke.
Petronille was still in a fragile state from the death of her
young son, Baldwin, a few months before. Although of tender years, Baldwin had been of a very pious nature and his
father, Richard de Humez, had sent Petronille and their
daughter, Alinor, to Lincoln in the hope that both would
recover a little more easily from their grief if they were away
from the familiar surroundings of their Stamford manor
house. They had come to stay just before the season of
Christ's Mass, for the holy season was a time when the absence from home of the son, and brother, they had loved so
well would be particularly hard to bear. Richard hoped this
latest tragedy would not be too distressing for his aunt.

The maidservant he had directed to bring up a flagon of
watered wine had come up the stairs behind him and Richard bid her fill three cups before straddling his long legs
over one of the stools by the table at which the two women
were sitting.

Nicolaa and her sister listened with grave attention as he
told them of how Ernulf had found Tercel's body, and where,

that morning. "He was shot with a quarrel from a crossbow," he added and saw the eyebrows of both women rise.

Petronille had drawn her breath in sharply when told of the death of her servant, but she kept her composure and asked, "Surely that is a strange weapon to use in such a confined space? I have not been up onto the walkway of the old tower since the days of my youth, but if it has not been altered in the intervening years, I remember it as a closely walled area, and not at all suitable for firing a bow."

"You are correct, Aunt," Richard said, "but this arbalest is not one that would normally be employed during battle. It is a much smaller weapon and not intended for such a deadly purpose."

Realisation dawned on Nicolaa as her son was speaking. "Are you saying that the crossbow your grandfather gave me is the one that was used?"

When Richard nodded, his mother rose from her chair and paced a few slow steps, thinking as she did so. "I haven't handled it for more years than I care to remember and neither has anyone else, except for the castle bowyer. I would not have thought there were many people even aware of its existence. How, then, did the murderer come to know it was there?"

"You are mistaken, Mother, in thinking it has been forgotten," Richard said. "The tale of how you fired it when Grandfather presented it to you is the sort of story that makes good recounting, especially to newcomers to the bail. I am certain that not only our household, but most of the townsfolk of Lincoln are familiar with the weapon's rather colourful history."

Nicolaa nodded. "So you think the murderer asked Tercel to meet him up on the ramparts, and then lay in wait with the arbalest, shot him and afterwards replaced the bow in its box?"

"It would appear so," Richard replied.

"A strange place to choose for an assignation," Nicolaa mused. "Was Tercel armed?"

"There was no weapon on him. But it could have been removed by the murderer."

"If it wasn't, then that means Tercel thought he had nothing to fear. So the person who killed him must have been someone he knew, and trusted," his mother opined. "Do you have any idea of about what time this took place?"

"Sometime early last evening I would judge," Richard replied. "The death rictus has just begun and, with the coldness of the night, would have been delayed for an hour or two. He must have been killed about three or four hours before midnight, or mayhap even a little earlier."

Petronille nodded. "I do not recall seeing Tercel at all last evening. It is likely he was murdered whilst we were eating."

"Aunt," Richard said, "what sort of a man was he? Beyond being aware that he was one of your attendants, I know little about him."

"I am afraid I am unable to tell you much," Petronille said, "for he has been in your uncle Dickon's service only a short time. Our household steward is getting on in years and Tercel was being trained as his assistant. While Alinor and I were preparing for our journey here, Dickon suggested Aubrey come with me, and gave the monies we brought with us into his care so he could act as my cofferer. Tercel is, or *was*," she corrected herself, "an illegitimate relative of one of Dickon's acquaintances. He had been well educated and so was considered suitable for the post. I found him to be diligent and of a seemingly amiable nature. I cannot fathom why anyone would wish him dead."

"During his time in your service, Aunt," Richard asked, "can you recall any occasion when he gave offence to anyone, especially while you have been here in Lincoln?"

Petronille thought for a moment and then shook her head. "None that I recall," she replied. "But you would do better to ask Alinor. She is far more conscious of the comportment of our servants than I."

Richard exchanged a smile with Nicolaa. His cousin Alinor was more like the castellan than her mother. She had the same coppery red glints in her hair and was of an even more determined nature. At eighteen years of age she had not yet had time to learn the tact that was Nicolaa's forte but, even so, it was readily apparent that Alinor was cast in the same mould as her aunt. They could be certain that she would have taken care to ensure that none of the servants took advantage of Petronille's complaisant nature and it was possible that, while doing so, she may have observed if there was any person who harboured an animosity for the dead man.

"I will ask Alinor about the matter, Aunt, just as soon as she has risen," Richard said and got up from his chair. "I had best go down into the hall and wait for Pinchbeck. Hopefully, he will not be too long."

Nicolaa followed her son to the door. "I will join you shortly," she said. "Since I am the one to whom the murder weapon belongs, I intend to be present at the inquest."

Richard nodded. "As you wish, Mother, but you had best dress warmly," he advised. "The wind up on the ramparts is bitterly cold."

Four

✦‑I‑✦

WHEN RICHARD DESCENDED TO THE HALL, LAST NIGHT'S guests were beginning to take seats at the tables to break their fast. The visitors were all leaders of various guilds in Lincoln town, and had come, accompanied by their wives, to the castle the previous evening so that they could proffer the donations they had collected for the upkeep of the foundling home Nicolaa had established at Riseholme, one of the properties included in the vast demesne she had inherited from her father. The castellan had decided to show her grati-tude for their largesse by marking the occasion with a feast and had invited all of those who wished to do so to stay over-night in the castle rather than risk a mishap on the treacher-ous ice-covered cobbles of the streets as they returned to their homes in the darkness of a late winter evening. Only two of the guests had declined to take advantage of her offer, but the rest had accepted the invitation and had been ac-commodated in chambers either within the main keep or in the old tower.

Richard took a seat at the high table and a page came forward and asked if he wished to be served with food, but Richard shook his head and told the boy to bring him a cup of unwatered wine. Although it was not his habit to imbibe such a strong vintage this early in the morning, preferring instead only a small measure of ale, he hoped the potency of the drink would help bring his disordered thoughts into some semblance of clarity before the coroner arrived. As the page scampered away to fetch the wine, Richard saw his cousin, Alinor, coming across the hall. Her face wore a strained look and Richard thought she must already have been told of Tercel's death, and the manner of it. This was confirmed when she came up the shallow steps to the dais and took a seat beside him.

"Mother has told me of Tercel's murder, Richard, and how it was accomplished," she said grimly. "What the devil was he doing up on the ramparts on such a cold night? And who had reason to kill him?"

"Those are questions to which I must try to find the answers, Cousin," Richard said mildly. "And, to that end, perhaps you can help me. What did you know of your cofferer—was he one to make enemies?"

Alinor shrugged. She was a handsome girl, her features a little too sharp for beauty, but her eyes gleamed with intelligence. Even though his cousin was headstrong, Richard was very fond of her; he had a healthy respect for her cognitive powers and found her strong family loyalty commendable. "I know little about his background beyond what my mother has already told you," she replied, "that he was baseborn and had been well schooled. He seemed to be competent enough in his duties but, on a personal level, I did not like him."

Richard raised his eyebrows in query at the unexpected statement and Alinor answered him in her forthright fashion. "The expression in his eyes did not reflect the words that came out of his mouth," she said bluntly. "There was a smugness about him that I found distasteful."

"Perhaps his murderer felt the same," Richard said thoughtfully. "Although I think it would take more than mere dislike to prompt a man to commit murder."

"I understand that Aunt Nicolaa managed to pull the crossbow," Alinor replied. "Perhaps the murderer was a woman."

"It could be so, I suppose," Richard replied thoughtfully. "A rejected lover or perhaps a jealous one? Was Tercel prone to dalliance?"

"Aren't most men that way inclined?" Alinor responded sharply and then gave a slight shake of her head to take the barb out of her remark. "Yes, he was. I know of one occasion at least, at Stamford, when our steward berated him for spending too much time in conversation with one of the maidservants. But as to whether or not he had engaged the affections of a maid since we have been in Lincoln—I am reasonably certain there could not be one within the castle household, for he would have known that your mother would never permit such a liberty, but in the town—it could be so."

At that moment, Nicolaa and her sister came through the door of the north tower into the hall and made their way to the high table. As they sat down, Richard saw Ernulf enter the room, thread his way through the servants laying platters of cold viands and small wicker baskets piled high with loaves of bread on the tables, and approach the dais. When he stood before them, he saluted Nicolaa and then said to

Richard, "Coroner Pinchbeck will be here within the hour, lord. When I told him it was Lady Nicolaa's weapon that was used in the killing, he was most obliging, and said that if there are enough witnesses present, he will hold an enquiry into the death today."

Richard gave a wry grin. "As I expected, Mother, he is most anxious to collect the value of the deodand from your coffers."

"I would wish that he were as eager to conduct investigations," Nicolaa replied sourly. "But, as usual, he will most likely claim he is too busy. It is therefore possible, Richard, that you will have to look into the matter in your father's stead."

"I had already expected that would be required of me, Mother," her son replied.

PINCHBECK DECIDED THAT HE WOULD HOLD THE INQUEST ON the spot where the dead man had been found and asked that the men-at-arms who had been on duty during the time he was killed, along with those who were present when the body was discovered, be brought forward to give witness. Despite the weak rays of the late winter sun, the temperature up on the ramparts was still frigid as the coroner, a short stout individual with an officious manner, quickly examined the body and the bolt from the crossbow. He then questioned the men-at-arms as to the times all of them had been on the ramparts and asked whether any of them had seen and heard anything pertinent to the death, barely waiting for their responses in his desire to escape the bitter wind that was blowing from the east. Pinchbeck's clerk, a reedy-faced individual with a dewdrop hanging from the end of his long pointed nose, recorded the answers on his wax tablet with fingers that were blue with cold.

"It is my judgement that this man was murdered by a person unknown, and that the instrument of death was a weapon belonging to Lady Nicolaa de la Haye, hereditary castellan of Lincoln castle and wife of Gerard Camville, sheriff of Lincoln," Pinchbeck intoned with indecent haste, adding that he gave his permission for the body to be removed to a place where it could await burial. The formal statement pronounced, even though somewhat swiftly, the coroner turned to Nicolaa. "If I may now view the crossbow, lady, I shall set a value on the deodand."

As the attending men-at-arms, under Ernulf's direction, picked up the corpse and carried it through the arch into the old tower and then down the stairs toward the small chapel in the castle precincts, Richard took his mother's arm and they led Pinchbeck down to the lower floor where the armoury was situated. The box containing the crossbow was then brought out for the coroner's inspection.

Pinchbeck's flabby face lit up with a smile when he saw the rich ornamentation. Running his pudgy fingers lovingly over the silver on the stock, he said, "This is a fine piece, lady. Your father must have been a most generous man."

"He was, and also one who was assiduous in his duty," Nicolaa replied with a touch of sarcasm, but the criticism of Pinchbeck's indolence passed unnoticed by the coroner.

"I would rate the worth of this piece is at least ten pounds, lady," he said. "And since, by your own admission, it is the weapon that was used to kill your sister's unfortunate servant, I must levy a fine in that amount upon your good self."

Nicolaa gave a brief nod. "I will have my secretary arrange for that sum to be sent to your home before the day is out, Pinchbeck. And I expect to receive a signed receipt from you in return."

"Of course, of course," Pinchbeck replied airily. "Now, as to further investigation into the death, I am not well-placed at the moment to have time to attend to all the details. And, since the death took place here in the castle, it might be more practicable if Sir Richard, as his father's deputy, took over the initial enquiry—that of questioning Lady Petronille's other servants to see if any has knowledge pertinent to the crime and so forth."

Richard gave a nod of assent, an expression of resignation on his face as Pinchbeck continued, "It is unfortunate that the Templar knight who was in your retinue is not still within the ward," Pinchbeck opined. "He was a resourceful man and had a talent for seeking out those who commit secret murder." He looked up with a query on his face. "But I heard that he has rejoined the ranks of the Order. Is that correct?"

"It is. Sir Bascot was awarded the office of draper in the Lincoln commandery and is now second-in-command to the preceptor, Everard d'Arderon," Richard told him.

"Ah, a worthy post, I am sure, but it is a pity he is not here to give you the benefit of his insight. He seemed to have remarkable perception in such matters." Pinchbeck drew his furred cloak closer about him and signalled to his clerk that he was ready to leave. "Well, I must hasten. I have many other duties to attend to. Please keep me informed of the progress you make in discovering the perpetrator of this crime, Sir Richard. And please remember that if, during the course of your enquiry, you should need the aid of my advice, I shall be only too happy to supply it. Call on me at any time."

With this final pronouncement, he swept out the door, his long-suffering clerk at his heels. Richard gave a mirthless chuckle. "His suggestion that I call on him is worthless. The only help Pinchbeck will give me is to sit by the warmth of his fire while he pontificates on the need for evidence, after which he will bid me go out and find some."

Receiving no response from his mother, who was standing still and silent at his side, Richard glanced at her. "Are you alright, Mother, or is the cold too much for you?"

Nicolaa shook her head from within the depths of her fur-lined hood. "No, I am warm enough," she answered. "I was just pondering on what Pinchbeck said about the Templar. His help in this would be most advantageous, Richard. As our lackadaisical coroner has just opined, Bascot de Marins has proved himself, in the past, to be unusually capable in solving crimes. I am wondering if he would be willing to lend us his assistance this time."

"But the previous cases occurred while the Templar was in your service, Mother. Now that he has rejoined the Order, his allegiance lies elsewhere. It is most unlikely that Preceptor d'Arderon would give his consent for de Marins to become engaged in such an enterprise."

Nicolaa gave her son a look that was filled with a glint of the inherent determination that had also passed down to her niece. "It will not hurt to ask, Richard. If one does not make any venture to gain an advantage, it will never be realised."

Five

✦✝✦

AT THAT MOMENT, THE TEMPLAR KNIGHT OF WHOM THEY WERE speaking was tallying columns of figures on a sheet of parchment in a small chamber in the Lincoln Templar enclave. He was of medium height and build and wore a leather eye patch over the socket of his missing right eye. Although not yet forty years of age, grey strands were already mingled with the dark hair on his head and in his beard, a legacy of the torture he had undergone while incarcerated for eight long years as a prisoner of the Saracens in the Holy Land. After escaping from his captors, he had returned to England and been sent to Lincoln castle to regain his bodily strength and his devotion to Christ, both of which had greatly diminished during his imprisonment and from the shock of learning that all of his family—mother, father and elder brother—had perished during his absence. Over the two years he had spent in the retinue of Nicolaa de la Haye, he had slowly recovered not only his health but also his faith and it had been at Eastertide of the year before that he had returned to the Templar ranks and been awarded the post of draper. It was a demanding position, and entailed assisting the preceptor, Everard d'Arderon, in overseeing the many properties that had been donated to the Order in the Lincoln area and helping train new initiates into the Templar ranks. Part of his duties included ensuring that all of the brothers were outfitted in a manner that conformed with the Order's Rule and keeping an inventory of the clothing and equipment with which they were provided. During the summer months there was much activity within the enclave as supplies were sent to commanderies overseas and new entrants to the Order were trained for active duty, but now, in the depths of a cold spell that had descended on the middle and north of England for the last three weeks, there was little work to be done and Bascot was using the time to bring the enclave's records up to date.

Despite the brazier burning in a corner of the small room, the air was cold and the Templar felt his fingers grow numb as he added up monies received for some of the commodities the Order traded in—precious spices that had been imported from Outremer and boiled sugar lumps called *Al Kandiq,* or *candi*, that were made from sweet canes in the Holy Land and had proved immensely popular with the English populace. As he totalled the column, he was gratified by the amount. The funds would be used to supply much needed arms and equipment to brothers in commanderies in Outremer and the Iberian Peninsula and assist them in forming the first line of defence against the persistent attempts of the infidel to encroach on Christian lands.

As he prepared to enter the sum into a ledger where the final totals were recorded, his thoughts drifted to Gianni, the mute Italian boy he had persuaded to become his servant as he had travelled back to England after his escape from the Saracens in 1199. Bascot had first come across the boy on a wharf in Palermo, in Sicily, while waiting for a boat that would take him and his mount on the final stages of the journey back to his homeland. The boy had been starving and near death from malnutrition. His pitiful state had tugged at Bascot's heart and, after overcoming Gianni's suspicions of his intent, he had convinced the lad to accompany him to England as his servant. They had arrived in Lincoln just over three years ago, in the depth of a winter that had been just as cold as the present one. Over time, Bascot had taught the lad to read and write and the boy's quick intelligence had come to the notice of Nicolaa de la Haye. When the Templar had rejoined the ranks of the Order, she had taken Gianni under her protection and given him a place in her retinue, working as a clerk under the direction of her secretary, John Blund. Leaving Gianni behind when he rejoined the Order had been a wrench for Bascot, for he had come to love the lad almost as much as if he were his own son.

Bascot looked again at the profit that had been made from trade in the imported *candi*. Again his thoughts drifted to Gianni, for the boy loved the sweets. Although Bascot would have preferred to be overseas on active duty rather than stationed in Lincoln, it was some solace to him that his present posting meant he remained in close proximity to the boy. Although he did not often see the lad, the knowledge that he was nearby was a comfort.

His thoughts were interrupted by a sudden gust of cold air as the door was opened and Preceptor d'Arderon came in. D'Arderon was an older knight, now past his sixtieth year, who had spent many years on active duty in Outremer. His broad face was pinched with cold above his short greying beard.

"There is a message come from the castle," the preceptor said as he walked over to the brazier and held out his hands to its warmth. "Lady Nicolaa has sent a request for your assistance in a murder investigation."

"Someone in the town?" Bascot asked, laying down the quill he had been using.

"No," the preceptor replied. "In the castle."

Bascot's face tensed and d'Arderon castigated himself for his clumsy speech. The preceptor knew how fond his fellow Templar was of young Gianni, and that his first concern at the news would be that the boy was in danger. Hastily, he reassured him that his fear was unwarranted.

"Gianni was not involved in the death. The man who was murdered was a servant in the retinue of Lady Petronille, the sister of the castellan. She and her daughter have been on a visit to Lincoln since just before Christ's Mass. Apparently someone shot the servant with a crossbow up on the ramparts. Richard Camville has undertaken an investigation into the killing and, if you are willing, asks my permission for your assistance."

IT WAS LATE IN THE MORNING BY THE TIME BASCOT LEFT THE preceptory outside the eastern wall of Lincoln town and rode through the Minster grounds in the direction of the castle. His duties were minimal at this time of year and d'Arderon had given his consent for Bascot to aid Richard Camville in the search for the person who had killed Aubrey Tercel.

"I can manage here while you are gone," d'Arderon had said. "Although I will leave the rest of the accounting for your return," he added with a wry chuckle. "That shall be your penance for being absent from your duties."

Bascot appreciated d'Arderon's indulgence. While it was true that, due to the cold weather, there was little activity in the enclave just now, the daily routine still had to be observed—horses led out for exercise, equipment inspected, meals prepared and observance of services in chapel. The Templar men-at-arms regularly based in the preceptory all knew their duties well and carried them out without need for much guidance, as did the lay brothers and servants, but it was part of Bascot's mandate, as second-in-command, to ensure that all ran smoothly. It was considerate of d'Arderon to allow him time away from his responsibilities.

Notwithstanding the practicalities, Bascot knew that the preceptor's indulgence was primarily due to the fact that d'Arderon was appreciative of the gift that his confrere had for solving secret murders, and was convinced it had been sent by heaven for a purpose. The year before, when Bascot had solved the mystery surrounding the murder of a young harlot found strangled in the Templar chapel, a sacrilege which had threatened to blight the reputation of the Order, the preceptor had afterwards spoken very solemnly of the matter. "This is not the first time that you have resolved a case of murder, de Marins," he had said, "but in this instance, all of our brothers will give thanks to God that He bestowed this ability on you. If it is the Lord's will that you are ever again called upon to be used as an instrument of His justice, it will be my joyful duty to give you my whole-hearted support."

Although d'Arderon had not voiced it, Bascot knew that this sentiment was the main reason for the preceptor's acqui-escence and hoped, as he had done each time he had been asked to investigate an unlawful killing, that he would not fail in his commission of the task. The slaying of another human being without just cause was heinous; not only was it an offence to God, but also to mankind. Now, as he left the Minster grounds and guided his horse across Ermine Street towards the castle, he sent a humble plea heavenward for guidance.

As Bascot neared the eastern gate into the bail, a straggling group of men and women on horseback were leaving the ward. All were sumptuously attired in heavy cloaks of fine material as they guided their rounceys over the slippery cobbles that led to Bailgate. The Templar recognised one or two—the head of the cordwainer's guild and that of the armourers—and they nodded in his direction as they passed. Their faces were solemn and, near the end of the procession, one young woman was crying copiously. An older man wearing a richly furred hat atop a shock of greying hair rode by her side and he reached across to pat her arm consolingly. The message Nicolaa de la Haye had sent to the preceptor had included the information that the murder had occurred during a feast the castellan was hosting in the keep and that the guests had been guild leaders from the town, some of whom had stayed overnight. Bascot assumed that these were the burgesses who had spent the night in the castle and were now making their way back to their homes.

When Bascot reached the hall Eudo, the Haye steward, quickly came forward and said that he had been instructed to ask the Templar, if he arrived, that he attend the castellan in the private chamber she used as an office. Bascot crossed the hall, threading his way through servants setting up the trestle tables that would be used for the midday meal, and made his way to the doorway of one of the four towers that formed the corners of the keep.

Nicolaa's office was situated in an upper storey and, when Bascot knocked at the door, a masculine voice bade him enter and he found that Richard was with his mother in the room. The castellan's son was standing near a small table with a cup of wine in his hand, while Lady Nicolaa was seated behind the oak table she used as a desk. A brazier burned in one corner and the room was filled with warmth.

"You are well come, de Marins," Richard said warmly. "I hope your presence here means that Preceptor d'Arderon will allow you to spend some time assisting us with the investigation into this murder."

Bascot confirmed this was so and accepted the offer of a seat and a cup of wine. When he had made himself comfortable, Richard told him of how Tercel had been found and that a small crossbow given to Nicolaa by her father had been the instrument of his death.

"From the progression of the death rictus, I would estimate that he was killed sometime yesterday evening," Richard added, "possibly while the feast was still in progress. The meal for the guild leaders, which was, of course, of sumptuous fare, was served a little later than usual, just before Compline, and went on for some hours, while our household, including my aunt's retinue, ate at the regular time and occupied the tables at the back of the hall. All of the townsmen and their wives, with one exception, stayed in the hall until near midnight. We have questioned all of the servants—both our own and my aunt's—and the last time Tercel was seen was just as the first course of the servants' meal was being brought out, when he left the table allotted to my aunt's retinue and made his way to the jakes at the back of the hall."

Bascot nodded his comprehension of the sequence of events and Richard continued his recounting. "As mother mentioned in her note to you, because of the inclemency of the weather, she told all of her guests that if any wished to stay overnight, accommodation would be provided for them. Most accepted the offer. I have interviewed all of those who remained to ask if they noticed anything untoward, but the majority of them did not know the murdered man. . . ."

Just then, there was a knock at the door and Richard paused to give permission for the person outside to enter. To Bascot's pleasant surprise, Gianni came into the room, some sheets of parchment in his hand.

The boy's eyes widened at seeing Bascot and he gave the Templar a smile that was full of glad welcome. Bascot had not seen the lad for some months and was surprised to observe that Gianni had matured considerably in the intervening time. The lad did not know his age but Bascot thought he had been about twelve years old at the time they had travelled to England together. Now, three years later, that estimate was proved reasonably accurate for there was a faint shadow of shorn facial hair above Gianni's upper lip and, with his unruly mop of brown curls trimmed into some semblance of order, he was acquiring a manly look. His liquid brown eyes remained the same though, and sparkled with delight at the Templar's presence.

Gianni went over to where Nicolaa was seated and, with a deferential nod, handed her the papers he was carrying. She thanked him and told him to take a seat at the small lectern that stood in the corner of the room, the place where her secretary, John Blund, usually sat to take dictation.

"We are making good use of Gianni's talents, de Marins," Nicolaa informed the Templar. "He has been present during all the interviews Richard conducted and has made notes of any pertinent details. Unfortunately, there has not been much for him to record." She held up the sheets of parchment. "He had just made a fair copy of the results, if you wish to look at them."

The Templar thanked the castellan and, when he saw the clear script in which the details were written, gave Gianni a nod of approval. Nicolaa noticed the gesture and, with a warm smile, said, "Gianni has done well since he began his training under Master Blund. He has now completed his formal lessons and I have given him a permanent post as clerk in the scriptorium."

As Gianni reddened under the praise, Bascot felt his heart swell with pride. When he remembered the frightened young boy he had rescued from certain death in Palermo, he thanked God that he had been the instrument of the lad's survival.

As he glanced over the list, he saw that alongside the names of two of the guests—a furrier, Simon Adgate, and his wife, Clarice—was a note that they, along with another couple, an armourer and his wife, had been allotted sleeping chambers in the old tower, just below the spot where the murder took place. It was also appended that, when questioned by Richard, none of the four people had either seen or heard anything while they were abed. Beside Clarice Adgate's name, mention was made that she had retired to the chamber early, before the feast had started, due to feeling unwell. She must be the one guest that Richard had mentioned as not staying in the keep until the celebration was over.

The Templar tapped the notation with a forefinger. "Is Simon Adgate an elderly man with greying hair?" he asked.

Surprised, Nicolaa confirmed the description and asked if he had made the acquaintance of the merchant. "No, I have not," Bascot replied, "but I passed some of the guests leaving the castle as I arrived and one of them was attired in a particularly fine fur hat, and had with him a young woman wrapped in a vair-trimmed cloak. Since it says here that Adgate is a furrier, it is likely he and his wife would be attired in clothing of such richness. When I saw them I assumed that the woman was his daughter, because of her youth. She seemed to be in much distress."

"She was," Nicolaa told him. "The thought that she had been sleeping so close to where the murder was carried out upset her greatly and she reacted with a great outpouring of tears. Her dismay seemed a little excessive, I thought, but her husband told me she has a very sensitive nature, and apologised for her outburst."

"She was in close proximity to where the murder took place, and at the right hour, and you have said that it could have been a woman who used the bow," Bascot observed. "Have you discounted her as a suspect?"

"We have," Nicolaa replied. "Clarice Adgate is, I fear, a rather empty-headed young woman and, whatever the cause of her distress, it denotes a hysterical nature. For the murderer to successfully lure Tercel up onto the ramparts and shoot him, determination and a steady nerve were required. The furrier's wife does not seem to me to be possessed of either of those attributes."

Bascot accepted Nicolaa's assessment without hesitation. He knew the castellan to be an astute observer of human nature and had rarely known her judgement to prove faulty.

"I have yet to make enquiries of the two guild leaders and their wives that did not remain in the castle overnight," Richard told him. "But since it is most likely that they, in common with most of the others, would not have known Tercel personally, I do not suppose any of them will have taken particular note of his movements."

"I presume there was much activity in the hall last night, lady," Bascot said to Nicolaa. "With the number of people that were present—the guests, your own household and your sister's retinue—it would have been easy for the dead man to leave the hall relatively unnoticed in the throng."

"That is true," she agreed. "Attention was also distracted by a minstrel I hired. He proved to be an excellent jongleur who kept us enthralled with his songs. But as far as we have been able to determine, no one was noticeably absent except Adgate's wife. And the only one that saw Tercel leave the hall was one of our household servants, and that only because he almost bumped into him as he was on his way to the latrine."

"Your sister has been in Lincoln for some weeks now, I understand," Bascot said. "During that time, Tercel might have made an enemy in the town. It would have been easy for an extra person to have slipped in amongst your guests when they arrived. Mayhap the murderer came from without the bail and left after he had completed his mission."

Nicolaa gave the notion some thought and said, "It is possible, I suppose. Petronille is an easy mistress; all of her servants have been given leave to attend services in the cathedral whenever they wish, or to go abroad in the town if their absence does not cause a disruption in the commission of their duties. It is conceivable that Tercel might have made an enemy among the townspeople during his forays into

Lincoln." She looked at her son. "My sister's servants will have to be questioned again, to see if any of them know where he went, and whom he met, on those occasions that he left the ward."

Richard nodded. "It is as good a place as any to start, I suppose. Will you assist me, de Marins?"

"With pleasure," the Templar replied.

Six

✠

I T WAS NEARING MIDDAY BY THE TIME SIMON ADGATE AND HIS
wife, Clarice, arrived at their fine stone house situated near
Stonebow, the principal gate at the lower end of Lincoln
town. Their journey from the castle had been slow; even
though the sun was shining, its meagre warmth had not
completely melted the coating of ice on the cobbles and the
streets were still slippery. They had been forced to guide
their horses down the sharp incline of Steep Hill with great
care until they reached the main thoroughfare of Mikelgate.
Once away from the castle ward, Simon had ceased his attempts to comfort his wife and become aloof. By the time
the couple had reached the turning where their house was
located, Clarice's crying had been reduced to quiet hiccup-
ping sobs and she was timorously glancing sidelong at her
husband's stern face. His grey eyes were hard and the deep
furrows alongside his mouth seemed as though they were set
in stone.

Adgate's business premises adjoined his house. Since he

knew that his assistant would be in the shop attending to any customers that had come out on this cold morning, he guided their horses around to the small stable at the back of the building and, after giving the animals into care of a groom, led his wife directly into the house. The middle-aged maidservant who supervised Adgate's household heard their entry and came forward to take their outer clothing.

"There is a good fire in the hall, Master Simon," she said with a worried glance at Clarice's tear-stained face. "Shall I bring some mulled wine to warm you?"

Simon shook his head. "Take your mistress up to our bedchamber," he instructed tersely, "and help her disrobe and get into bed. She has had a bad shock and is in need of rest."

As the servant took Clarice's arm and led her up the stairs to the upper storey, Simon went into the room that served as a small hall. It was a graciously appointed chamber containing a highly polished oak table and chairs and padded settles. There were tapestries on the walls depicting hunting scenes, and many of the animals whose furs he sold were portrayed in the background—foxes, squirrels, rabbits and the weasel from which ermine was obtained. On the floor, in front of the hearth, was a fine wolfskin rug on which lay two pairs of soft shoes—one pair for himself and the other for Clarice—lined with lamb's wool. Simon walked over to an open-faced cupboard at the end of the room and took down a silver goblet, into which he poured a full measure of wine from a flagon on the table. Then he sat down heavily on one of the settles near the fireplace, hardly feeling the warmth of the flames. It was as though the ice that covered the town had invaded his heart.

Clarice's outburst of tears had shocked him, and it had

taken only moments for him to realise that her grief for the death of a man she was supposed to have known only in the most casual fashion was inordinate. The implication of her unseemly weeping hit him like a hammer blow and, with a sense of desolation, he realised she had been intimately involved with Aubrey Tercel. As the other guild leaders and their wives had turned to stare at her in puzzlement, his first reaction had been to protect both her and his own reputation and so he had led her apart from the group. But the effort of keeping his anger in check and forcing himself to show a solicitous concern towards her had placed him under a great strain, especially as it had been compounded with a personal fear of quite a different nature.

As he sipped the wine, he tried to still his racing thoughts. Had his protestations that his wife's anguish was due to her delicate nature been accepted by Lady Nicolaa and Sir Richard? He was not sure, for he had seen the dawning of speculation in their eyes. But that was the least of his worries, he thought, and again dread gripped him. There was far more at stake than the loss of his good name; if what he feared was true, then the well-being, indeed the very lives, of people that were dear to him hung in the balance. Fervently, he offered up a prayer that even if Clarice's adulterous affair should be discovered, the other connection between himself and the dead man would remain a secret. If it did not, the consequences could be disastrous.

IN THE CASTLE BARRACKS, ERNULF WAS ALSO IN A STATE OF agitation, but for an entirely different reason. As serjeant of the garrison, it was his responsibility to ensure that the castle and its inhabitants were safe, and he felt that since the men under his command had not been alert enough to catch the murderer it was he, as their senior officer, who was at fault. Whether the murderer had come from without the walls, or within, his entry up onto the ramparts should have been seen by one of the guards and challenged. After the inquest, and following the coroner's questioning of all of the men-at-arms who had been on duty, Ernulf had subjected them to a second inquisition in the barracks, voicing his displeasure for their lack of vigilance.

"How could you have missed someone being killed right under your noses?" he thundered. "What if this miscreant had been an enemy come to breach the walls? I reckon he could have led a troupe of soldiers inside the bail while you was all standin' around scratching your arses."

The two guards who had stood the night watch on the stretch of the ramparts where the murder had taken place withstood the tirade without speaking while the rest of the men-at-arms glanced at them uncomfortably. The pair were all too aware they had been lax; even if it was reasonable to claim that the murderer could have slipped by them during the few minutes that their route took them away from the area near the old tower, they should have found the body long before the serjeant did. No matter that the night air had been so cold it numbed a man's senses, or that the bitter wind had forced them to keep their heads down lest their breath freeze in their mouths, the door that gave admittance to the tower should have been regularly checked to ensure that it remained locked. If they had gone across the catwalk to perform that simple task, they would have found the corpse and raised the alarm long before dawn's light. The delay of those few precious hours might well have enabled the murderer to escape. Ernulf had every right to be furious. They eyed him warily; it was entirely possible they would be dismissed from their posts.

The serjeant gave a curt nod in their direction. "You two will be docked half a month's salary for this night's shoddy work," he said curtly and then glared at the other men standing in front of him. "And the rest of you had better take heed. Let me catch any of you idle cowsons sleepin' at your posts again and you'll be standin' on the outside of the bail, looking for work."

When they were finally dismissed, all of the men gratefully threw themselves down on their pallets to get a few hours rest before the next shift of duty, the errant pair who were at fault thankful they still had employment. Ernulf, his broad face set in a scowl, stomped to the small cubicle at the back of the building that served as his personal quarters and, pulling aside the leather screen that served as a door, went inside.

Muttering to himself discontentedly, he seized a leather jack of ale from where it stood in a corner and poured himself a full mug, heating it by plunging into its depths the tip of a metal poker that had been sitting in the burning embers of a brazier. When the murky liquid had been scalded, he threw himself down onto a stool and took a long pull.

As the tension slowly drained out of him, he began to ruminate on who had access to Lady Nicolaa's crossbow and when it might have been taken from its case. Richard Camville had spoken to the castle bowyer while they had been waiting for Coroner Pinchbeck to arrive and the bowyer had said that he had replaced the bowstring on the weapon two weeks before and had not had occasion, since that time, to handle it again. If the murderer was someone who lived within the ward—and Ernulf shuddered at the thought that it could be someone known to him—then the bow could have been removed at any time since then and kept hidden until it was used to kill Tercel. But, if the person responsible for the death had been one of those who came to the feast—a much more preferable assumption to the serjeant—then it would have to have been removed sometime during yesterday afternoon or evening.

Rubbing a hand over the stubble on his jaw, Ernulf felt a renewed sense of frustration. The only thing that was certain was that the bow had been returned to its usual place after the murder, for it had been there a few hours later when Richard and Ernulf had gone to the armoury after the discovery of the body. If he was to recall anything that would help identify the murderer, it would be profitless to try and determine when the bow had been taken, for it could have been removed at any time over the last fortnight; he must try to remember if he had seen anyone near the armoury during the time it was replaced.

Most of the guests had arrived earlier in the afternoon and had been in the keep by the time of the evening meal, the earliest hour at which Tercel could have been killed. Ernulf focussed on the few minutes after he had eaten and had left the hall to return to the barracks. It had been dark by then, with only the flaming torches set along the perimeter of the ward to lighten the gloom, and most of the people he had seen in the ward merely dim figures well wrapped up in cloaks and hoods. While he could not recall seeing any of them near the door to the armoury in the old tower, he had to admit that he had assumed all of them were members of the castle household who slept outside the keep; the blacksmith in the smithy, the grooms in the stable and those such as the cowherd and goose girl who slept in small shacks alongside their charges. Now he wondered if had been mistaken. Could it be that one of the closely shrouded figures had been the murderer? Concentrating his attention, he tried to re-create the scene in his mind, but for all his efforts, the only person he could recall with any clarity was the furrier's wife; and he had recognised her only because the white fur on the hood of her cloak had shone bright in the gloom as she tripped across the bail. While it was true she had been heading in the direction of the old tower, her presence there, according to Sir Richard, had been accounted for.

After that, he had spent the remainder of the evening in the barracks polishing his boots with goose grease and repairing a rip in his tunic before taking a final walk around the bail to ensure all was in order for the night. By then it had been close onto the midnight hour and he had stayed in the ward until the eastern gate had been barred behind the four guests that had left. Once assured that everyone was abed, he had gone to his own pallet for a few hours' rest. At no time had there been any occurrence that had seemed untoward, nor could he now call any helpful detail to mind.

Annoyed that his mental exercise had proved futile, the serjeant poured himself another cup of ale and again heated it with the tip of the hot poker. Sir Richard had told him that he was going to ask Bascot de Marins to assist in the murder enquiry and Ernulf fervently hoped the Templar would be able to do so. The serjeant had come to know Bascot quite well during the two years he had stayed in the castle as part of Lady Nicolaa's retinue and had a high respect for his ability to seek out those who perpetrated secret murder. Ernulf prayed the Templar would once again prove his competence and catch the sneaky bastard who had crept up onto the ramparts and killed Lady Petronille's cofferer.

* * *

As the guild leaders who had stayed the night in the castle went back to their homes, all of them—with the exception of Simon Adgate—felt gratified by the success of the previous evening's celebration. The unfortunate incident of the murder had dimmed their enjoyment a little, but none of them had been personally acquainted with the dead man and so his demise did not trouble them unduly. Once they were safely within their own walls and had seated themselves at their respective tables to enjoy the midday meal, uppermost in their minds was the project they had supported and the glow of satisfaction they were still deriving from their participation.

The day before had been the designated date for the monies the guild leaders had collected in support of Nicolaa de la Haye's scheme to be handed into her care. She had, a few days before the appointed time, sent a message to all of them that the occasion would be marked by a celebratory meal which they, and their wives, were invited to attend. The castellan's gesture of appreciation had pleased them all, especially the women, and they had dressed in their best finery for the occasion.

It had greatly increased their joy when they had found, on their arrival at the castle in mid-afternoon, that William of Blois, prebendary and precentor of Lincoln cathedral, was also in attendance, seated on the dais beside Nicolaa and her sister. William had been elected by the Lincoln cathedral chapter to fill the office of bishop, left vacant by the death of Hugh of Avalon in 1200, but due to a dispute between the chapter and the king, had not yet been consecrated in the office. This event, however, was expected to take place in a

few months' time and the precentor had come to the castle
to give his wholehearted support to the establishment of
Lady Nicolaa's foundling home. William was an elderly man
and frail but, nonetheless, his voice had been filled with vigour as he spoke of his approval for the scheme.

Once the guild leaders and their wives had all taken their
seats at tables set up just below the dais, Nicolaa had given
a signal to her steward and five young children had been led
into the hall and told to stand in front of the guests. All of
the youngsters were clad in rags and their faces pinched with
hunger. The company had naturally been dismayed at their
condition, and many of the women present gave audible
gasps of dismay for the children's piteous state.

Nicolaa had then risen and spoken to the assembly.
"These are the first of the orphans that have been chosen by
priests within the town as deserving of assistance," she said.
"None of them have a parent or adult protector to care for
them and, as you can see, are in desperate need of food and
shelter. It is for the support of such as these that all of you,
and the members of your guilds, have contributed funds.
Due to your generosity, these children, and those that will
follow them, will be provided with food and clothing for
months to come. You may be assured that you have, by your
beneficence, saved them from starvation and certain death."

She gave a slight pause to let her next words have more
impact. "I am sure Precentor William will agree with me
when I say that Bishop Hugh is certain to be looking down
from heaven at this very moment and pronouncing a bene-
diction on all of those who have participated in this act of
charity."

There was a collective sigh of contentment at her words.
Hugh of Avalon had been unceasing in his efforts to help the

poor of Lincoln. They all well remembered how he had harangued the more affluent citizens of the town into giving alms for the indigent and monies for the upkeep of the lazar house in Pottergate. Of abstemious nature himself, he had sternly reminded them of the passage in the Bible that stated how difficult it was for rich men to enter the kingdom of heaven and, by the forceful dint of his personality, inveigled them into opening their purses on behalf of the needy. There was no question that the late bishop had been the most devout of men and all of them had heard the rumour that he would soon be nominated for sainthood; to receive his blessing for participating in this charitable venture, especially from beyond the grave, would ensure the remission of many sins. All of the townsmen felt that the monies they donated would be well-spent.

Nicolaa let the children linger a moment longer to reinforce the mood she had invoked and then gave her steward a signal to lead them from the chamber. Almost immediately, the guild leaders rose from their seats and, hefting bags filled with silver pennies, approached Nicolaa's secretary, John Blund, who was seated at a small table near the dais waiting to receive the pledges and issue written receipts. As they passed in front of the high table, Precentor William rose to his feet and, after exchanging a surreptitious smile of accomplishment with Lady Nicolaa, added his individual blessing to the enterprise.

Although the precentor left before the feast began, the joyful mood continued throughout the evening, enhanced by Nicolaa's pronouncement that the total sum of their largesse had proved great enough to pay for the hire of a few local tradesmen to give the boys among the orphans instruction in basic crafts such as carpentry and cobbling.

"Also," she added with a gesture to where Petronille was seated beside her, "my sister, although no longer a resident of Lincoln, has added a generous donation of her own which she wishes to be used for the hire of a sempstress to give lessons in simple sewing to the female children."

This information was met with a round of appreciative applause from the townsmen and Petronille bowed her head in gracious acknowledgement. She knew how much the success of this enterprise meant to Nicolaa and had gladly given her support. Her sister's determination to sponsor a refuge had been precipitated by an event that occurred during the winter of the previous year when the bodies of two children, one of them not much more than an infant, had been discovered near a huge refuse ditch just outside Lincoln's town walls. Nicolaa had been extremely distressed by the incident and had formed a resolve to do her utmost to prevent any other destitute children within the precincts of the town from suffering such a dire fate. She had quickly set to work enlisting the aid of Precentor William, telling the clergyman that, as an example to others, she was willing to donate the use of one of the buildings on her own estate, and the servants to staff it, for use as a foundling home. The precentor had admired her determination and, acknowledging the dire need for such an establishment, had added his efforts to hers, instructing the clergy of the town to do their utmost to persuade Lincoln's leading citizens to donate funds for the project.

The merchants and tradesmen had been slow to respond at first but then, when they realised that Nicolaa would look with disfavour on any who did not support her plan, had been quick to come forward. For many of them, the castle was their foremost customer and the loss of income they would suffer if Lady Nicolaa decided to purchase the wares and services they provided from another source would make a severe impact on their revenue. Finally, at the season of Christ's Mass, the promise of their pledges had enabled Nicolaa to put the finishing touches on her plans and she had ordered that the barn on her property at Riseholme be made ready to receive its first recipients. Petronille felt joy in her sister's accomplishment, as did the townsmen who, once they had overcome their initial disinclination to part with their hard-earned silver, preened themselves on a wave of benign self-righteousness.

Now, as these same citizens settled themselves comfortably in their homes and prepared to enjoy the midday meal, there were not many who regarded the death of Aubrey Tercel with much interest. Although most felt some sympathy for Lady Petronille in the loss of her servant—a few of the older townsmen remembered her from the days of her youth when she had been growing up in the castle—the general feeling was that since the dead man had not been from Lincoln and was largely unknown throughout the town, it was not a matter that need concern them unduly. None of them could foresee that it would not be long before all of them would be drawn into the murder investigation, and in a manner they could never have anticipated.

Seven

✦✛✦

IN THE CASTLE, IT WAS DECIDED THAT PETRONILLE'S SERVANTS should be questioned after the midday meal was over and Nicolaa invited Bascot to take a seat at the table on the dais and dine with them. Before they went to the hall, however, the Templar asked Richard if he could view the corpse.

"Since I did not see Tercel while he was alive," he explained, "it might be helpful to familiarise myself with his appearance before we interview the servants in your aunt's retinue. That way, I can put a visage to the person of whom we are speaking."

Richard agreed and the pair went down to the small chapel on the lower floor of the keep where the body had been placed in a coffin and laid in a niche.

"I have sent a man-at-arms to Stamford with a message informing Uncle Dickon of what has happened. I assume he will wish the body returned to Stamford for burial, but it is best to be sure before I arrange transport. Since the weather is so cold, Tercel's flesh will not deteriorate unduly while we await my uncle's reply."

The chapel was, indeed, very cold and both Bascot and Richard felt the heaviness of the chill as they walked to where the corpse was lying. Candles had been placed at each end of a temporary bier and by their flickering light the face of the dead man could be seen. The death rictus had not yet faded but, due to the fact that Tercel had fallen in a prone position at the moment of his demise, his body lay relatively flat and in a semblance of rest.

"The remains will be taken outside the ward to the church of St. Clement this evening," Richard told Bascot. "The priest will hold a Mass for the care of his soul and my aunt and Alinor, along with the other servants in their retinue, can go and offer their respects if they wish. The body will remain there until we know where it is to be buried." St. Clement was the small church just outside the castle walls to the north and the one attended by the soldiers of the garrison as well as most of the household staff.

Bascot removed the cloak covering the corpse. The murdered man looked to have been in his mid-twenties, of slim proportions, and well muscled in a wiry fashion. Although the jaw gaped open, it could be seen that his features had been pleasing, with high cheekbones and a strong chin. The mouth, despite the unnatural contortion of the death stiffening, still retained a sensuous fullness. But it was difficult, without life's animation, to determine the personality of the man that had once inhabited what was now only a deteriorating earthly shell.

The Templar noticed that he seemed to have taken care of his appearance. His reddish blond hair and short beard were neatly trimmed and had been smoothed with a pomade that had a strong aroma of sage. His clothes, which were of a moderate quality becoming to an upper servant in a baron's household, had been carefully chosen. He was clad in a dark blue tunic of heavy wool that complemented his pale colouring and the belt around his waist was of soft red leather tooled with spiral decorations, as were the shoes on his feet. Only the gaping hole made by the crossbow bolt in the cloth over his chest, and the traces of blood surrounding the tear, marred the neatness of his aspect.

Bascot noticed a glint of gold at the neck of the dead man's tunic and pushed the collar aside to examine it more closely. It was a gold chain and when he pulled it free, discovered a ring depending from it, a heavy gold band surmounted by the design of a crossed knot. "An expensive piece of jewellery for a servant," he remarked to Richard, and then, as he turned the ring to the light of the candles, noticed there was an engraving on the inside of the band—a crescent moon with the points facing upwards and half encircling a small star. Both symbols were often used separately by the noble class, but it was not common to see them in concert. The Templar remembered seeing this combination only once before, and, when he passed it to the sheriff's son, so did Richard.

"That is the design Lionheart used on his great seal," he exclaimed, using the soubriquet by which the late King Richard had been commonly known. "Why would my aunt's cofferer be wearing a ring engraved with a royal motif?"

Bascot shrugged. "Lionheart was generous and it would not surprise me if he had given the ring to a retainer as a reward for service, even if the recipient was a commoner. Perhaps Tercel came by it as a gift of inheritance from some family member."

"You could be right," Richard agreed. "I shall ask my aunt about it."

"Was his scrip on him when he was found?" Bascot asked.

Richard nodded. "Alinor has taken charge of it. The money that was given into his care was all accounted for, with the expenditures that had been made on my aunt's behalf since she arrived in Lincoln listed on a piece of parchment and kept with the coins that remained—a sum of just over two pounds."

"Then, since the money was not taken, robbery could not have been the motive for the murder," Bascot said and pulled the cloak back up to the dead man's chin. "We must seek elsewhere for the reason."

They left the chapel and went back up to the hall where the serving of the midday meal was just about to begin. Making their way to the table set on the dais, Richard took a seat alongside his mother, and Bascot a place between Petronille and her daughter farther along the large oaken board.

The castellan's sister welcomed him warmly. The Templar had been of great assistance to her family in the past and she expressed her relief that he had come to their aid once again. "I cannot fathom why anyone would wish my servant dead, Sir Bascot," she said. "But I hope you will be just as successful in seeking out this murderer as you have in catching similar villains in times past."

"So do I, lady," Bascot said with heartfelt sincerity. "To take another's life without just cause is an abomination."

As the first course, wooden platters of sliced venison set round about with a selection of boiled vegetables, was placed in front of them, the Templar let his eye roam over the company at the tables below. He saw Gianni seated among the upper servants of the household alongside John Blund and

Lambert, the latter a senior clerk who was Blund's assistant. The boy gave the Templar a shy smile which Bascot returned. At the table reserved for the household knights, he saw an unfamiliar face and asked Petronille if the stranger was attached to her retinue.

"Yes," she replied. "That is Hugh Bruet. My husband gave him charge of leading our escort to Lincoln and staying here with us until it was time for our return to Stamford."

"And the rest of your entourage, lady," Bascot asked, "how many are they?"

"We came with four men-at-arms under Bruet's direction, and I brought with me a maidservant who is also my sempstress, along with another young maid that is attendant to Alinor. Originally there was also, of course, my dead cofferer."

"Richard says he will use his father's private chamber for interviewing our servants," Alinor said to Bascot from her seat beside him. "I have told them to go to the back of the hall after the meal is over and wait until they are summoned.

"I shall sit in with you and my cousin while you speak to them, Sir Bascot," Alinor added determinedly. "As Tercel was a member of our household, his murder is an affront to my father's good name and, since my mother has given her permission, I intend to stand in his place in the matter."

Bascot smiled inwardly. Although his young son's death had deprived Richard de Humez of a male heir, Alinor, like her aunt, had more than enough courage to step into his place.

THE FIRST IN PETRONILLE'S RETINUE TO BE INTERVIEWED WAS Hugh Bruet, the knight that Bascot had noticed at table in the hall. Gianni had been summoned to take notes of any relevant details and was perched on a stool in the corner with his wax tablet on his knee. The chamber they were in was a large one, containing a bed covered with wolfskins, spare tack for horses and, on a table to one side of the room, a magnificent chessboard set with playing pieces. When Bruet came into the room, he glanced around him and gave a nod of appreciation for the masculine accoutrements.

He was a man of middle years with a stocky build that swelled with hard muscle and it was easy to see why de Humez had chosen him for the task of escorting his wife and daughter on their journey. Bruet had a battle-hardened look about his person that would quickly deter any outlaws foolish enough to attack the cavalcade he led. He stood easily in front of Bascot, Richard and Alinor and, when asked about his knowledge of Tercel's activities during the time the de Humez party had been in Lincoln, admitted that he had little.

"The only times I had occasion to be in the cofferer's company was on our journey here and, after our arrival, when we all attended services in the cathedral during Christ's Mass," he said gruffly. "If he went into town I would not be aware of it; my duties lie in overseeing the safety of Lady Petronille and Lady Alinor; all else is without my province and beyond my interest."

"And you never heard report of any friends, or enemies, that Tercel may have made while he was here?" Richard pressed.

"No, lord, I have not," Hugh replied shortly. "As I said, our paths did not often cross."

Richard dismissed the knight and, as they waited for the first of the men-at-arms to come up to the chamber, discussed what the knight had said.

"I am sure that Bruet, like myself, did not approve of Tercel," Alinor told her cousin and the Templar. "I think that Hugh, too, sensed that there was something about him that was false, a slyness that was a mixture of diffidence and conceit."

"But your father must have trusted him, lady," Bascot objected, "else he would not have given him the appointment to act as cofferer during your visit."

"I do not say he was dishonest, Sir Bascot," Alinor replied, "only that he seemed to wear a mask over his inner thoughts. He reminded me of a mummer in a play, acting the role of a person that was not truly himself. I mentioned it to my father once, just after Tercel arrived, and he told me that I was imagining it and not to be foolish."

The Templar, unlike her father, took heed of Alinor's words and, as he glanced towards Gianni, saw that the boy was making a notation on his tablet using the curious shortened form of words that Lambert had taught him to employ when taking dictation. Someone had killed Aubrey Tercel and there had to be a reason. Alinor's suggestion gave him pause for thought. It was not uncommon for people to display alternate facets of their personality according to the requirements of different situations. Perhaps it had not been the man with which his companions had all been familiar who had engendered enough hatred to cause his murder, but the disparate character who lurked beneath the cofferer's mask.

Eight

✛

NEXT IN PETRONILLE'S RETINUE TO BE INTERVIEWED WERE THE men-at-arms. Each was questioned individually but although all of them had seen Tercel leave the ward on quite a few occasions, none knew where he was bound or the identity of any people he may have become acquainted with. As the most senior of the four soldiers had said to Richard, "We've bunked in with the garrison since we came and mostly spend our time there, helping out with the regular duties in the ward. We had no cause to speak to the cofferer, and so we didn't."

Once the last of the men-at-arms had been questioned, only the two female servants remained. The first of these was a sempstress, Margaret, a senior household servant who had been with her mistress since before the time of Petronille's marriage and her removal to Stamford, and who had, over the years, risen to the status of companion. Now approaching middle age, she was soberly dressed in dark grey and had a staid manner. When asked about her knowledge of the victim's movements during the time they had been in Lincoln, she replied that, except for one occasion, she had none.

"Aubrey and I sat together at mealtimes," she said, "and sometimes exchanged a few pleasantries, but beyond that the only contact I had with him was when he brought me some pelts of vair he had chosen as being suitable for Epiphany gifts from my mistress to her sister and daughter. Lady Petronille had sent him into town to obtain some samples and told him to bring those he had selected for my approval before the final purchase was made. Later, I stitched those that I chose for Lady Alinor onto the sleeves of the bliaut she is now wearing."

She nodded in the direction of Petronille's daughter who, over her gown of moss green, wore an overgarment of heavy red wool with sleeves that fitted close to the elbow and then flared out to fall in a gracious drape to her knees. The cuffs were trimmed with the bluish grey squirrel fur called vair. "Lady Nicolaa's sempstress did the same with those milady gave to her sister," Margaret added.

Bascot and Alinor both glanced at Richard and saw that a frown had appeared on his face. Simon Adgate, the burgess whose wife had been so distraught upon learning of the murder, was the head of the furrier's guild. Had it been from his shop that Tercel had purchased the furs for his mistress? They listened with interest as Richard posed his next question to the sempstress.

"There are five or six furriers in Lincoln," Richard said to Margaret. "Did Tercel mention which establishment he got them from?"

The sempstress shook her head. "He brought a selection of perhaps a dozen furs. I do not know if they all came from the same furrier, or from two or three different ones."

* * *

AFTER MARGARET WAS DISMISSED, THEY TOOK A FEW MOMENTS
to discuss what she had told them before they sent for the
young woman who was Alinor's maid.

"When you interviewed Adgate earlier this morning, was
he one of those who denied being acquainted with the victim?" Bascot asked Richard.

Richard shook his head. "No, he was not. He admitted he
knew who he was, but gave me the impression it was no
more than awareness of his identity." The castellan's son
paused as he mentally reviewed his conversation with the
furrier. "I did not know, then, that my aunt had sent Tercel
into Lincoln to buy furs, so I did not ask Adgate if they were
purchased from his shop. And Adgate did not volunteer the
information, although he did not strike me as being particularly evasive."

"Then he needs to be asked that question," Bascot said.
"Even if they did not come from Adgate's premises, he may
know from whom they were purchased. It is the first intimation we have of a place in the town that Tercel visited
during the time he was in Lincoln."

Alinor had looked thoughtful while they were speaking
and now added her own contribution to the conversation.
"Perhaps Adgate's wife, Clarice, should also be interviewed
again," she said slowly.

"Why?" Richard asked.

"Well, primarily because you told me that she seemed
inordinately upset when she heard about the murder."

Both men nodded and waited for her to continue. "I
know that my aunt said she thought Mistress Adgate's outburst was due to her unstable nature, but it still seems exces-

sive and makes me wonder if her reaction was provoked by something other than hysteria."

Alinor took a breath and expanded on her notion. "We know she retired early from the feast because of her indisposition and so was abed in her chamber in the old tower at the time the murder took place. What if the cause of her distress was because she saw, or heard, something that she did not realise was important until hours later, when she learned what had happened?"

"But, surely, she would have told me of it when I spoke to her," Richard protested.

"Maybe she was too frightened to do so and that is why she burst into tears," Alinor replied. "If she knows something that will identify the murderer, she may be fearful of speaking out lest she put herself in danger."

"It could be so," Bascot said contemplatively. "And, if it is, raises the question of whether or not her husband is aware she is hiding her knowledge."

"Then she, along with Adgate, must be interviewed again," Richard agreed. "And let us hope we learn something useful by doing so. So far, we have little to lead us in the direction this investigation should take."

Having made that decision, he sent the servant on duty outside the chamber door to fetch up the last servant in Petronille's retinue, the young woman who was Alinor's maidservant. She was about twenty years of age and came into the chamber confidently, her manner sprightly. Before she entered, Alinor told them that the maid's name was Elise, and that she was the daughter of the de Humez butler at Stamford.

"I chose her as my personal maid because she has a pleasant demeanour and is enthusiastic in her tasks," Alinor added. "She also provides me with a lively turn of conversation. Her cheerfulness has helped me get through many a sad hour since my brother's death."

True to Alinor's description, Elise answered their questions forthrightly, saying that although she had not engaged in much conversation with the murdered man, she was sure he had a paramour in the town. "Not long after we came to Lincoln, he started going to a barber in the town to get his hair and beard trimmed," she said with a cheeky grin, "and I sometimes smelled some kind of perfume on him when we sat down to our meals in the hall. Men don't usually take such care with their appearance unless there is a woman they want to impress, but I don't know who she was. It is not a matter which he would have confided to me, for I rebuked him once for being over-familiar and, after that, he kept himself apart from my company."

Alinor frowned. "You did not tell me that he gave you offence, Elise."

"There was no need, lady," Elise replied with a confident air. "I left him in no doubt that I thought him a coxcomb and he did not trouble me again."

Barely concealing a smile for the direct manner in which Elise had answered their questions, Richard dismissed her and turned to the Templar. "From what the maid has told us, it seems there is a good possibility that Tercel had a paramour in the town. It could be this liaison is at the root of the murder."

"Maybe that is what Clarice Adgate is keeping secret," Alinor said suddenly. "She is a young and handsome woman married to an elderly husband. Perhaps she was not ill last night, but used that stratagem as an excuse to leave the feast early—knowing her husband would be engaged with the company in the hall for some hours—so as to meet with Tercel, who was her lover."

"She would be taking a great risk of discovery," Richard said. "Her husband could have come to the guest chamber at any time to see how she was faring."

"But is not danger part of the attraction of an illicit love affair?" Alinor replied. "And maybe there is more that she is hiding. Perhaps Adgate did come to check on her, found Tercel making him a cuckold, and killed him in a fit of rage."

But even as she made the postulation, Alinor was shaking her head in negation, recalling what Richard had told her of the interviews he and his mother had conducted earlier that morning. "No, that cannot be so. You told me that the other couple who were given lodgings in the old tower—the head of the armourer's guild and his wife—stayed with Adgate for the duration of the feast and that they all left the hall together when it was time to retire."

"Besides that, Cousin," Richard said, "if Adgate had found his wife and Tercel in flagrante delicto, it is more than likely he would have attacked the cofferer in the chamber where he found them and, if he murdered him, done the deed there. And we know that cannot have happened because there is no doubt Tercel was murdered up on the ramparts. The bolt that killed him was embedded in the door post behind him and gives irrefutable evidence that the bow was fired from within the walkway."

"Also, the choice of such a weapon must be considered," Bascot added. "We know that the killing must have been premeditated. Whether the crossbow was taken from the armoury in the days since the bowyer last maintained it or just a short time before it was used for the murder, whoever fired it planned his actions carefully. It was not, as you suggest, an act done in the heat of sudden anger. If it were so, Adgate would have used a knife or his fists."

At Alinor's downcast look, the Templar hastened to assure her that her proposal was not entirely without merit. "Nonetheless, you may be correct in your assumption that Tercel was having an adulterous affair, and even if it was not with Clarice Adgate, it might have been with one of the other women who attended the feast. If that is so, and her husband knew of it, he may have formulated a plan to kill his wife's lover under cover of the celebration." He turned to Richard. "Besides the furrier, do any of the other guild leaders have young and attractive wives?"

"No," Richard replied. "All the townsmen are of mature years and, except for Adgate, married to women of similar age."

Bascot posed his next question reluctantly; it was a sensitive one but had to be asked. Before he did so, he explained to Richard his reason for asking it. "We should also consider that the murderer may be a resident in the castle, one of the men in your household, perhaps, who had developed a fondness for a maid and was angry because she had become amorously involved with another man. Or, since it is conceivable that a woman could have fired the bow, a female servant that Tercel had taken advantage of and then spurned."

At Richard's nod of acceptance, the Templar said carefully, "Are there any, among your mother's household servants, that could be suspected of such an entanglement?"

Richard shook his head, his eyes gleaming with amusement at the Templar's discomfiture, and told Bascot that they had already considered such an eventuality and deemed it unlikely. "As you well know, my mother would dismiss any servant found guilty of lewdness, but that does not mean it did not happen, just that it had not yet caught the attention of her eagle eye, or of Eudo's, our steward. But my mother is a good mistress and I do not think any of our women servants would take the chance of losing their position, no matter how persuasive Tercel might have been."

Bascot accepted Richard's assessment and, leaving the possibility that a paramour was somehow involved in the murder, they turned their thoughts to other ways it might be possible to gain information.

"The two guests that did not spend the night within the ward remain to be questioned," Richard said. "It is a slim hope, but they may have seen or heard something that might help us. I shall send a message asking them to return to the ward. . . ."

"It might be best to interview them in their own homes or business premises," Bascot interjected. "A formal interrogation can be intimidating and stifle the remembrance of small details. Since there is little more that can be done here I will, if you wish, go into town tomorrow morning and speak to both of them. I can also go to Adgate's home and ascertain whether or not it was from his shop that Tercel purchased the furs for your aunt. And, at the same time, try to discover if his wife is, in fact, hiding some detail that may be useful to us."

Richard accepted the Templar's offer gratefully. "I must admit that I have had my fill of playing inquisitor and will be glad of a respite, even if only a brief one. Your help is greatly appreciated, de Marins." The castellan's son looked over to where Gianni was sitting. "I will have Gianni transcribe a record of the interviews we have just conducted in

case you wish to review them. Is there anything else you re-
quire?"

The Templar nodded. "Yes, with Lady Nicolaa's consent,
I would like Gianni to accompany me into town tomorrow
and be present while I interview the other two guild leaders.
He has been with me on such ventures before and can make
notes of the conversations, as he has done in the past."

Gianni's face broke into a grin as Richard, on his mother's
behalf, gave permission for the lad to be absent from the
scriptorium. The boy could think of nothing finer than to be
in his former master's company as they once again attempted
to track down a secret murderer. From his answering smile,
Gianni knew the Templar felt the same.

Nine
✦✚✦

THE NEXT MORNING, AFTER THE SERVICE AT TERCE, BASCOT rode out of the commandery and across the Minster in the direction of the castle. Stalls selling heated wine and roasted chestnuts had already been set up in the area around the cathedral and the aroma of hot meat pies wafted in the air as roving vendors hawked their wares among the small crowd that had attended the morning service. Even though the temperature was slightly warmer, the Templar was well wrapped up in his cloak and wore a black quilted arming cap on his head for protection against the chill. As he passed out of the Minster grounds and crossed Ermine Street, there was already foot traffic and wagons on the main thorough-fare, all making their way towards Northgate, Lincoln's northernmost exit, and the one that led out into the open countryside.

When Bascot reached the castle gate, he saw Gianni waiting for him just inside the entrance, eyes alight with excitement. On his head the boy had a fur-lined cap that had been given to him by Ernulf a couple of winters before. The last time he had seen Gianni wearing it, it had been too large, but now it fitted snugly over his curls and, with a heartrending pang, Bascot was once more made aware of how much the boy had grown.

With a lighthearted step, Gianni ran forward and handed a piece of parchment to the Templar. On the paper were written the names of the two townsmen that had yet to be interviewed. One of them was known to Bascot, a barber-surgeon he had met three years before when a priest had been stabbed in St. Andrew's Church. Bascot had not made the acquaintance of the other, who was, according to the note Gianni had made beside his name, head of the chandler's guild.

"We shall see these two citizens before we go to the furrier's shop," Bascot said as he motioned for Gianni to scramble up and ride pillion behind him. "The barber, if I remember correctly, is an observant man. Mayhap he will recall something that can help us learn more about the victim."

He felt the boy give two light taps on his shoulder, a signal for "yes." As they rode out of the castle ward and onto Ermine Street, it was as though time had turned backward and they were as they had once been, master and servant on a quest. It gave both of them a great feeling of satisfaction and, had it not been that it was the occasion of a murder that had caused them to be once again in close company, they would have found great joy in the reunion.

The streets of the town were sparsely populated and those who were out in the cold air were well wrapped in cloaks and hats. The barber, whose name was Gildas, had his business premises on a narrow turning just off Danesgate, near the church where Bascot had first met him. Gildas' shop was a large establishment employing three assistants and had the sign associated with the trade—a brass cup atop which stood a pole wound about with bandages—outside the door.

When they went inside, the shop was crowded with customers, all sitting on chairs with elongated backs that ended in wooden headrests. Some of the patrons were having their faces shaved or hair trimmed, while one or two were being bled, some by the opening of a vein on the inside of the elbow, others by dry cupping, where a heated circular vessel was applied to the skin and, as it cooled, drew the blood to the surface. Another, attended by Gildas himself, was stripped to the waist and had leeches affixed to his chest. Piles of bandages, jars of leeches, pairs of wicked-looking pliers for drawing teeth and small, sharp knives were neatly stacked on shelves along the walls and the air was heavy with heat from braziers burning in each corner. The strong scent of perfumed oil was overlaid with the metallic tang of blood and the floor was littered with tufts of hair and soiled bandages.

When Bascot entered the shop, Gildas immediately left his customer and came forward to greet him. The master barber was as the Templar remembered him; a rotund little man of short stature with greying hair and a merry smile. Around his neck hung a thin silver chain threaded with extracted teeth.

"Sir Bascot—you are well come, well come indeed."

Gildas' customer, noticing he had been deserted, gave a shout of alarm and the barber motioned for one of his assistants to attend to the man before turning back to his visitor.

"I expect you have come about the murder that took place in the castle the night before last," he said knowingly.

"We have," Bascot confirmed. "You were, I understand, one of those who attended the feast that evening?"

Gildas' chest swelled with importance. "Yes, as head of our guild, I went there to take the monies I and the other barber-surgeons in the town had collected for donation to Lady Nicolaa's foundling home."

"But you did not stay the night?" Bascot asked.

Gildas shook his head. "I had an important client coming early the next morning and had to be in my shop to attend him. My wife did not relish the journey home on so cold a night, but she understands that the needs of my customers must come before personal comfort."

"The man who was killed was named Aubrey Tercel," Bascot said, "and was a servant in Lady Petronille's retinue. Did you know him?"

"I did not know his name, but I believe I know which man was murdered," the barber pronounced. "Did he have fair hair and wear a dark blue tunic with a red leather belt?"

Surprised, the Templar said that the description fitted the dead man. Gildas gave a self-satisfied smile. "When the news of the murder spread throughout the town yesterday and it was said the victim had been a servant of Lady Nicolaa's sister, one of our guild members, a barber by the name of Hacher, said that a member of Lady Petronille's retinue had come to his shop twice in the last few weeks to have his hair trimmed." Gildas gave Bascot a wide smile. "Now, Sir Bascot, I pride myself on being able to recognise the work of every one of our guild members and, when I arrived at the castle, I immediately noticed the man I have just described passing through the hall. I knew at once that he had been to Hacher to have his hair dressed. I would not have taken note of him otherwise. Hacher's style of work is unmistakable—

cut just below the ears and at the sides and long in the back. . . ."

Bascot had forgotten that Gildas, while observant, was also garrulous and gently cut the barber off in mid-flow. "Then I need to speak to this other barber. Tercel may have said something while in his shop that could be pertinent to the murder investigation. Where can I find him?"

"Just on the other side of Spring Hill, by the church of St. John," Gildas replied, his round face showing the pleasure he was deriving from being able to help. Bascot had no doubt that, by the end of the barber's working day, every customer would be regaled with the details he had been able to supply. As he watched one of Gildas' assistants pick up a pair of vicious-looking pliers and prepare to draw a tooth from a man whose face was contorted with misery, he hoped the story would distract the unfortunate customer from his pain.

BASCOT AND GIANNI FOUND HACHER'S SHOP IN A LITTLE SIDE street just behind St. John's church. It was smaller than the one Gildas owned and the barber was the antithesis of the talkative guild master. Tall and skinny, Hacher had a cadaverous face that looked as though it would crack if its owner broke into a smile. There were only two chairs in his shop, one occupied by a man having his luxuriant beard trimmed by an apprentice and the other empty. Hacher was sitting on a stool at the back, surveying his almost-deserted shop with a lugubrious expression. Here, as in Gildas' premises, the air was filled with pungent aromas but overlying the tang of blood was the strong scent of sage, the same cloying perfume that had emanated from Tercel's corpse.

As Bascot and Gianni came through the door, Hacher

rose from his seat, and, with a hopeful raising of his sparse eyebrows, enquired how he could be of assistance. When the Templar related why he had come, gloom once again settled over the barber-surgeon's features, but he confirmed that Aubrey Tercel had come to him twice over the weeks since Christ's Mass, and had his hair trimmed both times.

"He was a fussy customer," Hacher added dolefully. "Complained I hadn't cut his hair short enough the first time and declared he wasn't prepared to pay the cost of a second trimming. But he did buy some scented oil to keep his locks smooth, so I suppose I gained some profit from his patronage."

"While you were attending to his needs, did he make any mention of acquaintances he had made in the town?" Bascot asked. "Perhaps a lady whom he wished to impress?"

Hacher thought for a moment. "He didn't say much, just told me he was only in Lincoln until Eastertide and was in the retinue of Lady Nicolaa's sister. The next time he came, he said he was in a hurry, and we spoke little."

"Are you sure he said nothing else—where he was going after he left your shop, for instance?" Bascot pressed.

When the barber gave a woeful shake of his head, the Templar and Gianni, disappointed, left the shop. But once they were again out in the street, Bascot paused for a moment. "Hacher's information does not help us much," he said to Gianni, "but it does give us some indication of Tercel's personality. It appears he was a vain man, and parsimonious with it. You must have seen him while he was staying at the castle, Gianni. What was your impression of him?"

Gianni immediately struck a pose, arms akimbo, feet wide apart and head thrown back. The implication was obvious and confirmed Bascot's judgement of Tercel's conceit.

The Templar smiled at the boy's mimicry, but it quickly faded as he thought that the man the boy was parodying was now dead. A coxcomb he may have been, but he did not deserve to have his life taken by another.

He looked at the other name on the piece of parchment Gianni had given him. "The chandler's shop is on Mikelgate, between here and Adgate's premises. We will go there first and then to the furrier's."

As BASCOT AND GIANNI WERE ON THEIR WAY TO THE CANDLE makers, the five young foundlings destined to be taken to Riseholme were being shepherded into a capacious wain. The day before, after spending the previous night sleeping on straw in the stables, they had all been thoroughly washed by the castle laundress in the room where she kept a large vat of water boiling to wash the napery used in the hall. The washer-woman was a raw-boned female with arms that swelled with muscle. For all her frightening appearance, she had been gentle with the children, lathering them with soap made from wood ash and tallow and sluicing them down with warm water before she removed the lice from their undernourished bodies. She had then clad them in warm clothes—remnants of old servants' tunics cut down to smaller sizes by the castle sempstresses—and given them a bowl of warm broth to eat. Now, their pitifully thin frames wrapped up against the cold and their shrunken bellies filled, they were to be taken to their new abode.

They were all frightened. The youngest, a girl of about five years of age, was weeping and clinging to the hand of her sister, a girl only a couple of years older than she. The pair had recently lost their only protector, an elder brother who had succumbed to a fever, and both were frightened at being sent to live among strangers. The older sibling was valiantly trying to present a brave face for the sake of her little sister, but her lower lip began to tremble as a castle maidservant instructed them to get up into the back of the cart that was to take them to Riseholme.

As the five-year-old was lifted up, she began to wail. "We's not bein' taken to be murdered, are we, like that man that was killed?" she cried out in terror. All of the children cringed as she gave voice to her fear. The third girl in the group, a child of about seven who answered every question put to her with only a shake of her head and a muttered "Dunno," abandoned her resolute silence and let out a small moan.

It was oldest of the boys that brought calm to the situation. He was a ten-year-old named Willi with a thatch of hair the colour of carrots and freckles sprinkled liberally over the bridge of his nose. As the maidservant fussed and tried to comfort the girls, he took the smallest one by the hand and said stoutly, "Don't be daft, little 'un, 'course they ain't going to kill us. Now, stop your grizzlin' and do as you're told." Mollified, the child took his hand and allowed herself to be lifted up onto the bed of the cart.

The maidservant gave him an approving smile and guided the other children up into the wain before climbing up beside them. Willi and the only other lad in the group, a blond-haired boy named Mark, a couple of years younger than Willi, moved a little apart from the girls and the maidservant, sitting on the floor of the cart with their backs to the driver.

As the equipage trundled out of the castle gate and headed north on the two-and-a-half-mile journey to Riseholme, Mark spoke to Willi in a whisper.

"You don't reckon that girl is right do you, and that we're all going to be murdered once we get to wherever we's goin'?"

"'Course not," Willi replied firmly. "D'you think it likely they'd have given us food if they wus going to kill us? Be a waste of good grub, that would."

Mark saw the wisdom in his words, but remained unconvinced, the intelligent blue eyes in his bony little face screwed up in concentration as he did so. "Still," he said finally, "there wus a murder in the castle t'other night and it must've been someone in the ward that done it." Keeping his voice low so the girls would not hear, he added in a whisper, "How do we know the murderer ain't the groom that's drivin' this cart? Or that maidservant they sent along with us?"

"'Cos I saw the murderer, that's why, and it wasn't either of these two," Willi replied, keeping his voice low so that neither the maidservant nor the groom would hear what he said.

Mark's eyes grew round. "You saw him? When was that then?"

"When they wus takin' us across to the stables. I saw someone comin' out of that old tower on the other side of the bail. All wrapped up in a cloak and skulkin' along in the shadows. Can't think of any reason for a person to be actin' like that if they wasn't doin' anythin' wrong. Must of been the murderer."

"Are you goin' to tell anyone about it?" Mark asked fearfully.

"Why should I? It's nuffink to do with me."

"You might get some extra food if you wus helpful," Mark suggested. "They'd be right pleased if you told them what you knows."

"Nah," Willi replied with a shrug of his shoulders. "They'd only start askin' me all kinda questions and I wants to keep my head down low 'cause I'se not staying long at this place they're takin' us. I only come with the priest that brought me to the castle 'cause I was hungry. Me da said I wus to wait where he left me and if he comes back and finds me gone, he'll give me a right good thrashin' for not doin' what I wus told."

"How comes you're here if you've got a da?" Mark asked in puzzlement. "All the rest of us is orphans. The priest where I went to get alms asked me that partiklar like. Said I couldn't go to the home if I had someone to look arter me."

"I lied, didn't I?" Willi replied breezily. "My da went lookin' for work and told me to stay where I wus and get alms from the priest at St. Peter's church. He said he'd only be gone a day or two, but he was gone longer than that and I wus starvin' so bad my stomach hurt. So when the priest asked me if I had a ma or da, I told him I didn't so's I'd get somethin' to eat. But I didn't 'spect I'd be sent to the castle, nor that I'd be taken outside the town, so I'm not gonna stay at this place they're takin' us for long. Soon as I gets a chance, I'm goin' back to Lincoln so's I can find my da."

Mark thought over what Willi had told him. "You wants to be careful," he cautioned. "If that murderer saw you lookin' at him and finds you wanderin' around the town, he might just kill you so's you can't tell no one it wus him you seen. You'll be safer out at Riseholme."

Willi looked at Mark and realised his newfound friend had made an assumption that was erroneous. He started to correct him, but then changed his mind. The less the other boy knew, the better. Instead he gave Mark a glare and said, "I ain't told no one what I saw 'cept you. And if you tells on me, I'll say you saw the murderer as well. Then you'll be in just as much danger as me."

Mark quickly assured Willi that he would not reveal what he had been told but, after he had done so, added, "I'd still be right chary of going back to town if I wus you. If you isn't, you might just end up dead as well."

Ten

***

WHEN BASCOT AND GIANNI WENT INTO THE CHANDLER'S manufactory they were met, as in the shops of Gildas and Hacher, with a comforting blast of heat. From the front entrance, the chandlery opened out into a huge workshop lined with troughs containing melted beeswax. Alongside each trough was a line of workers holding rods from which depended rows of linen wicks. Slowly and carefully they lowered the rods and dipped the wicks into the melted wax until a layer formed around each one. The rods were then hung up so the wax could dry and, as soon as it was hardened, the process was repeated until each candle was of a desired thickness. Some of the finished products were narrow and tapered, some broad and shallow while others, tall and fat, contained exactly enough wax to burn for twenty-four hours. These last would be scored with lines, each one denoting the passage of one hour, and used as a guide for the passage of time. It was a simple task but one, nonetheless, that required delicacy and a certain amount of expertise to

ensure that each candle was of a perfect weight and smooth-
ness.

To one side was a small hearth where honeycombs were
being dissolved. Two young men attended this process and
the aromatic scent of the crushed herbs they were adding to
the melting beeswax was pleasing to the nostrils. Standing
at the back of the large chamber were immense racks hung
with finished candles. These needed to dry for at least eight
days and, in good weather, would be trundled outside to allow the sun to bleach the wax to a fine brightness. Overseeing all of the work, and pacing back and forth as she did so,
was a girl of about eighteen years of age dressed in a dark
grey gown over which was draped a voluminous apron.

The chandler, a man appropriately named Thomas Wickson,
came bustling forward when he saw Bascot and Gianni enter. He was a narrow-shouldered man with an ample belly
swelling the front of his elaborately embroidered dark red
tunic and it soon became obvious that he was puffed up not
only by his girth, but with self-importance. When asked
about Aubrey Tercel and whether he had noticed the cofferer's movements during the feast, Wickson said that since he
had not been aware of the victim's identity, nor his appearance, he had not had any reason to take note of his activities.
Wickson made it clear, by the dismissive way in which he
spoke, that he considered the murder to be outside his realm
of interest, and Bascot changed the direction of his questions, asking the chandler why he had not taken advantage
of Nicolaa de la Haye's offer to spend the night in the castle.
With a little moue of regret, Wickson explained that his
wife had been indisposed and therefore unable to accompany
him to the feast, and he had been impatient to get home and
see how she was faring.

"My daughter, Merisel, went with me in my wife's stead," Wickson said, waving a hand in the direction of the young girl standing by the men dipping wicks into the troughs of melted wax. "My marital union has not been blessed with sons, but Merisel is a daughter to be proud of," he said, "and will one day inherit my business. She will bring a goodly dower to the man who is fortunate enough to take her to wife," he added with a satisfied smile. "And, I can assure you, her hand in marriage will not be lightly given."

At the sound of her name, Merisel looked up. She was not overly comely, but was fresh-faced, with pale hazel eyes and a determined chin. As she noticed the Templar looking in her direction, she dipped her head in respect.

"Since your daughter was present at the feast, I would like to speak to her," Bascot said to the chandler, "and ask if she knows anything about the murdered man that may prove useful."

Wickson looked as though he was about to object, but the stern glance the Templar gave him did not brook refusal, and the chandler called Merisel to come forward.

Standing quietly in front of the Templar, she listened without interruption as Bascot explained his purpose in being there and then posed his questions—had she ever made the acquaintance of Aubrey Tercel and, if so, had she observed his movements during the time she had been in the castle?

Merisel responded politely in the negative to each of the questions, meeting his gaze with seemingly frank and open honesty. Only when he asked if she knew of anyone in the town who had a connection with the murdered man did Bascot have a doubt about her denial. Her glance slid sideways for a fraction of a second before she said that she did not.

"Are you certain, mistress?" Bascot insisted. "It is reasonable to assume that the murder has been a topic of conversation among your friends and customers and if someone has mentioned, even only in passing, that they had spoken to him, I would be interested to know of it."

This time her answer came steadily enough and the Templar wondered if he had imagined the uncertainty in her previous reply. "I seldom have time for idle gossip, lord," she said. "All of my days are spent here, in the chandlery and, because of my mother's recent illness, I also have the responsibility of her household duties, so I have had little opportunity to engage others in conversation."

Aware that the girl had neatly sidestepped a direct answer to his question, Bascot was reluctantly forced to leave the matter there. In some fashion, he thought, the girl was not telling the complete truth. It may have only been that, in front of her father, she did not want to admit that she had noticed Tercel's handsome appearance and perhaps admired him, or discussed him with other girls her own age. She was of an age that is ripe for marriage; it would be unnatural if she did not cast her eyes on any personable young men who chanced to be in her company. But even if that was so, it did not mean that she had any information that might prove pertinent. Nonetheless, he told Gianni to take note of her name and put a question mark beside it.

Even though the temperature had risen a little during the morning, it was still chilly outside when the pair left the chandlery. As it was now almost the noon hour, Bascot went into the shop of a nearby baker and purchased two pastries filled with cooked meat and onions for their midday meal. They ate the food standing in the street just outside the baker's door and, when they had finished, Bascot extracted a couple of *candi* from the pouch at his belt. Gianni's face broke into a wide smile as the Templar tossed one to him and the lad popped it into his mouth and crunched the sweet with obvious relish.

The business premises of the furrier, Simon Adgate, was a little farther down in the town, on a street that led off Mikelgate, and hard by the church of St. Peter at Motston. The church bell had just finished tolling the hour of Sext when they reached the shop. Dismounting, the Templar tied his horse to a post in front of the door and they went up to the entrance.

As Bascot pushed open the heavy panel of oak, he found a guard standing in the enclosed entryway just inside. The watchman wore a metal studded jerkin and carried a cudgel tucked in a belt around his waist. Noticing the Templar badge on Bascot's shoulder, he respectfully asked the one-eyed knight his name and the nature of his business. When told that he had come on behalf of Lady Nicolaa and wished to speak to the furrier, the guard led him through a door and into the shop, recommending him into the care of a man who was, the watchman said, Simon Adgate's assistant.

The assistant, a youngish man with a foppish manner, obsequiously assured the Templar that, if he would care to wait, he would fetch Adgate from upstairs. As he scurried away, Bascot and Gianni looked around the room into which they had been shown. Furs of every kind were carefully hung on hooks placed around the walls of the shop. There were soft pelts of sable, bluish grey furs of vair and snow-white ermine, all dressed and ready to be attached to an assortment of garments, and a few which had already been sewn onto cloaks and tunics and spread across a wide display counter. Two large coffers, the lids thrown back, also held a wide variety of pelts—marten, rabbit, fox and wolf spilled over the edges of the chests. There was much wealth in the generous display of goods and Bascot could understand the need for a guard. An intruder would have no need for stealth, he would merely need to snatch a handful of expensive furs and beat a hasty retreat to make his daring worthwhile.

Gianni lightly touched Bascot's sleeve and inclined his head towards a pile of squirrel skins lying on top of a counter. They were similar to the ones that the sempstress had sewn on Alinor's gown.

A moment later, Simon Adgate came into the room. Seen close to, Bascot noticed that despite the fact that Adgate's hair was so pale a grey it was almost completely white, it topped a face that had retained its youthful vigour, with alert eyes and a full, mobile mouth. His frame, beneath the lavishly furred overtunic that he wore, was robust and his hands were large and strong. The furrier was extremely hale for a man that must be approaching sixty years of age.

"Greetings, Sir Bascot," Adgate said in a reserved manner. "My assistant tells me that you wish to speak to me on behalf of Lady Nicolaa—how may I help you?"

"We have been told that Aubrey Tercel, the man who was murdered while the feast was in progress, purchased some furs for his mistress, Lady Petronille, a few weeks after their arrival in Lincoln. Was it from your establishment that he bought them?"

With a glance at his assistant, who was within earshot and, by his inquisitive attitude, listening to their conversation, Adgate said that it was.

"Why did you not mention this to Sir Richard when he asked if you were acquainted with him?" Bascot asked.

"I must apologise for my neglect," Adgate said with

seeming contrition. "It was merely a business transaction and so I did not think it of any importance."

"Did you attend to him personally?"

"Yes, I did," Adgate said uneasily. "When my assistant realised that the purchase might prove to be a substantial one, he sent for me and I showed Tercel a selection of the furs that I carry."

"As I understand it," Bascot pressed, "he came into the shop on more than one occasion. Did you see to his requirements each time?"

Adgate nodded, and the Templar could sense mounting tension in the man. "Surely, during three times of meeting, you must have spoken of matters other than the furs," Bascot suggested. "Did he tell you anything about himself, or the places he had been in the town?"

Adgate shook his head and walked over to the pile of furs that Gianni had pointed out earlier. Bascot noticed that the furrier walked with a slight limp. Picking up a pelt of sable, Adgate brought it back and showed it to the Templar. "As you can see, my goods are of the finest quality," he said, running his fingers caressingly through the rich, dark fur. "I have no need to engage in idle chatter with a customer to persuade them to make a purchase. Tercel saw the quality of my goods and so, I assume, did Lady Petronille when he took the squirrel furs to show her. Our conversation dealt entirely with the business transaction. We spoke of nothing else."

The furrier's little speech seemed earnest but Bascot was not gulled. There seemed to be a hint of desperation behind Adgate's facile words and, glancing at Gianni, the Templar saw the boy surreptitiously curl the tips of the fingers of his right hand and quickly release them, a gesture that denoted apprehension. He had noticed the furrier's uneasiness as well.

Bascot considered Adgate's limp. Was it an old injury or a recent one? Could it be that there was some merit to Alinor's wild assumption that the furrier had discovered his wife and Tercel together and fought with him, and that their struggle had resulted in an injury to Adgate's leg? But the furrier had been overlooked all that evening by another guild leader, the armourer and his wife who had sat beside Adgate and accompanied him to their respective guest chambers in the old tower. Still, there must be a reason for the furrier's seeming alarm and perhaps, as Bascot had discussed earlier with Richard Camville and Alinor, it was related to his wife.

Feigning acceptance of Adgate's explanation, the Templar said, "I need to ask a few questions of your wife. Now that she has had time to get over the shock of being in such close proximity to where a murder took place, I would like to ask her whether or not she has recalled any information that may help us."

Bascot felt, rather than saw, Adgate stiffen. "I am afraid my wife is indisposed," he protested. "She has taken a chill and is keeping to her bed in an effort to recover from it."

But Bascot did not intend to be so easily thwarted. "Be that as it may, I must insist on speaking to her, else it will be necessary for her to come to the castle so that Lady Nicolaa or Sir Richard can ask their questions directly."

Faced with the unacceptable alternative, Adgate acquiesced to Bascot's demand, asking only that the Templar give his wife a few moments to don suitable attire before coming down.

Bascot nodded and the furrier left the room, instructing

his assistant to show the Templar into an adjoining chamber and pour him a cup of wine. The room into which Bascot was led, with Gianni at his heels, was a sumptuous one; a gleaming oak table set with candlesticks and condiment dishes of silver graced the middle of the room and richly embroidered tapestries hung on the walls. In front of a fire blazing in a capacious hearth were ladder-backed chairs and settles and a thick rug lay on the floor. There were two casements and the shutters of both had been partially opened to reveal square panes fitted with thinly shaven horn that allowed light to enter but prevented coldness from seeping into the room. The assistant bid the Templar be seated and poured wine into a silver cup and placed it in front of him.

His duty completed, the servant left the room and Bascot looked at Gianni and raised an eyebrow. "There is much wealth here," Bascot mused. "If Tercel was making Adgate a cuckold, the furrier has more than enough riches to pay for the hire of an assassin."

Gianni nodded in solemn agreement as the door opened and Adgate returned, leading his young wife by the hand. Clarice was a very handsome woman, with clear skin and a ripe red rosebud mouth, but now her pretty face was withdrawn and there were dark hollows under her lovely green eyes. She came forward hesitantly and seated herself on the edge of a chair.

Bascot regarded her for a moment before he spoke. She did not look up at him while he did so, directing her gaze downwards to where her hands were tightly entwined in her lap. "On the night of the feast, mistress, you told Sir Richard that you left the hall early and, after going to the chamber in the old tower which you and your husband had been allotted, went immediately to bed and slept undisturbed until morning. Are you absolutely certain all was quiet during all that time?"

Clarice answered in a voice so low it was barely audible. "Yes, lord, I am."

"And earlier, when you crossed the bail, did you see anyone lingering around the entrance to the old tower when you went in—a servant, perhaps, or one of the guests?"

Clarice shook her head and said nothing, keeping her eyes downcast. Bascot, irritated by her withdrawn attitude, decided to act on instinct and said sharply, "But you were acquainted with the man who was murdered, mistress, were you not?"

Clarice's gaze flew up to Bascot's face and he saw fear in her eyes. Adgate, who had been hovering behind his wife's chair, placed a hand on her shoulder and answered in her stead. There was a touch of panic in the protective movement and, the Templar noted with surprise, also a fleeting curl of distaste on the furrier's full lips when his fingers touched his wife's body.

"My wife might have been in the shop on one or two of the occasions when he called—she is often in there helping me display some of the ladies' furred cloaks to prospective customers—but that can hardly be called an acquaintance-ship."

The Templar ignored the furrier and, once again, spoke directly to Clarice. "When he came into your husband's shop, mistress, did you engage in conversation with him?"

Clarice remained mute and looked helplessly up at her husband. Adgate once again gave a reply to the question. "As I have said, Sir Bascot, she may have seen the dead man once or twice, but that is all. Now, I must insist that you allow my wife to return to her bed. She is ill, as you can see, and the memory of how near she was to death is very distressing to her."

Bascot stood up. "Very well, furrier. I will leave my questions there—for now. But I, or Sir Richard, will want to speak to both you and your wife again. Be ready to present yourselves at the castle tomorrow at mid-morning. Perhaps your wife will have recovered sufficiently by then to answer my questions more fully."

Adgate started to protest, but the Templar cut him short. "I find it hard to believe that your wife would be so stricken with distress for the death of a man you claim she barely knew, or that she was so indisposed that she heard nothing while this same man was being murdered in the building where she was abed. I would advise you both to reflect on the matter until tomorrow and, when you come to the castle, be ready to tell the truth."

Clarice let out a great sob as Bascot and Gianni left the chamber. Once outside the shop, Bascot untied the reins of his horse and, as they both settled themselves atop the animal, said to Gianni, "Lady Alinor was right, there is something that both Adgate and his wife are not telling us. It only remains to discover what it is."

LATER THAT EVENING, HER WORK IN THE CHANDLERY FINISHED for the day and the household set in order, the candle-maker's daughter, Merisel, slipped into the chamber where her ailing mother lay in bed. The illness that had seemed slight on the day of the feast had taken a turn for the worse and Mistress Wickson now lay on her pallet, grey-faced and short of breath.

Merisel went to her side and, reaching out a hand,

smoothed her mother's disordered hair back from her brow. Edith Wickson did indeed look ill, large dark circles had formed under her soft brown eyes and her mouth was tremulous. She had always been of an energetic and dithering nature, flittering from one task to another in an effort to please her demanding husband; to see her lying so still was worrying. "Are you feeling any better, Mother?" Merisel asked.

"A little," Mistress Wickson replied. "Have you attended to all that needs to be done?"

"I have," Merisel replied. "Do not worry, you will soon be well and able to see to the tasks yourself."

Edith Wickson fiddled nervously with the heavy braid of greying brown hair which lay over her shoulder and said, "Your father told me that a Templar came today to question him about the murder in the castle. And that he spoke to you as well. What did he ask?"

"Only if we knew the man who was murdered in the castle and if we had seen him speaking with anyone in the town."

"And what did you tell him?"

Merisel shrugged. "The truth, of course. That I had neither made his acquaintance nor knew of anyone that had."

Mistress Wickson took her daughter's hand and pressed it as tears welled in her eyes. "You are a good girl, Merisel, and serve your father and myself well. You know that I only want what is best for you."

Merisel smiled. "I am glad you feel so, Mother," she replied, but a shiver of unease rippled through her. It was unlike her mother to be so melancholy. She reached for a small phial sitting on a table beside the bed. "Come, take the medicine I got from the apothecary. It will help you sleep more peacefully. If you do not get enough rest, it will take you longer to recover."

Obediently, Mistress Wickson sipped the foul mixture from the spoon her daughter held out to her, then lay back and closed her eyes. But as Merisel doused the candle and left the room, the girl could not erase the conversation she had with the Templar from her mind, nor the anxiety her mother had shown when she had asked about it.

Eleven
✠

ᴇARLY THE NEXT MORNING, SOME FIFTY MILES SOUTHWEST OF
Lincoln, Richard de Humez, Petronille's husband, was pacing the floor of a small chamber in his manor house near
Stamford, agitatedly running a hand over the thinning hair
on his pate. Seated on a chair across the room was a local
knight, Stephen Wharton, whose small demesne abutted
the fief de Humez held from the king. They had been friends
for many years but now de Humez' face was filled with con-
sternation as he stopped his pacing and faced Wharton.

"I find it hard to believe that what you have just told me
about Tercel is true. Why did you not apprise me of these
facts when you urged me to give him a post in my household?"

Wharton, a man of about fifty years of age with an open,
honest face and mild blue eyes, tried to find words that
would pacify the baron. De Humez was a fussy and precise
individual who was a little too conscious of his high position,

but he was a decent man and they had been friends for a long time.

"Truly, Dickon, I did not think the matter of any importance. . . ."

De Humez's response was full of irritation. "Of no importance! How can you deem it a falderal that a retainer of mine—one I took into my service on *your* recommendation—believed himself to be the bastard son of a man who was once king of England! And that he might have been murdered to prevent him substantiating that claim!"

"It may seem as though I have deceived you, Dickon, but truly, that was not my intent," Wharton said abjectly. "I thought his notion was merely a passing fancy, one that he would soon dismiss when he saw the futility of pursuing it further. But now that he has been killed, I fear he may have been asking questions in quarters where they would not be well come. . . ."

"And was murdered to ensure his silence," de Humez finished gravely. The baron walked over to the table and poured himself another cup of wine. When he had drunk deeply from the cup, he sat down heavily on a padded chair beside the roaring fire in the grate.

"You had better tell me the whole sorry tale, Stephen. And then, if you value my friendship, you will go to Lincoln and repeat it to my sister-by-marriage, Nicolaa de la Haye." His eyes narrowed as he added, "And God help you if this so called fantasy of Tercel's has put my wife and daughter in danger. I am not normally a vengeful man, but you can be assured that in this instance I will ensure you pay to the fullest measure for your actions."

Wharton took a nervous swallow of his wine. De Humez

held a large fief from the king and was far above him in wealth and social standing. He hoped that what he was about to relate had nothing to do with Tercel's death but if, by some rare chance it did, he prayed that his own role in the matter would be overlooked, at least by the man seated across from him.

Bascot arrived at the castle just after Terce. He had spoken at length with Richard Camville and Lady Nicolaa the afternoon before, relating the little he had learned from the barber-surgeons and the chandler before revealing his suspicions about Simon Adgate and telling them that he had commanded the furrier and his wife to come to the castle for further questioning at mid-morning. Nicolaa had requested that Bascot be present at the interview and the Templar had willingly consented. Now, as he left his horse in the castle stable and made his way into the hall, the Haye steward, Eudo, came forward and told him that the castellan and her son were in the solar and had asked that, when he arrived, he joined them there.

As Bascot went up the stairs in the western tower, Gianni came from the landing that led off to the scriptorium, his wax tablet in his hand. Together they ascended to the top storey, where the solar was located. When they entered the chamber they found Alinor seated alongside her aunt and cousin. From the purposeful set of her mouth, Bascot could see that she had been told of his suspicions about Clarice Adgate and agreed with them.

She gave him a smile as he took a seat beside her. "Well done, de Marins," she said. "It would seem you have already discovered the murderer. Adgate's wife must have been having an affair with Tercel and somehow the furrier managed to kill him for his trespass."

Bascot shook his head. "I am not certain of that, lady, only that Adgate and his wife are hiding something. It may be," he added, remembering the momentary look of revulsion on the furrier's face as he touched his wife's body, "that Clarice Adgate is the woman your maid supposed Tercel was involved with but, beyond that, it does not necessarily follow that her husband is the one who killed him. Adgate was overlooked for all the hours during which the murder was committed."

"It could be that the furrier hired an assassin to do the deed for him," Alinor opined.

"He certainly has enough wealth to do so," Bascot agreed. "But surely such an act would be more easily accomplished within the confines of the town. And it would be a haphazard assassin that would not come armed with his own weapon and instead have need to take one from the castle armoury."

As everyone nodded their agreement, Bascot leaned forward and spoke to Nicolaa. "Lady, I think it would be more profitable if we spoke to Adgate and his wife separately. When I spoke to her, she continually looked to the furrier for guidance. If it is her intimate connection with Tercel that the pair is hiding, she may be more forthcoming if he is not on hand to protect her from any reckless admission."

Nicolaa nodded and, at that moment, a servant came into the solar and told the castellan that the furrier and his wife had arrived and were downstairs in the hall. "Send the woman up first," she instructed the servant. "And tell the husband he is to wait below until he is called."

A few minutes later Clarice Adgate came hesitantly into

the room. She was dressed in a sober gown of dark grey and her coif was of plain white linen. The only ornamentation on her person was a simple gold chain about her neck bearing a small pendant etched with the image of the Virgin Mary. She fingered this nervously as she gave a small curtsey of deference to Lady Nicolaa and the other nobles. Her eyes flicked from one to the other in apprehension.

By unspoken agreement, the castellan began the questioning. The management of her huge demesne had given her years of experience in dealing with situations similar to this one, when it often became necessary to ferret out the truth between the conflicting claims of tenants and villeins.

"Mistress Adgate," she said in a deceptively kind tone, "you have come here to answer further questions about the night my sister's retainer was killed. Previously you stated that you retired early because you were feeling unwell. What was the nature of your indisposition?"

"My head was aching dreadfully, lady," Clarice replied, relieved at the innocuous nature of the question. "It was the excitement of the day, I think, that brought it on."

"And you went to the room you had been assigned, got into bed and immediately fell asleep?" Nicolaa went on.

"I did," Clarice replied.

The castellan leaned slightly forward as she posed her next question. "I am surprised that slumber came so quickly when you were suffering such pain. Did you take a medicament to ease it?"

The question took Clarice by surprise and she stumbled over the answer. "A medicament? I . . . I . . . yes, I did. I had a potion with me, a draught of poppy juice."

Nicolaa leaned back in her chair, seemingly satisfied with the answer. "I thought you must have done; that is what made you sleep so soundly. If you will give us the name of the apothecary from which you obtained it, we will have no further questions for you."

Clarice's face went white as she realised the trap into which she had been led. She was, as Nicolaa had said previously, a rather foolish woman. It had not taken a great deal of expertise on the castellan's part to lead her in the direction they wanted her to go. "I do not know which apothecary it was, lady," she replied, her lower lip beginning to tremble. "My . . . my husband got it for me."

"Then I will send for your husband and ask him where he bought it. I am sure he will be able to provide us with the answer," Nicolaa replied, raising her hand to motion to the servant standing at the door.

"No, lady, please!" Clarice burst out, her agitation increasing. "Simon will not know. . . . I was mistaken. . . . It was my maidservant that got it, not my husband. . . ."

"I do not understand your confusion, mistress," Nicolaa said sternly. "Juice of poppy is a powerful sedative; surely you can remember how you came by it. Or is it, perhaps, that you did not have any? That you did not go to the bedchamber because you were ill and needed to rest, but for some other purpose?"

Clarice burst into tears and the castellan pressed her advantage. "Aubrey Tercel was your lover, was he not?" Nicolaa charged ruthlessly. When the furrier's wife nodded her head in a forlorn fashion, Nicolaa sought to confirm the details of their suspicions. "And the reason you left the hall early was not because you were ill, but to engage in dalliance in the very bed you were later to share with your husband?"

Clarice's answer took them by surprise. "No, we did not meet in the guest chamber," she said miserably. "Aubrey told me to come to another room, one at the top of the tower. He said it was safer there and that if my husband should decide to retire beforetime, he would not discover us together."

Gianni and Bascot glanced at each other. There was only one chamber large enough to be used for such a purpose and it was one that the Templar and the boy had shared while Bascot had been staying in the castle before his return to the Order. And it was located just a few steps below the walkway that led to the ramparts.

Richard now took charge of the interrogation and spoke in harsh tones to the furrier's wife. "You have lied to us, mistress, and I do not take it kindly. If you value your freedom, and your life, you had best tell us the truth."

Clarice nodded and slowly the whole story came out. She had, she said, formed a friendship with Tercel shortly after Christ's Mass when he had come to her husband's shop to purchase furs on Lady Petronille's behalf. Simon Adgate was often away from his premises while he went to the tanning pit he owned in the lower part of the town and it was at those times that Tercel had come to the shop and engaged her in conversation and, finally, enticed her to meet him in a room he had rented above an alehouse in the town. When the feast was proposed, her paramour had suggested Clarice take advantage of her husband's preoccupation with the celebrations to join him in the old tower and she had agreed.

"But when I left him, he was alive," she said tearfully. "Truly, I did not know he was dead until the next morning."

"And where did you leave him, mistress?" Bascot asked. "Was he still in the chamber where you had met, the one at the top of the tower?"

"No," Clarice replied. "He was standing outside the door.

He thought he heard a noise while we were . . . while we were inside the room, and feared it might be my husband. He bade me go down to the bedchamber below and stood at the top of the stairs while I descended."

"And was it your husband?" Bascot asked.

"No, there was no one there; at least, I don't think there was anyone. Aubrey did not light a candle. I went down the stairs in the darkness, feeling along the wall to guide my steps. After I entered the bedchamber, I got into bed. A few minutes later I heard footsteps pass the door and thought it was Aubrey returning to the hall."

"By that time, mistress, he was dead," Bascot said harshly. "And the footsteps you heard belonged to his killer."

"I know," Clarice replied miserably. She lifted her tear-stained eyes to the company. "That is what I realised when I learned that Aubrey had been murdered—that I could just as easily have been killed as well."

They asked her a few more questions and when Alinor suggested the murderer had been her husband, Clarice startled them all with a flash of hitherto unseen insight. "But it could not have been Simon," she said. "My husband is lame—he broke his leg as a child and it never mended properly—and the footsteps that went by my door were unfaltering. He would be incapable of making such a swift passage."

That, at least, explained Adgate's limp and further negated him as a suspect. When the suggestion was made that Adgate had hired someone to carry out the deed for him, she again shook her head. "My husband was not aware that I had taken a lover until after Aubrey was found dead," she said miserably, her tears welling anew, "so he would have had no reason to do so."

Bascot asked her if Tercel had, during their times together, spoken of any enemies he had made in Lincoln and Clarice shook her head. "None that he mentioned. We did not . . . did not have time for much casual conversation together."

Finally, Nicolaa dismissed her and told the servant to admit her husband into their presence.

Twelve

✦

WHEN THE FURRIER SAW CLARICE WALKING ACROSS THE HALL to where he was seated, he knew by the look on her face that she had admitted her adultery. Not for the first time in the last few days, he asked himself why he had chosen to marry such a vacuous young woman. And again, the answer echoed hollowly in his head—vanity. He had watched Clarice grow up in the tanner's yard he owned, and where her father was employed, and had seen her beauty develop from the time she had been a small child. When she had reached the age of maturity, he knew it had been no coincidence that he had suddenly convinced himself that he should marry again and try, before death overtook him, to beget an heir to inherit his prosperous business. There were other women in Lincoln that he could have offered for, and would have suited him admirably for his purpose—young daughters of other merchants and tradesmen—but he had not taken the time to give any of them consideration; he had taken notice only of Clarice and her lovely green eyes, dwelling on the façade of her beauty and dismissing the emptiness that he had, even then, sensed lay within. And, if he further examined his conscience without self-deception, he knew that it had not been lust that had driven him, but the envy with which other men would regard him for having such a desirable woman in his bed.

Not even for one moment had he ever considered that Clarice, coming from such an impoverished background, would dare to stray from his bed. He had thought she would be grateful that he, a respectable and wealthy merchant, had taken her in marriage, and that he had cajoled her into loving him by the expensive clothes and furs with which he had adorned her lovely body. How wrong he had been. While it was true that she carried out her duties in his shop well enough, he had soon realised it pleased her mercenary heart to touch and display the fine furs that he sold. Her soul was grasping, seeking only the gratification of her senses. She had no thought for anyone other than herself.

With a surge of regret he remembered his first wife, his dear Martha. They had been wed such a short time before she was taken from him by death, and they had been so much in love. After she had died, fond memories of her had made him unable to countenance the thought of marrying again and the years had slipped by without notice. Now, with the folly of an aging man, he was wed to a woman who had proved no better than a whore. How ironic it was that if, by some chance, Clarice was with child, there was a more than a probable chance that the heir he had longed for had been sired by another man. For all his success in business, Adgate knew he had been a fool in his private life.

Clarice came up and stood nervously beside him as the servant who had accompanied her back to the hall told

Simon he was wanted in the solar by Sir Richard and Lady Nicolaa. Adgate gave his wife not a glance or a spoken word, just followed the servant across the hall and up the tower stairs. Before he went into the chamber, he tried to square his shoulders and exude a degree of confidence. He had no other option now but to tell the truth; that he had not been aware of his wife's infidelity until the moment when he and Clarice had been told of the murder. Had it not been for his wife's tears and tender murmurings of the dead man's name when she heard the news, he would, even now, still be in ignorance of her unfaithfulness. Pushing aside the pain the memory caused him, he reflected that honesty had always been his guide in business; he must trust it would suffice now. If he was careful with a recounting of the facts, questions about any other entanglements he had with Tercel might not be asked.

When he walked into the solar, the circle of nobles daunted him for a moment and he checked his stride. After a moment's hesitation, he summoned up the courage to stand determinedly in front of them, and he kept his manner deferential as Richard Camville told him that his wife had admitted she had gone to keep a tryst with Tercel in an upper chamber of the old tower on the night he had been killed.

"She also told us, furrier," Richard added, "that she met with him on several previous occasions. Are you certain you had no suspicion of this liaison?"

"No, lord, I did not," Adgate said. "Not until the morning after he was killed."

"I find that hard to believe," Richard said bluntly.

"Nonetheless, lord, it is true," Adgate asserted.

"You will have to convince me of the validity of that

statement," Richard declared. "The man who made you a cuckold has been murdered; that gives you a prime motive for killing him."

Adgate recoiled against the accusation, but he held Richard's gaze firmly as he replied. "It was not I who murdered him, lord. From what I understand, Tercel was slain early in the evening. I never left the hall until I retired to the chamber my wife and I had been assigned by your steward. The other guild leaders I sat beside at the feast can confirm that."

"You could have paid someone to do the deed for you, Adgate," Richard replied. "Lincoln is no different than other towns; one can always find a man who is willing to carry out such a service if the fee is handsome enough."

Adgate did not lose his composure at the suggestion. "As I said, Sir Richard, I had no knowledge of my wife's infidelity. How then would I have reason to hire an assassin?"

Bascot admired the man's imperturbability, but he noticed that beads of sweat were forming on the furrier's brow. Evidence of tension was entirely understandable in Adgate's situation; to be accused of murder is not a matter to be taken lightly, whether guilty or not. Still, the Templar wondered if his agitation was due merely to the ordeal he was undergoing or if it stemmed from some other cause.

Richard continued his questioning. "We have only your word to support your claim that you were unaware of Mistress Adgate's unfaithfulness. And I find it hard to believe that you did not notice her attraction to Tercel during the times he came to your business premises. You are a successful merchant and therefore not, I would think, a man who is easily gulled. How is it that your wife was able to do so?"

"I fear I was too complaisant in my affection for her," Adgate replied tightly. "I was married before, and happily, to my first wife and remained so until she died. While I have experience in commerce, I have little in dealing with women, other than those who come with their husbands to buy my wares. Had I paid Clarice more attention, perhaps she would not have sought comfort elsewhere. Although my wife's actions were inexcusable, I must admit that I am perhaps partly to blame."

The words galled him, but he had to admit they contained a modicum of truth. He should have been more observant and noticed that his pretty young wife had an inclination for licentiousness. Then he could have made an effort to forestall her infidelity.

"Your answers are glib, furrier, and do not entirely satisfy me," Richard proclaimed. "Nonetheless, I will accept your protestation of innocence—for now. You may go, but hold yourself ready to be questioned further in this matter."

It was with great relief that Adgate turned and left the room.

After the furrier had exited the solar, Nicolaa, Richard, Alinor and Bascot discussed what they had been told.

"I think Mistress Adgate is now telling the truth," the Templar said, "but I am not so sure about her husband. Still, his testimony that he did not leave the hall is borne out by the others who were in his company, so unless he is lying about being unaware of his wife's adultery and did, in fact, hire an assassin—and I must admit I think that unlikely—we must look elsewhere for the murderer."

"But where?" Nicolaa responded. "Who else would have had reason to wish Tercel dead? He had only been in Lincoln a short time. . . ."

"But, even so, we must remember that he went quite often into the town," Bascot reminded her, "and had time enough to make the acquaintance of any number of people within the city walls. It could be one of these that led to his death—suppose he took another lover besides Mistress Adgate and the other woman became jealous at sharing his attentions with the furrier's wife, for example; or he struck up a friendship with a citizen in the town which became rancorous for some reason or another. There are many possibilities and the only way we can discover if any of them are worthwhile considering is to try and trace Tercel's movements since he came to Lincoln—where he went and to whom he spoke."

"Not an easy task, de Marins," Nicolaa said repressively.

Bascot agreed, but added, "The chore may be made a little lighter, lady, if your own servants and that of Lady Petronille were asked if he mentioned, even if only in passing, any of the places he went in the town; whether he was in the habit of visiting a certain alehouse, or had a favourite pie shop, for instance. Any small detail they can recall may assist us."

Nicolaa rose from her seat with a sigh. "You are right, de Marins. Every possibility must be pursued if we are to prevent this murderer from escaping retribution. Richard and I will question all of the servants again and let you know when you return tomorrow if anything of import has been uncovered."

As THE COMPANY ALL LEFT THE SOLAR, STEPHEN WHARTON, fifty miles to the southwest, had returned to his demesne and was preparing to travel to Lincoln. He did not look forward to the trip; it would take him the better part of two days and involve a stop overnight, probably at Grantham, but it was not the distance that was bothering him, it was what lay at the end of the journey. Richard de Humez had listened to his tale in near silence, the baron's irritation gaining momentum long before the story was told. Wharton hoped Nicolaa de la Haye would be more understanding, for he truly had not intended any harm by concealing the flight of fancy in which Tercel had engaged. Now, as one of the grooms brought out his horse, saddled and ready for him to mount, he wondered if he had been too credulous in his deceit.

Thirteen

❖

AT RISEHOLME, ALL OF THE CHILDREN, EVEN THE RELUCTANT Willi, marvelled at the comforts they were experiencing. The refurbished old barn was snug and secure, with lime-washed walls and a dirt floor that was clean and hard packed. A fire blazed in the middle of the large space, the smoke escaping through a hole in the newly thatched roof, and over the embers hung a huge cauldron filled to the brim with an appetising broth thickened with barley and root vegetables. Each child had a pallet stuffed with clean straw and, best of all, a blanket to cover them at night. Twice a day they were each given a cup of milk—a rarity that some of the children had never tasted before—and three small loaves of coarse bread to share. In their short and desperate lives, they had never before been so well fed or warm and each of them revelled in their good fortune. Even the youngest, little Annie, had stopped grizzling and her older sister, Emma, was beginning to blossom at being relieved of the little girl's demands. The other girl, Joan, although still maintaining her near silent demeanour, now accompanied her monosyllabic responses with a tremulous smile.

After they had first arrived, the bailiff, a stern-faced man who, despite his intimidating demeanour, spoke to them kindly, had shown them around the property and told them where they were allowed to roam and where they were not. All of the buildings—a small and sturdy stone-walled manor house, a newly built barn used for storing grain and root vegetables, a large byre with a dozen milch cows, an enclosure with a few pigs and a shed where cheese was made—were out of bounds for the present, he explained. Once they had become used to their surroundings, the boys would be expected to muck out the cowshed and pigsty and the girls to tend a vegetable plot at the rear of the main building. He also told them that, when the summer came, they would help to gather apples and plums from the fruit trees in a large orchard that abutted the inner compound and assist with gathering the harvest from the fields of wheat and barley to the south. But until then, he said, and while they put some "meat on their sparse bones," they would be expected to keep the barn in which they were living clean and tidy; their pallets were to be rolled up neatly every morning and the boys were to fetch fuel from the woodshed and tend the fire while the girls were to empty their slop bucket once a day and sweep the floor.

As the bailiff, a man named Stoddard, looked at the thin little faces of the youngsters, his heart swelled with pity. Lady Nicolaa had promised all of the Riseholme servants a bonus each Michaelmas for the extra work the children would cause but, even if that had not been so, Stoddard would have welcomed the chance to help these poor unfortunates and he knew the rest of the servants felt the same.

Now, on their third day at Riseholme, as the children rolled up their pallets and were looking forward to breaking their fast, Mark motioned to Willi to come a little aside and said, "It's a good place here, inn't it?"

Willi was forced to nod his head in agreement, and Mark, who felt he owed it to his new friend to dissuade him from a foolish course of action, said, "You knows as how you'd be a right silly beggar to leave and go back to Lincoln, don't you? We's got everything we needs here. Why go back there and be hungry and freezin' cold again?"

Willi set his mouth in a stubborn line. " 'Cos I'se got to go and find my da, that's why. How will he know where I am? Only orphans is allowed to come to this place and I ain't one, so he'll never think to look for me here, will he?"

"But what if that murderer sees you?" Mark asked. " 'Specially if your da ain't come back yet and you got no one to protect you. You could be killed stone dead like that man up on the ramparts."

"I'll have to take my chances," Willi replied stoutly, but despite his brave words, the young boy was fearful. The person he had seen near the tower had looked straight at him as their glances met and was sure to know him if their paths chanced to cross again. Mark was right; it would be more sensible to stay at Riseholme, but Willi was desperate to find his father who, if he had chanced to earn a few pence, might spend it in an alehouse if Willi was not there to dissuade him. His father had not always been a tosspot. They had lived in a village not far from Lincoln until last spring when Willi's mother had died of a fever. Up until then, his father had worked hard at his trade of thatching and they had a little cot to live in, provided by the high-ranking cleric who held the land in return for the fee of his father's labour for two days a week. But when Willi's mother died, his father had taken to drinking all his hard-earned pennies away in the village alehouse and had not turned up for work. When the cleric had threatened eviction if the terms of the fee were not met, Willi's father decided he would go to look for work in Lincoln, and so they had come to the town. But thatched roofs were not, due to the town's bylaw, in common use within the town and prospective employers had not been plentiful. On the few occasions that his father had been fortunate enough to earn a few pennies repairing thatch on small buildings such as barns or outhouses in the suburbs, the coins had been squandered in an alehouse before Willi could persuade his father to spend them on food and shelter. Finally, they had been reduced to begging in the street or lining up with other indigents for alms from the church. It had been then that his father had declared he would go back into the countryside to find work and told his son to wait in Lincoln for his return. Willi knew he had to be in the town when his father came back for him; if he was not, they might never see one another again. He would rather take the chance of being murdered than losing his da forever.

As the two boys parted company to attend to their chores, neither of them noticed that Joan, maintaining her usual silence, had crept up close to them and listened to their conversation.

IT WAS ALMOST MIDDAY WHEN STEPHEN WHARTON ARRIVED at Lincoln castle. His horse and that of the groom who had accompanied him were flecked with foam from the hard riding they had been put to that morning. After stopping overnight in the guesthouse of an abbey a few miles north of

Grantham, Wharton had decided they would start out before first light and the pair had spurred the horses hard for the remaining twenty-odd miles. Wharton was anxious to get his unpleasant errand done with.

After instructing his groom to tend to their mounts, he walked wearily up the steps of the keep's forebuilding and, upon entering the hall, asked the servant in attendance at the door to inform Lady Petronille that he wished to speak to her urgently.

A little over an hour later, while Richard and Bascot were ensconced in Gerard Camville's chamber discussing the paucity of information that had been obtained from re-interviewing all of the servants, there was a knock at the door and the Haye steward, Eudo, entered.

"Lady Nicolaa has sent me, Sir Richard," he said, "with a request that you and Sir Bascot attend to her in the solar. She told me to tell you that the matter is most urgent."

Fourteen

✦—✦—✦

W HEN RICHARD AND THE TEMPLAR ENTERED THE SOLAR THEY found Nicolaa, Petronille and Alinor seated at the far end of the room in the company of a man who was a stranger to both of them. He appeared to be of middle age and, by the sword he wore at his belt, was of knight's status. On his face was an expression of apprehension. A little behind Nicolaa's chair, Gianni sat unobtrusively on a stool, his wax tablet and stylus in his hand, glancing apprehensively at the company around him. The strained look on the countenances of the two sisters bore evidence of tension and Alinor's delicately arched brows were drawn down in a glower. In her hand, Nicolaa held an unrolled sheet of parchment.

"This is Stephen Wharton, a friend of my brother-by-marriage," Nicolaa said, introducing the man to her son and the Templar as they approached. "He is also the person, Richard, who recommended that your uncle Dickon give Aubrey Tercel a post in his retinue."

She paused for a moment as the men all nodded at one

another. Then, her voice taking on the determined note that
Bascot knew so well, continued, "Wharton has come to tell
us a very strange tale about the background of the murdered
man. While there is no proof of anything he will relate, the
important aspect is that Tercel believed it to be true and, in
so doing, may have given someone reason to wish him dead."

After Richard and Bascot had got over their surprise at
Nicolaa's words, they looked towards Wharton expectantly.
The knight took a nervous swallow of wine before he began
to recount his tale for a second time. Although neither
Nicolaa nor Petronille had evinced any censure of him for
keeping Tercel's fanciful conclusions a secret, Alinor had
been furious and still was. She, like her father, saw the re-
pression as a breach of trust and had accused Wharton of
placing her mother and herself in possible danger. As the
visitor looked at the two men facing him, he felt very nervous of their reaction to his story; would they, like Alinor,
find his actions irresponsible?

Taking a deep breath, Wharton began his recounting.
"When Aubrey was just a few weeks old, my younger
brother, Lionel, brought him to my manor house. Although
Lionel never confirmed it, I believed the boy to be my brother's illegitimate son. He asked me to keep privy the fact that
he had given the babe into my care, so together we con-
cocted a tale that the child was the posthumous offspring of
my falconer, Bran Tercel, who had taken a chill and died of
a congestion in the lungs a couple of months before. We said
that my falconer had told me on his deathbed that he had a
paramour in Stamford town who was enceinte with his child
and begged me to care for the babe after it was born. To explain the absence of the mother, we said that she had died
giving birth and her family had given their consent for the

boy to be placed in our care. It was a flimsy tale, but it was accepted, and no one questioned it during the years that Aubrey grew to manhood."

Wharton took another swallow of wine and, knowing the next part would be the hardest to relate, continued. "About the time that I recommended Aubrey be taken into Dickon's service, my brother had a fatal accident. While out on a hunt, Lionel's horse stumbled and fell, and in the tangle that ensued, landed on my brother with the full force of its weight, crushing his vital organs. He lived for only a couple of hours and died in extreme pain."

The knight looked up at the company; his eyes had darkened as he had spoken of his brother's death. "Since Lionel had never wed, it fell to me to go through the few possessions he kept at the dower property he inherited from our mother. Among them, I found a small package containing a letter that was addressed to me"—he gestured towards the parchment Nicolaa was holding—"and which I have brought with me. It was written some years before, about the time that Lionel left England to follow King Richard on crusade to the Holy Land. I think my brother penned it in case he should not return and, when he came safely back, forgot that it had been written, and left it lying in the chest where I found it. In the letter, among instructions for disposal of his property, there was mention of Aubrey. It said that although Lionel knew I had assumed the boy to be his bastard, this was not the case. It went on to say that Aubrey had been given into his care by someone 'to whom he owed a debt of loyalty' and that the reason he had allowed me to be misled as to the boy's parentage was to prevent the child's true heritage from becoming known. There was a ring enclosed with the papers that Lionel said would provide a small inheritance for Aubrey and was to be given to him if, and when, I deemed him worthy of receiving it."

"Was it a gold ring with an engraving on the inner side of a crescent moon encircling a star?" Richard asked.

"Yes, that's the one. After I read the letter, and had given much soul-searching thought to the matter, I showed the letter to Aubrey and gave him the ring. My main reason for doing so was that he should know his father had not been, as he had been led to believe, of common stock, but had most likely been a friend of my brother's and therefore a man of knight's rank."

"Did your brother name the father?" Bascot asked.

"No. He said in the letter that it was of no consequence; the lie had been told to protect Aubrey's mother. She had been a maid of Winchester, Lionel wrote, and a woman of good repute, who was the daughter of a merchant and promised in marriage to a burgess of Lincoln. Since her future husband could not be expected to accept her as a bride if he discovered she had borne a child sired by another man, it was decided to keep the matter secret and my brother was asked to take her to a convent where she could be immured until the birthing. After that event, he said, it had been requested of him that he find a good home for the babe, so the woman could go to her betrothal as though she were a virgo intacta. As far as I can tell, all went as planned. Lionel brought the child to me and the mother married the merchant. Since I had believed the boy to be my own kin, even though of bastard stock, I contrived to have him educated and cared for as best I could. It was a shock to learn, so many years later, that my reason for doing so was fallacious."

"Did your brother never ask after the child's progress?" Nicolaa asked.

"Lionel was seldom in England during the years after he left Aubrey with me. Lionheart gave him a small fief in Aquitaine and it was there that he spent most of his time, and where he died, the manner of it told to me in a missive sent by the priest who was his confessor. I sometimes received a letter from Lionel to let me know how he fared, but that is all. But his news dealt mostly with his own activities or, after Lionheart died, with the political situation across the Narrow Sea, and made no mention of the boy. I must admit, to my shame, that I gave little thought to Aubrey myself until I found the letter I have brought you. His tutor was one I had hired to school some of the children of my upper servants and I left him to the cleric's care, and that of my steward. On the rare occasions I spoke to him, he seemed a personable lad, and intelligent."

Richard leaned back in his chair. "As interesting as all this is, Wharton, I cannot see what connection it has to his murder."

"The tale, in itself, would have none," Wharton said. "It is what Aubrey made of it that has brought me here. I wish now that I had kept the secret hidden from him. He made much of the ring and the mention of Winchester in the letter, for around the date of his conception, which would have been during the month of April, 1176, the late King Richard, then a prince, was in the town at a meeting with his father, King Henry."

Wharton paused to allow everyone to cast their minds back to that year and remember how King Henry had, in response to the constant plotting of rebellion by his wife and recalcitrant sons, imprisoned his queen, Eleanor, at Salisbury in 1174. Although she had been kept in close confinement by her gaolers, her incarceration was not unduly harsh and, two years later, in 1176—the year of which Wharton was speaking—she had been taken to Winchester at Eastertide for a reconciliatory meeting between the son and his father. Prince Richard had been amenable to the conclave, for he hoped, with his mother's help, to persuade his father to give him assistance in controlling the rebellious nobles in his duchy of Aquitaine, a part of the territory Eleanor had inherited from her own father and which she had persuaded Henry to cede to their son a few years before.

Once assured that all of his listeners recalled the circumstances of which he was speaking, Wharton continued his tale. "Aubrey cobbled the information together in a most unlikely fashion. He said the coincidence of the prince being in Winchester at the time of his conception, coupled with the fact that my brother had been in his service, could lead to no other conclusion than that his father had been Lionheart himself. The ring, he said, confirmed this because it bore a design that was often used on his badge, both while he was a prince and when he later became king."

"A rather dramatic summation," Richard opined sceptically. "The ring could have belonged to any of the nobles in Lionheart's retinue. Even when a prince, he was known to be generous in rewarding his followers, and remained so after he took the throne. To give such a token would not have been unusual. And your brother's mention of loyalty could have meant that due to friendship with a fellow knight."

"That is exactly what I tried to explain to Aubrey," Wharton agreed eagerly, "but he would not listen. Although he was intelligent, he could be rather inflexible in his opinions."

Alinor gave a snort of derision. "You understate it, Wharton. Tercel was smug and self-opinionated." The knight looked abashed and made no comment in response.

"How long was your brother in Lionheart's service?" Richard asked.

"Almost three years," Wharton replied, "and had accompanied the prince to Winchester in 1176. I was surprised to see my brother when he turned up with Aubrey, for I had believed him to have returned to Aquitaine, but he said he had been sent to England with messages for Queen Eleanor and was due to return to his duties across the Narrow Sea, hence the urgent need for my help."

The knight leaned forward now, his reticence forgotten. "When I saw how Aubrey reacted to the information contained in Lionel's letter, I tried to dissuade him from his notion. I told him that his father was most likely another knight, like my brother, in Lionheart's service, one who was my brother's friend and had asked for his help, but Aubrey would have none of it. His father must have been the prince, he said, of that he was certain, and the only way he could prove it was to find the woman who had been his mother. When I taxed him with how he proposed to do that, he said he would go to Lincoln as soon as opportunity provided and seek her out. I thought he would have no chance to do so while in Dickon's service and would soon forget his ridiculous notion, but I did not foresee that Lady Petronille would subsequently decide to travel to Lincoln and that Aubrey would be included in her retinue."

"He practically begged my father to come with us," Alinor said angrily. "Now we know the reason why."

Richard shrugged. "Well, I cannot see what Tercel hoped to gain by proving the prince was his sire or how he would be considered a threat if he managed to do so. Lionheart acknowledged a couple of bastard sons, both of them in lands he held on the continent, but only one of them, Philip of

Cognac, benefitted by his acknowledgement, for he was given an heiress to wed. Even so, all Cognac received on the death of his father was one mark, which King John, in accordance with his brother's will, awarded him. Tercel could hardly have expected any financial reward."

"I think his interest was more in confirming that he was of royal blood than in the expectation of material gain," Wharton said. "He became obsessed with the idea and believed it would enhance his stature in society. That aim, even though self-serving, would have been innocent enough, but in order to achieve his goal, he would need . . ." Wharton, reluctant to speak aloud the implication, let his words trail off.

"To discover the identity of his mother and, in so doing, reveal the fact that she had borne an illegitimate child before her marriage," Bascot finished for him.

Nicolaa nodded in agreement as the Templar continued. "Whoever Tercel's father was, his mother has now been married—if she still lives—for twenty-six years, her shameful secret hidden from all the world. No matter whether her former lover was king, merchant or peasant, to have such knowledge bruited abroad would create a terrible scandal, one that would affect not only her, but those with whom she has since become closely connected, such as her husband and any legitimate children she has borne since her marriage. Such a revelation would be disastrous."

A silence fell over the company as they realised the import of Bascot's words, all of them reluctant to speak aloud the inescapable conclusion they led to. Filicide—to kill one's own child—was the most dreadful of crimes, and none of them wished to admit that such a thing could have happened within Lincoln's society.

It was Petronille who, as understanding came to her, broke the silence. Her voice trembling with disbelief, the words burst from her, "Surely you are not insinuating that his mother is responsible for Tercel's death? Such an evil is impossible to contemplate."

Wharton was abashed by her obvious distress. He had not wanted to speak of his fear in front of a woman still grieving for her recently dead son, but there had been no other recourse.

Nicolaa leaned forward and laid a hand on her sister's arm. "Please do not upset yourself, Petra. It may not have been the mother herself who committed the murder, but someone who wishes to protect her. A family member who was privy to her secret, perhaps, and did not wish to see her good name sullied, or even her husband who, for all we know, could have later discovered her transgression."

"Even so," Petronille said, her face ashen, "the mother would have to be complicit. I cannot believe there exists any woman who would willingly countenance such a terrible act."

"I agree, Petra; most women would not," Nicolaa said softly, "but not all females are imbued with a maternal instinct, as history tells us well enough. Did not Medea and Jocasta in Ancient Greece consent to the slaying of their offspring? And the women of Rome, in bygone days, allow unwanted babies to be left on the hillside to die of exposure?"

"But those were not Christian women," Petronille objected fiercely.

"Nonetheless, they were mothers," Nicolaa reminded her gently. "If we are to apprehend the murderer, we must give due consideration to every possible motive, no matter how distasteful."

A tear rolled down Petronille's cheek and she bowed her head. Finally, with some reluctance, she made a response. "I suppose you are right, sister. The devil lurks in the most unexpected of places. He can taint even a love that should be sacrosanct, that of a mother for her child."

Rising from her chair, she dashed the tears from her eyes, and then faced the others. "I do not think my continued presence here will be of assistance to the investigation," she said, her voice unsteady. "Indeed, at the moment, I think it would be detrimental. If you will excuse me, Nicolaa, I will go to the chapel and offer up prayers for the soul of my dead servant. Alinor may remain if she so wishes and, if there are any decisions to be made, can make them on my behalf."

Silently, Richard rose and accompanied his aunt to the door. Once Petronille had left the room, he returned to his seat, his face like a thundercloud. "I hope, for my aunt's sake, that the mother was not involved in the death but, if she was, I will do my utmost to see her punished to the fullest extent of the law."

Fifteen

⊷—⊷

AT RICHARD'S ANGRY PRONOUNCEMENT, WHARTON WAS CON-
trite. "Dickon was right. I should have told him of Aubrey's delusion. None of this would have happened if I had
done so."

"That is not necessarily so," Nicolaa said tartly. "If he was
as adamant as you say about finding his mother, it would not
have been long before he found a way to come to Lincoln and
look for her. And if that search was the cause of his murder,
then he would still be dead, whether he was Dickon's retainer
or not. If any blame can be attached to you, Wharton, it is for
telling him the contents of your brother's letter in the first
place. It would have been far better to have left him in ignorance, content with the fictitious mother and father you provided him with so many years ago."

It was unlike the castellan to express herself in such a
harsh manner. Bascot thought Petronille's distress had probably fuelled her angry words. Even though their natures
were diverse, the two sisters were close and, he surmised,

had been so ever since their mother had died when they were both quite young. None of the company made any response to Nicolaa's acerbic observation. Stephen Wharton, chastened, looked down into the depths of his wine cup in embarrassment and Alinor, for once, was silent, her lips compressed together as she nodded in agreement with her aunt.

Richard was the first to move. He leaned forward and replenished his mother's wine cup and Nicolaa, after taking a brief sip and setting her mouth in a determined line, said, "Tercel's quest would have been a monumental one. There are above seven thousand people in Lincoln, and over a third of them are women. If we are to consider only those of the correct age, that still leaves approximately a thousand who could be considered suitable."

She looked around the company. "That is a formidable number among which to search for a woman whose name and appearance are not known, and it is highly unlikely that my sister's servant—who was unfamiliar with Lincoln and had been here only a few weeks—would have been successful. I think we must ask ourselves if there is any merit in following this trail, or if it may prove to be merely a waste of time."

"I agree that Tercel's enquiries might have been futile, lady," Bascot said, "but there is always the chance that the very act of his asking questions about his mother may have stirred up alarm in someone who knew her identity. Even if he did not find her, his searching may have precipitated his murder."

Nicolaa regarded the Templar for a moment and then said, "You could be right, de Marins. But to try and trace his movements and see if we can discover, among the many people he must have spoken to, which conversation prompted his death, will surely prove impossible."

"Such a detailed search might not be necessary, lady," Bascot said, "if we limit the parameters within which we make it, and we can do that by taking into consideration why it was that he was killed here in the bail and, more specifically, on a night when you had a large number of guests in the hall. Unless it was to take advantage of the distraction your visitors provided, it must have been because this was the only occasion when the murderer was in close enough proximity to Tercel to slay him. Should that be so, we can exclude your retainers, and those of Lady Petronille. All of them are normally in the ward and could have killed him at any time during his stay in the castle. We are then left with the visitors who were here throughout that evening. Were there any females among the guests that are of the right age to be his mother?"

Nicolaa took a sip of her wine and mentally reviewed the women who had been in the hall on that night. "There were a dozen guild leaders in the company and, with the exception of Thomas Wickson, all were accompanied by their wives. Over the last few months, and through encouraging them to contribute to the foundling home, I have come to know all of them more familiarly than would be my normal custom. Discounting Clarice Adgate because of her youth, the other ten are all of mature years. Five of them, to my certain knowledge, have either been married to their spouses far too long to be considered a candidate, or are widows who have married for a second time but were wed to their first husbands some time before the date of Tercel's conception. Of the remaining five, two of these, during the course of conversation, told me they were born and bred in Lincoln, so they could not have come from Winchester. We are then left with three whose backgrounds I am not aware of—one is the wife of the head of the goldsmith's guild, the second that of the draper's and the last, the sealsmith's."

"Tercel's mother may have died in the interim since his birth," Bascot said. "But that does not mean that her husband, if he knew the secret, would not want to protect her memory and, in doing so, his own reputation. You mentioned that some of the guild leaders have been married twice—what of their first wives? Could any of them have come from the south of England?"

"A good point," Richard conceded. "Adgate was married before. He told me so when I was questioning him about his current wife's infidelity."

"And at least two of the others were, the guild leader of the wine merchants and the man who is head of the baker's league," Nicolaa confirmed, and then paused. She shook her head at the proliferation of daunting possibilities but, as the Templar had said, they had decided to investigate only a small number of people. Good fortune may be with them. She turned to Wharton. "Tercel was, according to you, Stephen, born in January of 1177?"

"That is so," the knight confirmed. "He was only a few weeks old when he was brought to me a few weeks after Christ's Mass exactly twenty-six years ago."

"Then we are looking for a marriage that must have taken place later in that year or possibly the one after. And for a bride that came from Winchester. But if I summon all of the likely candidates to the castle and the guilty party is among them, our questions about the date of their marriage and the place from whence the wife came will give alert to our suspicions."

"I agree, lady," Bascot said. "It is a task that must be undertaken very carefully and not in a confrontational manner."

"Ernulf may be able to help," Nicolaa said musingly. "He was born in Lincoln and knows most of the townsfolk. He also has a prodigious memory. It is quite possible he will know the details we seek."

Bascot nodded. "He has helped me before with his knowledge. I shall speak to him directly. If there are any of whom he is not certain, we can look more closely into their background."

Alinor now leaned forward with a suggestion of her own. "It might be helpful if one of us had another word with Mistress Adgate," she said. "It is possible that Tercel, during his trysts with her, may have asked about, or mentioned, Adgate's first wife, or one of the other women at the feast, especially if he was trying to garner information about a particular individual. If he did, it might point our way more quickly."

As the others considered her proposal, Alinor added, "I would be more than willing to interview her, Aunt, and . . ." She paused and gave her cousin a measuring glance. ". . . perhaps it might be just as well if Richard were present. The furrier's wife appears receptive to a handsome face and figure; mayhap his company will prove an aid to her memory."

Alinor's jocular remark lifted, if only by a fraction, the gloom that had spread over them all since the body had been found. Although the castellan's handsome son was to be wed in a few months time, Richard had long had the reputation of being a womanizer and, as his mother and cousin were only too well aware, was a consistently successful one.

"I agree with Alinor's suggestion, Mother," Richard proclaimed and then added with mock seriousness, "and, in the hope that my capabilities will fulfill her high expectations, will gladly give her any assistance she requires in her interview with Mistress Adgate."

"I am quite certain your charm will not fail me, Cousin," Alinor replied dryly, "for if she should prove impervious to it, she will be the first woman who has ever done so."

AFTER THE COMPANY LEFT TO PURSUE THEIR VARIOUS LINES OF enquiry and Stephen Wharton went to make arrangements for his return to Stamford the next day, Nicolaa was left alone in the solar. After a few moments' reflection, she sent a servant to summon her secretary and went to her private chamber to await his arrival. Pouring herself a cup of cider, she paced the length of the room with the goblet in her hand, pondering whether or not to apprise King John of the possibility that his deceased brother might have spawned another bastard son. John, since his coronation, had been plagued by the rebellious actions of a legitimate nephew, Arthur of Brittany, the posthumous son of another Plantagenet brother, Geoffrey. Many of the king's subjects felt that Arthur should have been given the crown instead of John, and the dissention had been a thorn in his side for some time, especially since Philip, the king of France, had espoused Arthur's cause and encouraged him to take up arms against his royal uncle. Only last year, Arthur had attempted to seize his grandmother, the widowed Queen Eleanor, from her castle at Mirabeau and, had John not ridden valiantly to his mother's rescue, would have held Eleanor as a hostage against his claim for the English crown. To advise the king that he may have had yet another close relative, albeit an illegitimate one, and that he had been murdered, might not be welcome news to John, but given the monarch's suspicious nature, may be the most advisable course of action.

Nicolaa had always been open and honest with the king and she knew that he had never doubted her loyalty. But her husband, Gerard, on the other hand, was not viewed in such a favourable light. Many years ago, while Lionheart was on the throne, Gerard had formed an alliance with John in an act of rebellion against the monarch but, once the brief insurgence was over, their reluctant friendship had turned rancorous. If she did not apprise John of this latest development and he heard of it from another source, it could be that he would view the matter as an aborted attempt at subversion by Gerard. She decided that candour, as it had always been, would be prudent, and when her secretary entered the chamber a few moments later, told him that she wished to dictate a letter that was to be despatched to the monarch at his castle in Falaise, Normandy, where Arthur was being held prisoner. After that, she told him, she would also compose one for him to send to Gerard in London. Just in case there were any repercussions from the king, it was best that her husband be forewarned.

Sixteen

✠

IN THE SCRIPTORIUM, IT WAS ALMOST TIME FOR THE EVENING meal by the time Gianni had finished transcribing the notes he had taken during the morning's discussion between Nicolaa and the others. He had one more task to finish before he could go down to the hall and partake of some food; that of copying out the relevant passages in the letter penned to Stephen Wharton by his brother. Since Wharton intended to begin his journey back to Stamford the next morning, the copying had to be done by the end of the day so that the letter could be returned to the knight before he left Lincoln. Lambert, the other clerk in the scriptorium, offered to bring Gianni some refreshment from the hall while he completed the task and the lad enthusiastically nodded his head. He had barely had time to snatch more than a crust of bread and a small chunk of cold meat at the midday meal and his stomach was growling with hunger.

Unrolling the long sheet of parchment, he read through the opening paragraphs detailing various bequests to ser-

vants and disposal of property until he found the portion
that dealt with Aubrey Tercel. Anchoring the letter on his
lectern with two small blocks of wood, he set to work. He
had already noted that the letter, even though in a scholarly
hand, was informally worded and guessed that, as Lionel
Wharton had been about to embark on crusade, he had dictated it in haste to a priest or cleric. The passage about Tercel had been taken down in a similar fashion; the sentences
overlong and often repetitive. When he came to the part
that dealt with the woman who had been his mother, it was
written in the same rambling manner and Gianni had to
stop and read it twice to ensure the meaning. After he had
finished, he laid aside his quill and pondered on the fact that
there was a slight ambiguity in the words.

When Lambert returned with a platter laden with a
bowl of rabbit pottage, half of a small loaf of oat bread and
two cups of ale, Gianni showed the relevant portion to him
and, through the sign language that Lambert had taken the
pains to learn so he and his young colleague could communicate, asked his opinion as to the precise meaning of
the passage.

Lambert laid the platter down and read through the
document as Gianni hungrily wolfed down the stew and
bread. When the older clerk had finished, he rubbed a finger
along his prominent jaw and said, "I see what you mean,
Gianni. The way this is written—'The woman who became
enceinte was in Winchester'—could mean that she lived in
the town, which is the way Stephen Wharton construed it
but, conversely, it might just as well signify that she merely
happened to be in the town at the time she lay with her
lover. It does not necessarily indicate that she resided there."

Lambert's dark eyes lit up with appreciation. "You have

done well to spot that, Gianni," he said. "I think it might be worthwhile to bring it to Lady Nicolaa's attention."

LATER THAT EVENING, SIMON AND CLARICE ADGATE SAT IN the furrier's hall, the meal they had been served hardly touched. Uppermost in Clarice's mind was the message that had been brought earlier that day by one of Nicolaa de la Haye's men-at-arms, requesting her presence at the castle early the next morning.

"I do not understand why they wish to speak to me again," she said to her husband anxiously. "I have told them all I know."

Simon did not seem to have heard her and Clarice regarded her husband from beneath lowered eyes. He had been this way ever since the morning they had learned of her lover's death. When they had gone into the hall to break their fast on that dreadful day, and one of the other merchants had told them that Aubrey's body had been found up on the ramparts, she had burst out crying and had been too grief-stricken to take particular note of Simon's reaction. But later, as he had led her to a seat and brought her a glass of wine, she had realised, to her horror, that he had guessed of her entanglement with Tercel, for he had bent over her as he had given her the wine and muttered tersely, "Try to comport yourself in a more discreet fashion, Clarice, otherwise it will be obvious to others, as well as myself, that you knew the dead man far better than was seemly." Ever since that moment, he had been engulfed by an air of preoccupation.

But even so, and while his manner had been scornful, he had not once castigated her for her adultery, not even after that dreadful interview with the castellan and her son when she had admitted the affair. Although he had tried to protect her when the one-eyed Templar had come to question her, he had rarely spoken to her directly since he had become aware of her infidelity. She could not understand why he did not voice his anger, for it was within his rights as her husband to beat her for her lecherous behaviour or, at the very least, take away the furs and costly gowns with which he had so generously provided her. She was grateful that, so far, he had not done so and fervently hoped it would remain that way.

As THE CASTLE HOUSEHOLD WAS PREPARING TO SETTLE DOWN for the night, the two female servants in Petronille's retinue, Margaret and Elise, were sitting at a small table in the hall, drinking a cup of camomile cordial before they went to help their respective mistresses disrobe for the night.

The pair did not normally seek out each other's company. Their ages were too far apart for easy companionship and Elise found Margaret's reserved demeanour repressive while the opposite was true for the sempstress, who considered Elise's lighthearted manner too bold. But since the murder, the two had been drawn together, partly because the servants in the Lincoln castle household had become a little reserved in their company, almost as though they would, by association, become tainted with the tragedy, but mainly because they served the two ladies peripherally involved in the drama.

"I understand from Lady Alinor that her mother became very distraught after a meeting with Stephen Wharton today, although she did not tell me the reason," Elise said to Margaret, hoping to find out what it was that had so upset Petronille.

"Yes, she was sore distressed," Margaret confirmed and

then, to the young maid's satisfaction, related how it was thought that Aubrey's mother might be responsible for his death. "I agree with milady," the sempstress proclaimed in a self-righteous manner. "It is inconceivable that a woman would kill her own child."

Elise was as shocked as Petronille at the suggestion, but her outspoken nature compelled her to add, "Well, somebody murdered him. And if it wasn't his mother, and the furrier doesn't seem to be guilty, who else could it be?"

Margaret shrugged, a delicate lifting of shoulders clad in a sober dark gown. "All of us who shared Aubrey's company during the last few months at Stamford were aware of his predilection for amorous involvements. It is quite conceivable that he had another paramour beside the furrier's wife, perhaps even a woman here in the castle household. If she had a lover who was enraged by Aubrey's trespass on the affection of a woman he claimed as his own, it is quite possible he murdered him out of jealousy. There are not many men who would ignore such an insult."

"You think it is a man, then, that did the killing? It is said that a woman could have fired the bow."

Margaret gave a dismissive shake of her head. "A woman would have killed the furrier's wife, not her lover. It must have been a man."

Elise considered her companion's pronouncement. "It could be that Mistress Adgate was the true target and Aubrey was killed by mistake."

The sempstress drew down the corners of her mouth in disagreement. "I think it unlikely, Elise, and that you would do well to hope it is not so."

Elise looked at Margaret in surprise. "Why should I do that?"

The sempstress glanced around to ensure they were not overheard and lowered her voice. "Because it would indicate that the murderess was driven to her crime, as you have just said, by hatred of the women her lover found attractive." At Elise's continued look of incomprehension, Margaret explained her reasoning. "I am well aware that Aubrey often looked at you with lustful speculation. If I noticed it, I am sure others will have done so. If, as you surmise, the murderer is a woman that is driven by jealousy and is taking vengeance on the women her lover found attractive, it could be that, even though he is dead—or perhaps especially because he is . . ."

"She will want to kill me as well," Elise finished fearfully and shivered. She looked around the hall, focussing her attention on the female servants going about the task of clearing the huge chamber after the evening meal. Some were piling soiled napery into baskets while others were dousing the candles on the board or removing the wooden platters that had been used to serve food. Most of them were young and one or two quite handsome in appearance. She was sure Aubrey's lecherous nature would have prompted him to make advances to them as he had done to her. While she herself had rebuffed him, it could easily be, as Margaret said, that one of them had been beguiled by his handsome appearance and succumbed to his charms.

"But Lady Nicolaa said she was sure that none of her household staff was involved in the murder," Elise protested, remembering with relief what she had been told by Alinor.

Margaret pressed her prim lips together. "Lady Nicolaa is undoubtedly a woman of good judgement, but even so, she is not infallible." Then, as she saw the effect her words had on her young companion, she leaned forward and placed a consoling hand on the girl's arm. "I did not mean to alarm you," she said softly, her face contrite and her voice full of concern. "As I said, there is a only a slim chance that it was a woman, and even less that she is one of those here in the castle. I am certain the murderer was a man and, if it was, you have nothing to be frightened of."

Elise nodded silently, but her stomach churned with alarm. Even though Margaret had assured her that her fears were groundless, it would be wise to be watchful.

In the candle manufactory, Merisel Wickson lay on the pallet in her bedchamber pondering on her mother's illness. Mistress Wickson did not appear to be recovering from the strange malady that had overcome her; even the apothecary was nonplussed as to its source. Merisel had gone to him twice now, each time giving a further description of her mother's ailment and, in the end, he had finally opined that she had been taken with one of the maladies that often plague women as they approach the end of their childbearing years, saying he could do no more than give her an additional dose of the elixir that helped her mother to rest.

But Merisel was not satisfied with his diagnosis. Her mother, although often indecisive, was not usually physically weak and it was most strange that she had, in the space of one day, succumbed to a mysterious illness that had left her enervated and in a fragile state of mind. Uppermost in Merisel's thoughts was that this sudden ailment had come upon her mother just after she had received a visit from her cousin, Simon Adgate, behind the closed door of the hall in their home.

Simon did not come often to their house and, to Merisel's

uncertain knowledge, her mother had never gone to his. The
rarity of the furrier's visits was due to an argument that had
taken place a few years earlier during what had begun as a
casual conversation between Adgate and her father, when
Simon had declared that the rights of the tallow candle-
maker's guild was equal to that of Wickson's, who fashioned
their product from beeswax. Her father had not been head of
his guild at the time, but he was very prideful, especially
where his business was concerned, and his insistence that the
superiority of his product should give his guild more privi-
leges than one that was, in his opinion, inferior in status,
had caused hard words between them and he and the furrier
had rarely spoken since.

It was due to this incident that on the infrequent occasions when Simon came to their home, he timed his visits to
occur when the chandler was engaged in his workshop so
that he could visit his cousin without her husband's company. Adgate had always spoken kindly to Merisel each time
she had seen him, asking after her health and well-being
and, by the solicitous manner in which he addressed her
mother, was made aware that he was very fond of her.

But on this last occasion of his calling, Merisel had been
coming down the passageway next to the chamber in which
they were ensconced and had noticed that the tone of their
voices, even though muffled by the closed door, had a tinge
of urgency about them. There had also been a thread of anxiety in the few words she had heard her mother speak. Merisel had paused for a moment and listened, not out of a desire
to eavesdrop but because she feared her mother was in distress. But the door was of thick oak and the sounds had been
muted. She had not been able to catch the gist of the conversation, only part of an odd sentence here and there, but she

was certain she had heard the name of Tercel mentioned, along with the words "threat" and "be careful." A few moments later, the door had opened and her mother and Adgate had come out. Both of them had seemed flustered when they saw Merisel standing outside the door, her mother gasping in surprise and asking her daughter, more tersely than was usual, what she was doing there. Merisel had held up the soiled apron she was on her way to replace with a freshly laundered one and, with an expression of relief, her mother had dismissed her. Simon, too, had seemed reassured by her explanation, and had given her a friendly nod as she continued on down the passage to the clothes hamper where a supply of clean linen was kept.

Now, Merisel pondered on that meeting between her mother and Adgate. At the time, she had put it from her mind as having no import. But when a customer, the day after the murder, had told Merisel and her father about it and she had later related the conversation to her mother while taking her some soup at midday, she had been disturbed by Mistress Wickson's reaction. Her mother, her cheeks suddenly bloodless, had turned her face to the wall, murmuring that she was tired and wanted to rest. When Merisel had asked her if she had known the man who had been killed, her mother's reply had been barely audible as she said, "No, no, I never met him. Please leave me now. I am too weak to talk anymore." From that moment, Mistress Wickson's illness had taken a downward turn.

It was because of her mother's denial that Merisel had lied to the Templar knight when he had asked if she knew of anyone that had made the acquaintance of or had any connection with the dead man. Whatever the reason for her mother's falsehood—if it was one—Merisel did not intend to be the cause of involving her ailing dam in a murder investigation. But even though she had no intention of revealing what she had heard, Merisel could not forbear from ruminating on the implications of her mother and Simon Adgate's exchange and the fact that it had been just after their meeting, and the mention of Tercel, that her mother had proclaimed she was ill and could not accompany her husband to the feast. There must be a connection between the two events.

It was not in Merisel's nature to allow such a mystery go unresolved, especially one that might have made her mother ill, but she feared that if she questioned her dam directly, it might cause her further upset. The only recourse was to go to Simon Adgate and ask him to explain what she had overheard and why her mother had denied knowledge of the murdered man when Merisel had heard her speak his name. But even though the furrier had seemed, on the few occasions she had met him, to have an amiable nature, would he be willing to discuss with her matters that he and her mother so obviously wished to keep private? Or would he, despite his seeming kindness, castigate her for prying into affairs that were none of her concern? Well, she thought, if she did not ask, she would never find out and, summoning up the resoluteness that was part of her character, decided to go and see him the very next day.

Seventeen

❦

As Bascot rode to the castle the next morning, he wondered if finding Tercel's mother might not prove an impossible task. The previous afternoon he had sat with Ernulf in the barracks and they had gone over the names on the list that Nicolaa de la Haye had given him. Ensconced in the serjeant's cubicle, and sharing a jack of ale, Ernulf was anxious to help. He still felt some guilt for his men not apprehending the murderer, or at least finding the corpse long before sunup, and was anxious to redeem himself. He listened carefully as Bascot told him the circumstances of the dead man's background and how his unidentified mother, or one of her relatives, might be responsible for his death. The Templar cautioned him that the whole matter must be kept privily lest the guilty party be alerted and then Ernulf, with a grim nod, had given consideration to each of the guild leaders.

Bascot was already aware of Ernulf's wide knowledge of the townsfolk and their backgrounds—it had been of use to the Templar on more than one occasion in the past—and now he found that the castellan had been correct in stating that Ernulf also had an excellent memory. Completely unconsciously, the serjeant recalled seemingly disparate facts by associating them with those that were important to him and, after a few moments' cogitation, had been able to immediately eliminate two of the guild leaders—a baker and a goldsmith—and their wives.

"The baker was married in the same year that Lady Nicolaa's father had the gatehouse repaired—'twas the year before my lord's death—and I recall how everyone was complaining that the baker's wares were suffering because of his distraction with his young bride," Ernulf said with a smile. "Not that he didn't get himself right after a week or two when his energy began to flag, but we had a good laugh about it at the time. But that was at least a year afore the time you are wantin', so his wife couldn't be the girl you are seeking and, besides, she was the daughter of another baker in the town, so I know she isn't from Winchester."

As far as the goldsmith was concerned, Ernulf shook his head in denial. "He's his wife's second husband. She was a widow when he married her about ten years ago, and he was unwed afore that."

"And his wife—do you know the date of her first marriage?"

"Must be nigh on thirty years ago. Her first husband was a goldsmith, too. Right parsimonious cowson he was, as well. I remember the first time I saw them both, when I was nobbut a young lad and had just been taken into service here in the castle. Some miscreant had broken into the goldsmith's manufactory a couple of weeks before and stole a load of his stock. When the thief wasn't caught right away, the goldsmith come hotfoot to the castle to complain to mi-lady's father that the town guard weren't doing their duty and he should be recompensed for his loss." Ernulf smiled at the memory. "He got short shrift from my lord. Sir Richard told him that if he was too miserly to pay for a good watch-man to guard his wares then he couldn't expect the town guard to do the job for him. The goldsmith's wife was with him when he came and a right snooty piece she was then, and still is, I reckon. I was in the hall when they arrived, taking some food with some of the other men-at-arms after comin' off a shift of night duty and she looked at all of us men-at-arms like we was pig dirt under her shoes. She couldn't be the one you're looking for—she was married to her first husband far too long ago."

Of the three remaining couples on Nicolaa's list, Ernulf, after some careful thought, was able to reject another two couples. The head of the wine merchant's guild, the serjeant was certain, had been married under the requisite number of years. "Wed his wife no more than twenty years ago," he finally declared. "I remember it right well 'cause the town guard had to be called out to deal with some guests that had become unruly at the marriage feast," Ernulf said with a knowing grin. "Seems the wine merchant had been a little too openhanded with his stores at the celebration and some of the bride's young relatives who had travelled to Lincoln for the ceremony—she hails from a town in the north—had become so cup-shotten they had to spend the night in the town gaol."

"And the head of the draper's guild?" Bascot had asked. This townsman was one of those whose first wife had died a few years before and had recently remarried. The Templar hoped that Ernulf's memory would stretch to a recall of the details of his first betrothal and, after some cogitation on the serjeant's part, was pleased to find that it did.

"Seems to me the draper's first wedding was around about the time of the terrible earthquake we had in 1185," Ernulf said, scratching his stubbly grey beard as an aid to concentration. "I can call to mind that the draper had to put off his marriage until the lintel over the porch of All Saint's—that's the church where he and his bride were to take their vows—was made safe for them to stand under." The serjeant nodded his head as the details slowly became clearer in his mind. "Yes, that's right. He wasn't the only one who had to delay his wedding; there were two or three others who had to put off the ceremony. Lady Nicolaa sent the castle stonemason to help with the repairs about the town and the mason told me the draper's father was right upset about the postponement." Here Ernulf gave Bascot a knowing wink and added, "Seems as though he was in a rush 'cause the belly of his son's bride-to-be was swelling up right fast and he was afeared his first grandchild would be born afore they got wed."

"And the bride, she was a local girl?" Bascot asked.

"Aye," Ernulf responded. "Daughter of a friend of the draper's mother."

Disappointed, Bascot went on to the last name on the list, that of a seal maker, John Sealsmith. But, in this instance, Ernulf, for the first time, could not be of help.

"He set up his business in Lincoln about a dozen years ago, as far as I can recall," the serjeant said. "He's a surly bastard and doesn't give away too much about his private business. I did hear he had been in Doncaster before that, but as to the year he got married or whether or not he and his wife originally came from our town, I've no knowledge."

Deciding he had no recourse but to visit the sealsmith

and question him personally, Bascot shared a final cup of ale with Ernulf and made his way back to the preceptory. After attending the evening services in the Templar chapel and sharing the light collation that constituted the evening meal with his brothers, he had gone to bed and ruminated on what he had learned, but it had been to no avail and he had spent a restless night. It was with relief that he had risen at dawn for the service of Matins and, as he knelt in the chapel, had asked God for guidance in solving this latest mystery. Now, as he rode across the bail, he hoped that the visit to the sealsmith would be worthwhile. If it was not, he would ask Gianni for the notes the lad had transcribed and go through them carefully to see if there was some detail that had been missed.

When he went into the castle keep, Bascot found Eudo, the Haye steward, waiting for him with a request from Nicolaa de la Haye that he join her in her private chamber before he went into town.

Upon entering the room, the Templar was surprised to see that Stephen Wharton was with the castellan. Gianni was seated at his usual place at the lectern in the corner.

"I had thought you would be on your way back to Stamford by now," Bascot said to Wharton. "It is well past first light."

"It is at my request that Stephen has delayed his departure," Nicolaa said. "Gianni noticed a passage in the letter Wharton received from his brother that lacks clarity and it indicates that we may be wrong in assuming Tercel's mother was from the town of Winchester. She may only have been a visitor there—perhaps passing through in the company of other travellers bound for one of the ports on the south coast, or for the purpose of a visit to relatives—and, if that is the

case, she could have come from anywhere in the kingdom."
She handed Bascot the copy Gianni had made of the relevant
portion of Lionel Wharton's letter.

"My brother was not literate," Wharton said when Bascot
had read it. "He would have dictated this to a clerk or priest
to pen for him and, because he could not read what had been
written, may not have noticed the ambiguity."

The Templar handed the piece of parchment back to
Nicolaa de la Haye, and spoke to Wharton. "At the time
your brother brought the babe to you, did he say anything
that might help to clarify the meaning of the wording?" he
asked.

The knight shook his head in negation. "No. As I explained, I assumed the babe was his, a by-blow conceived on
a favourite leman and that, for reasons he did not wish to
disclose, he had chosen not to leave the child in her care."

"And Tercel made no comment on this passage when he
read the letter?" Bascot asked.

"No, he did not, and nor did I," Wharton replied. The
knight rubbed a hand over his face in exasperation. "We
were both distracted by the content, not the detail. Aubrey's
concentration was focussed on the ring, citing it as proof of
his royal paternity, and I was engaged in trying to dissuade
him from his ridiculous notion. If your young clerk had not
noticed the uncertainty in that passage, I would never have
questioned my assumption that Aubrey's mother came from
Winchester."

Nicolaa turned to Bascot. "If she did not—and of that we
cannot be absolutely sure—then the enquiries you are making will be to no purpose."

"It is still possible that our first interpretation is the correct one, lady," Bascot responded, "so all may not yet be

lost." He spoke again to the Stamford knight. "Describe for us, if you will, the night your brother brought the babe to you. Can you remember exactly what he said?"

Wharton reflected for a moment. "It was in the month of March and Lionel came late in the evening, rushing into my manor house and the chamber where I was going over some of the household accounts. He told me that he had a great boon to ask of me. . . ."

"Was he carrying the babe himself?" Bascot asked.

The Stamford knight looked at the Templar in astonishment. "Well, no, of course not. He had left the child outside. . . ."

"With whom?" Bascot asked. "A servant on your staff?"

"No, the boy was in the care of a wet nurse. Lionel left her and the babe in the hall."

"And did you see this woman? Could she have been the mother?"

Wharton grimaced. "I saw her after I had agreed to Lionel's request and he called for her to bring Aubrey to my chamber. I cannot credit that she was the mother. She was admirably suited to nurse the babe, plump and with an ample bosom, but she was also past the first bloom of youth and, by her dress, of servant stock. I do not believe she could have been sought after in marriage by a Lincoln merchant."

"But it is conceivable that the mother could have handed the babe into the nurse's care, so she would have seen the woman who bore Tercel, even if she did not know her name."

"I suppose so, yes," Wharton admitted.

"Did your brother call the nurse by name?" Nicolaa asked. "Did you notice anything about her that might enable us to find her?"

"No. After she brought the babe to my chamber, I sent

for my wife, explained the situation to her and she took charge of Aubrey. The nurse left the room once the child was gone. I presume that Lionel, when he departed, took her with him."

"So we have no clue as to who she may be, either," Nicolaa said with dissatisfaction. "Are you certain your brother said nothing on that night that may help us gain a clearer meaning of the place where the mother lived?"

Wharton raised his shoulders in a gesture of apology. "Not that I can recall, lady, I am sorry."

In THE SOLAR, RICHARD AND ALINOR WERE SHARING A FLAGON of watered wine while they awaited the arrival of Clarice Adgate. They had both been told of the possibility that Tercel's mother might not have been, as had first been believed, a resident of Winchester and were discussing how to alter their questioning of the furrier's wife accordingly. About an hour after Terce, a servant came to tell them that Adgate and Clarice were below, in the hall.

"Send the wife up first," Richard instructed and then said to Alinor, "She was more forthcoming the last time when left without her husband's presence. Mayhap it will be so again."

Clarice came into the chamber with a similar attitude as before, her steps hesitant and a look of apprehension on her face. Richard smiled at her warmly and the girl responded with a lightening of her expression. Alinor chuckled inwardly at the effect her handsome cousin had on women and let him take the lead in the questioning.

"We appreciate the candour you showed the other day in telling us of your liaison with my aunt's cofferer, mistress,"

Richard said smoothly, "and, while we do not have any more questions about that side of your relationship with him, we would like to ask if you and he spoke together of any matters not related to your affection for each other."

Clarice looked at him in bewilderment. "What matters, lord?"

"Anything at all," Richard replied easily. "Did he mention the people he had become acquainted with while he had been in Lincoln, for instance, and ask you about their families?"

The furrier's wife frowned in concentration. "I do not think so," she answered nervously. "We spoke little of other people besides us two . . . ," she added, her fair skin blushing a deep shade of pink. "And if he did mention anyone, I am afraid I cannot now remember it."

Alinor, her impatient nature surging to the forefront, said brusquely, "Then give it more consideration, mistress! If a woman has so much passion for a man that she betrays her husband to be with him, then she hangs on his every word, and savours every tidbit of conversation he offers. Cast your mind back and try to recall if he mentioned anything about the places he had been in Lincoln or the names of any of the people he met."

Cowed by Alinor's stern tone, Clarice's lip trembled, and she made an effort to reply. "He did say he had visited the shops of other furriers in Lincoln but had found none whose stock compared with Simon's. And I remember that he once remarked on the excellence of the wine sold by the merchants in Lincoln." She looked at Alinor anxiously. "Is that what you wish to know, lady?"

Before his cousin could make a response, Richard interjected, "That is just the sort of information that we are seeking," he assured her. "Did he happen to tell you which furriers or wine merchants that he visited?"

Calmed by Richard's understanding tone, Clarice turned to him gratefully but, nonetheless, shook her head in regret. "No, but on one of the occasions he came to my husband's shop, Simon took him through to the hall to share a cup of wine. It was . . . it was the day before the feast. I think Aubrey may have had another commission from Lady Petronille to purchase more furs; at least that is what I assumed, for he had mentioned that his mistress had been well pleased with the ones he had purchased previously. He and Simon were in the hall quite a long time and it is possible that, while they were speaking together, Aubrey mentioned the names of the other furriers he had visited, perhaps in reference to a comparison of prices."

With a sigh of relief, Richard instructed a servant to bring Simon Adgate to the solar and, wishing to discuss privily what Clarice had told them, instructed her to wait for her husband's arrival at the far end of the room. As she moved out of earshot, Alinor said to Richard in an undertone, "What a witless jade. I cannot understand why Adgate married her."

Richard grinned. "There are other attributes that a man looks for in a wife, Cousin, besides intelligence. And you must admit that Mistress Clarice is very comely."

Alinor gave Richard a sidelong glance of exasperation and said, "Be that as it may, Richard, I am still suspicious of Adgate and agree with the Templar that he may not be telling the complete truth. Let us see what he has to say about this conversation he and Tercel had behind closed doors."

Eighteen

✠

"I AM CERTAIN ADGATE IS THE ONE WHO COMMITTED THE murder," Alinor exclaimed later that afternoon as she and Richard sat in the solar with Bascot and her aunt. "Richard and I first interviewed his wife alone, and then had Adgate join us. Beforehand, Clarice told us that her husband had spoken at some length with Tercel in private, in the hall of their home, and may have mentioned something about the people with whom her lover had become acquainted with in Lincoln. But when we summoned Adgate and asked him about the conversation, he said that, contrary to his wife's recollection, they had been closeted together for only a short space of time, just long enough to discuss the cost of a fur hat Tercel wished to purchase for himself. The price had been far too high, Adgate said, and the conversation a brief one of only a few moments duration. I saw the bemusement on Clarice's face when her husband said this. It was not the truth, I am sure of it. Adgate is lying, I know he is, and why else would a man do so unless he has something to hide?"

"It may not be the act of murder he is keeping secret, Alinor," Nicolaa admonished her niece patiently. "And, even if it were, you have no proof of your accusation. The other guild leaders whom Adgate sat alongside at the feast have already testified that he did not leave their company until it was time to retire, so he was overlooked for the whole time when the murder was committed. It is impossible that he is the one who carried it out."

"Even if he could not, I am still not as certain as you that he did not pay someone to do it for him," Alinor insisted. "Someone who was already within the bail. It could be one of your own servants, Aunt, maybe one of the men-at-arms who were on duty on the ramparts that night."

Nicolaa's response was reproving. "I think that is highly unlikely. None of my household servants have ever given me the slightest reason for distrust. The same is true of the men-at-arms. Besides, as we said before, that would imply that Adgate knew beforehand of his wife's intended assignation in order to arrange the matter, and I am reasonably confident he did not. While I am aware that Mistress Clarice is not possessed of a great intelligence, I doubt whether she is brainless enough to let slip to her husband beforehand the details of the meeting with her lover, so how could he have been aware of it? And aware of it Adgate would have to have been if he was to instruct a hired assassin to wait for Tercel outside the chamber where he and Clarice had their tryst. And why go to all the trouble that such a scheme would entail? It would have been far simpler for a hired killer to murder Tercel while he was abroad in the town—slip a knife in his ribs while he was in a crowd or lure him down a deserted byway and do the deed there. We have been through all this before, Alinor, and discounted Adgate as a suspect. I know you are anxious to put an end to this matter, but you will not do so by grasping at will-o'-the-wisps."

Alinor got up and paced a few steps. "Mayhap that is so, but I can sense Adgate's guilt, rolling off him like a storm cloud." She sat back down, frustration written all over her face.

Nicolaa turned to Bascot. "Did you have any success today in your interview with the seal maker, de Marins?"

"Not insofar as to consider either he or his wife as suspects, lady," the Templar replied. "As Ernulf thought might be the case, they came to Lincoln from Doncaster some twelve years ago, and had never lived here before that. In addition, Sealsmith's wife told me that she and her husband were wed only eighteen years ago, not long enough for us to consider her as a candidate for the mother. But questioning them was not entirely in vain. Mistress Sealsmith gave me some useful information which, although gossip, I am certain is true."

The Templar paused for a moment as he silently reviewed his visit to the sealsmith's manufactory. It was a moderately sized establishment, with living quarters above, and located on the same street as Simon Adgate's shop. Although Sealsmith was called a seal maker, it was actually the matrices, the implements impressed with a design on one end for marking hot wax, that Sealsmith manufactured. When a manservant admitted Bascot and Gianni into his workshop, the seal maker was busy at a small forge melting silver for the base of a matrix. He was a burly man of middle height with a thatch of thick black hair and heavy eyebrows that joined one another across the bridge of his nose. When Bascot's rank and name were announced by the servant, it was obvious that Sealsmith was reluctant to leave his task, for he greeted his visitor with a sullenness that was barely concealed. Upon being told that Bascot had come to ask both him and his wife some further questions about the night that Tercel had been killed, he had answered brusquely and with an air of impatience.

"We saw nothing that had 'owt to do with the murder," he said in a broad accent. "Just like we told Sir Richard at the time."

"Nonetheless," Bascot said sternly, "I still wish to speak to both you and your wife."

His ill temper still evident, the seal maker gave the task of overseeing the molten silver to one of his young apprentices and, stomping to a door set in the interior wall of the workshop, called loudly for a servant to fetch his wife.

Imogene Sealsmith was a rather dowdy woman of middle years, with small dark eyes and an upturned nose that gave her the look of an inquisitive bird. Far more amenable than her husband, it was she, rather than the seal maker, who responded to Bascot's questions, repeating the same answers she had given Richard Camville; that she and her husband had never made the acquaintance of the victim or noticed him during the feast. It was not until Sealsmith, distracted by a clumsy movement of the apprentice tending the forge, darted over to take charge of the small ladle full of molten silver, that Imogene was more forthcoming.

"'Tis true that neither my husband nor myself had ever spoken to the man that was killed," she said quietly, "but from what I have heard since his death, I think it might have been him that I saw arguing with Simon Adgate outside our gates the day before we went to the castle for the celebration." She paused and gave the Templar a glance of satisfaction when she saw she had gained his interest. "Was he a man with fair hair, personable looks and a swagger of self-importance?"

Judging her a woman with a love of indulging in salacious gossip, Bascot answered cautiously, keeping his own voice low so that her husband could not overhear. "There are many men who would fit that description, mistress. Perhaps I could judge better if you tell me why you think the person you saw may have been the murdered man."

With a disapproving sniff for his seeming doubt of her claim, the sealsmith's wife could not deny herself the enjoyment of relating her reason for making it. "All of us who live hereabouts knew that Clarice Adgate had taken a lover; she was seen leaving her home on several occasions when her husband was away from his shop, all dressed up in fine furs and without a maidservant or a basket for shopping or the like. And one of our neighbours saw her slipping into an alehouse in the town, one that has rooms above that can be rented for an hour or two, so we knew she was meeting someone she shouldn't. We had speculated on who her lover might be and when I saw Adgate arguing with that young man, I reckoned it was him that Clarice had been meeting and that the furrier was giving him a warning to leave his wife alone."

"Did you hear what was said between them?" Bascot asked, careful to hide his distaste for the relish she took in relating the tale.

Mistress Sealsmith shook her head regretfully and admitted she had not. "But I'm certain I'm right when I say he was Clarice's paramour," she insisted. "All of us who stayed in the castle overnight saw how she burst into tears when we were told of the murder and who it was that had been killed." She turned her birdlike eyes on Bascot with speculative glee. "And maybe I'm right again when I say it might have been Adgate who murdered him."

Now, to Nicolaa de la Haye and the others he told what Imogene Sealsmith had related. When he was finished, Alinor gave a smile of satisfaction. "It is as I suspected," she declared. "The furrier knew Tercel far better than he admits. I would wager Adgate knew of his wife's infidelity long before the night of the feast and it was he who arranged the death of her lover." She turned to Nicolaa. "You should summon the furrier to the castle, Aunt, and force him to tell you what he is hiding."

"Which may merely be that he was aware of his wife's adultery and did not want to admit it for fear we would suspect him of the murder," Nicolaa said wearily. "As I have said, the facts contradict his involvement in the death."

"Still, lady," Bascot said, "I think it would be worthwhile to try and find out more about Adgate." He turned to Richard. "I believe he told you that he was happily married to his first wife. If it was she who was Tercel's mother, then it could be that Adgate is trying to protect her memory, perhaps in collusion with a brother or other close male relative. If that is so, it could be the relative who, in fact, committed the murder."

Nicolaa considered the suggestion. "That is certainly a possibility. But if we question Adgate directly, he will be alerted to our interest, and his guilty partner, if there is one, will abscond before we can lay hands on him. We must find another way to obtain information about his first wife. If we begin to ask questions of those who live in his vicinity, our suspicions might reach his ears, so the only alternative is to search for details of their marriage in the parish records. But without knowing in which church the nuptials took place, it will be a tiresome task."

"I think, lady, that there might be an easier way," Bascot said. "And I know just the person who may be able to smooth the path."

LATE THAT EVENING, NICOLAA AND HER SISTER WERE IN THE castellan's bedchamber, preparing to retire. They had removed their outer clothing and, after donning furred bedgowns, were sitting in front of a glowing brazier enjoying a posset of heated wine mixed with camomile flowers to aid their sleep. Lest she upset her sister, the castellan had responded guardedly to Petronille's enquiry about how the murder investigation was progressing.

Petronille heard her sister out in silence and then sighed. "So, it remains uncertain who killed my poor servant, or the motive for doing so," she said and then, raising tired eyes to Nicolaa, added, "I am sorry I was so intractable the other day. I fear I allowed my grief for Baldwin to cloud my thinking."

"That is understandable, Petra," Nicolaa said quietly. She cursed the fact that this tragedy was upsetting her sister; Petronille had seemed to be recovering her spirits a little before Tercel was killed. Now, the unsavoury implications surrounding his death had prompted a resurgence of her grief.

"I have come to the conclusion that it might be beneficial for both of us to spend a short time away from this terrible business," she said, having earlier decided that a few hours away from the castle while Bascot tried to find out more about Adgate's first wife would cause no delay in the investigation. "And, to that end, have arranged that tomorrow we shall go to Riseholme and see how the foundlings are faring. My bailiff has given me good reports of their progress, but I owe it to the guild members who donated funds to give my personal attention to the children's welfare. The weather has warmed a little and is not too inclement. If we wrap up well, the air out in the countryside may prove a bracing tonic for both of us."

Petronille's face lit up. She had been enthusiastic about the foundling home and perhaps, Nicolaa thought privately, seeing firm evidence that five young lives had been saved from dire poverty might divert her sister's attention from thoughts of death.

Leaving their empty cups on a small table for collection by a maidservant in the morning, the two sisters climbed into the huge bed they were sharing. As Nicolaa laid her head on her pillow, Petronille said drowsily, "You know, I have been thinking much about Tercel and how he was when he entered our service. The first thing that struck me about him was that I had seen him before but, of course, I could not have done, for he had never left Wharton's demesne before he joined our retinue. Yet, since his death, the impression has returned more strongly. If his mother was from Lincoln, and her son resembled her, perhaps I might have met her in her youth, before I married Dickon and went to live in Stamford."

"It is almost certain she was of merchant class, Petra, and it is unlikely you would have done so."

"I know," Petronille replied. "But I cannot rid myself of the notion. It is most distressing. . . ."

As her sister's voice drifted off into sleep, Nicolaa once

again regretted that Petronille had been exposed to the terrible crime. She hoped the visit to Riseholme would lift her spirits. If it did not, as much as she valued her sister's company, she would urge her to return home before her planned departure at Eastertide.

Nineteen

✦╌✦

VERY EARLY THE NEXT MORNING, WILLI LAY AWAKE IN THE foundling home, staring up at the smoke hole in the ceiling. He had decided that this would be the day he would leave Riseholme and go back to Lincoln to try and find his father. He thought it would be best to go just before dawn so that he could steal away from the property in darkness and would have only a short time to wait before it would be light enough for him to find his way to Lincoln. There was only one problem with his scheme and that was the difficulty of judging the time. The small square opening above his head showed that it was still dark, but he had dozed somewhat after he had gone to bed at nightfall and could not tell how many hours remained until first light.

He looked toward the fire in the middle of the barn. It had been banked down the night before and was now just glowing embers. Alongside him the other children slept, Mark on the pallet next to this one and the girls beyond that. Over by the far wall the manservant that stayed with them every night was snoring loudly. Willi decided he would have to leave now, even though there might still be some hours until it was light. It might be necessary to wait in the greenwood until the darkness receded but it was better than leaving it too late and take the chance of someone seeing him. He had secreted a little food in his tunic over the last couple of days and his plan was to creep out of the small door at the far end of the barn and make his way quickly into the forest that lined the track leading from Riseholme to Ermine Street. The cover of the trees extended all the way to Lincoln; once within their shelter he could walk parallel to the main thoroughfare for the three miles to the town and enter Lincoln through Newport Arch, which was always opened early. If he could hide amongst the crowd of traders and other travellers that sought entry into the town every day, he would escape the notice of the gate wardens.

He turned slightly on his pallet and looked at Mark. The other boy was awake and his eyes gleamed in the small light from the fire. Willi had told his friend of his intentions yesterday and Mark had agreed to cover for his absence as much as he could by saying Willi was in the outside latrine or had gone to the kitchen, so as to delay the inevitable search that would be made. With a nod towards Mark, Willi rose from his pallet and carefully rolled up the rough woollen blanket that had covered him. It was still very cold outside; he would need the blanket to keep him warm.

Making as little noise as possible, he tiptoed across the open expanse of the barn, holding his breath and praying he would not be heard. With trembling fingers he lifted the wooden bar that secured the entrance and heaved a sigh of relief when it rose without a sound. The door had leather hinges that had been well oiled and it, too, silently slid open

wide enough for him to squeeze through. Carefully, he
pushed it shut behind him and looked around the yard. The
almost-full moon gave enough light for him to see his way
to the fence that surrounded the property. All was quiet.
There were a couple of dogs near to the building where the
servants lived, but they knew his scent and were not likely
to bark. With stealthy steps he crossed the yard. One of the
pigs in the sty grunted, but there was no sound from the
other animals—not the cows in their shed or the chickens in
the coop. A sudden shape loomed out of the darkness and he
jumped in alarm, but it was only one of the nanny goats,
staring at him with her protuberant eyes as her jaw moved
sideways in a chewing motion, making the tuft of hair on
her chin waggle. She continued to gaze after him as he ran
across the yard and climbed the fence. A few more steps and
he was across the track and into the cover of the greenwood.
Breathing a sigh of relief, he hoisted the rolled blanket onto
his shoulder and began to trudge his way through the deep
pile of leaves that had fallen to the ground the previous winter, heading for Lincoln.

NICOLAA AND PETRONILLE STARTED OUT ON THEIR JOURNEY
to Riseholme as soon as they had broken their fast. Hugh
Bruet, the knight who had accompanied Petronille to Lincoln, led the escort along with Ernulf and two men-at-arms
from the castle garrison. Bruet was pleased to be away from
the castle, for it alleviated the twinge of conscience he had
been suffering since the murder and dimmed his memory of
a minor happening that had caused him to wonder about its
import. He did not believe that what he had seen and heard
had anything to do with the death but, even so, he wondered

if he should have told Richard Camville about it. But to do so might bring another into disrepute, and cast aspersions where none were warranted. He was glad to be going to Riseholme; it would provide him with a brief reprieve from his dilemma. A ride in the brisk morning air might clear his thoughts.

Unaware of Bruet's concerns, Nicolaa and Petronille had mounted their palfreys and set off with a lightness of heart induced by a sense of revisiting the days of their youth. As adolescent girls they, along with their younger sister, Ermingard, had often accompanied their father on the trips he had made to inspect one or another of his properties. They had always looked forward to these excursions and the chance it gave them to ride out into the open countryside and away from the confines of the castle. And today they were reminded of the pleasure those trips had brought, for the cold snap had broken and a beneficent early spring sun was shining its warmth on their faces, just as it had then. As they rode, they chatted comfortably with one another. Although it was only a short distance to their destination, they passed a few fields being readied for the plough and once, through a gap in the forest, saw some newly born lambs gambolling beside their mothers. By the time they reached the turnoff that led to Riseholme, Nicolaa was pleased to see that her sister's cheeks had turned a rosy hue and a smile curved her mouth. It had been many weeks since Petronille had looked so happy.

As the party cantered along the turnoff to Riseholme, the castellan was surprised to see her bailiff and two or three servants searching among the bushes on the far side of the road. When the bailiff saw his mistress' party approaching, he quickly doffed the soft cap he was wearing and came to meet them.

"What is wrong, Stoddard?" Nicolaa enquired. "Have some of the animals got loose?"

The bailiff flushed a bright red. "No, lady, one of the children, a boy named Willi, is gone. We didn't notice his absence until we were all gathered to go to Mass in the village chapel. We are trying to find him."

"Gone?" Nicolaa exclaimed. "Do you mean he has run away?"

"It appears so, lady," Stoddard said with some embarrassment. "The boy was here last evening when all of the children went to sleep. He must have left sometime during the night, but the servant who was assigned to watch over the waifs didn't hear him go."

Turning to their escort, Nicolaa directed Bruet and Ernulf to take the men-at-arms and search the woods for the boy and then, urging her mount into a trot towards the gate into her property, spoke sharply to the bailiff. "I would have speech with this servant, Stoddard. It seems he has been remiss in his duties."

When Nicolaa, with Petronille following behind, entered the yard, the other children were standing huddled together in a group, the cook and a kitchen maid hovering alongside them. The unfortunate manservant who had slept in the barn was just emerging from searching the shed where the cheeses were kept and, when he saw Nicolaa, his face blanched and he quickly ran forward and fell to his knees. "I am sorry, lady. I should have been more vigilant, I know, but I didn't think as how any of the little ones would want to run away from where they were so well treated. He must have crept out while I was sleeping."

Nicolaa considered his words. She was a fair mistress and not given to harsh punishment, but all of her servants knew that if any of them proved to be lazy or disobedient, they could not expect a second chance, but would be dismissed from their posts without hesitation.

"Had you punished the boy for any reason?" she asked harshly.

"No, lady, there's been no need," the servant assured her and Stoddard, with a nod, confirmed his words.

"All of the children have been as quiet as mice since they came," the bailiff said. "We all thought as how they were happy here. I don't know what made Willi run away, but one thing I can promise you, it wasn't because he was abused."

Nicolaa gave a short nod. She had no cause to disbelieve Stoddard. He had managed the property for some years, as had his father before him. She looked toward the rest of the children. All of their faces were etched with fear and the smallest one was clinging to the cook's skirt and starting to cry.

"I will question the rest of the children and see if they know anything about this boy's disappearance," Nicolaa said to Stoddard as she dismounted from her palfrey. "Bring them inside the manor house. I will speak to them there, but first I wish you to attend me."

Nicolaa walked quickly into the building, calling for two cups and a flagon of cider to be brought into the small room that served as a hall. A manservant ran forward and placed two chairs in front of an unlit fireplace and then struck flint and tinder to some dried moss to set the logs burning. Although the chamber was unused by the servants, it was kept in readiness in case Nicolaa should visit. Now, a maidservant hurried to bring two pewter cups which she placed on a small table alongside a flagon of cider. At a nod from her mistress, she poured the fragrant drink into the cups and, sketching a bow of deference, served them to Nicolaa and Petronille.

The bailiff, who had been standing by the door, came forward at a gesture from his mistress, his cap in his hand.

"What did you observe about the boy that is gone?" she asked. "Did he seem discontent, or was he disobedient?"

"He appeared happy enough, lady," the bailiff assured her. "Tucked into the food right well and did the few chores assigned to him with a willing heart. I didn't notice anything amiss. If I had of done, I'd have taken him to task about it."

"And the other children—were they aware he was planning to run away?"

"They say not, lady, but Willi took a blanket with him when he went and now they seem to fear they will all be sent back to the streets of Lincoln because of the theft. It might be that fright is stopping up their tongues."

"Then they must be assured their situation will not change," Nicolaa replied. "Bring them in and I shall speak to them."

The bailiff turned to go but, before he went to do her bidding, he added, "Willi was friendly with one of the other children, a lad named Mark. It is possible he may have told him of his intention to leave and the reason for it."

"I will bear that in mind," Nicolaa assured him.

The children were shepherded in by the cook, with the little girl, Annie, still clinging to her skirt. When they were arrayed in front of her, the castellan said, "First of all, I want you all to know that none of you will be sent back to Lincoln. Even though we are concerned that Willi ran away, he was not a prisoner here and neither are the rest of you. If you wish to leave you will be allowed to do so, but if you want to stay then, providing you obey the rules that have been laid down for your conduct, you have a home here until you are old enough to fend for yourselves."

Relief was etched on the faces of the two older children, Mark and Emma, and the latter placed her arms around her little sister and said, "See, I told you, Annie. We won't be made to leave just 'cause Willi stole that blanket."

Annie hiccupped and looked up at the cook who gave her a reassuring pat on the head. Joan, in her usual non-committal way, said nothing.

"Now," Nicolaa continued, looking directly at Mark, "if any of you know why Willi left, or where he intended to go, I want you to tell me. Even though the weather is warmer, it is still too cold to be out in the woods alone. And if he should meet with a wild animal in the woods, he may be in danger of serious injury."

A silence followed her words. Mark stood with his lips pressed together and Emma shook her head. Annie, because of her tender years, was confused and looked at her sister in puzzlement, while Joan began to fiddle with the hem of her kirtle.

"Very well," Nicolaa said. "If none of you can help me, you may go with cook and break your fast. Since you missed Mass this morning, you will say two paternosters before you eat. . . ."

"He went to find his da," Joan suddenly burst out. "And he's going to be killed by the murderer."

Stoddard, who was standing by Nicolaa's chair, was the first to react to the astonishing statement. "What nonsense is this, Joan? Willi doesn't have a father; he's an orphan like the rest of you. And as for being killed . . ."

"He does so have a da," Joan burst out, her torrent of

words startling after she had been almost silent for so long. "*And* he saw the murderer, too, the one who killed that man in the castle."

"Joan, you must not tell lies. . . ." Stoddard began impatiently, but Nicolaa held up her hand.

"How do you know this Joan?" she said quietly.

"I heard him tell Mark," the girl said triumphantly.

Twenty

+†+

ANOTHER SILENCE FELL AS EVERYONE LOOKED AT MARK. THE boy was glaring at Joan, his small fists clenched at his sides. It was obvious the girl was telling the truth. Nicolaa, raising her hand, motioned to the bailiff.

"Stoddard, take all of the children except Mark to the kitchen and have the cook attend their needs."

As the bailiff and the other orphans left the room, young Mark stood forlorn in front of the two women, his hands now clasped in front of him and near to tears.

Nicolaa spoke gently. "Mark, what do you know of Willi's disappearance and this tale that he saw the man who committed the murder?"

The boy raised his head, his mouth trembling. "I gave my promise that I would not tell," he said, with an attempt at bravery.

"And you did not," Nicolaa assured him. "Joan did. But now that the secret is out, for Willi's own safety, you must tell us all you know."

"Willi does have a da," Mark said quietly, despair in his voice, "but he's been gone for a long time and Willi was hungry. When he went to get alms at St. Peter's, and the priest asked him if he had anyone to look after him, he lied, but it was only so's he could get some food. But when we was sent here, he was worried that when his da came back, he wouldn't be able to find him, so Willi decided to go back into town and look for him." The boy raised his fearful face to Nicolaa. "He only lied 'cause he was starvin', lady, he didn't mean no harm."

"Very well, Mark," Nicolaa said, "we shall let that pass for now. What of this claim that he made about seeing the murderer?"

The boy hesitated and the tears he had so far managed to stem spilled down his face. Petronille, her kind heart full of sympathy, recalled her own dead son. Baldwin had not been much older than this boy when he had died and, due to his illness, was almost as thin. She reached out a hand and said to Mark, "Come here, child, and stand beside me."

With stumbling steps Mark went to the chair where she was seated. She took his hand in hers and pressed it gently. Her skin was soft and a faint perfume of spring flowers rose from her clothes. "Do not be fearful," she said to him softly. "Neither you nor Willi are going to be punished. But you must tell my sister exactly what Willi said, for that is the only way we can protect him."

Reassured by her compassionate manner, Mark haltingly told Nicolaa what Willi had claimed. "It was the night we wus all taken to the castle, just after we'd been in that big room where all the townsfolk was sittin', and we wus being taken to the stables to sleep," he explained. "As we wus goin' across the ward, Willi said he saw someone lurkin' around that big old tower near the gate. The next day, after we heard that a man had been shot by a crossbow up at the top of the tower, Willi said he had seen the man what done it."

"He said it was a man and not a woman?" Nicolaa interrupted.

Mark screwed up his face in concentration as he thought back over what Willi had told him. He couldn't remember if Willi had said it was a man; Mark might have just assumed that it was. "I think so, but I'm not sure," he said honestly.

"Did he see the man's face?" Nicolaa asked.

"I don't know, lady," Mark replied earnestly. "He wouldn't tell me much 'cause he thought I might tell on him, even though I swore I wouldn't. But I warned him that if the killer had seen Willi lookin' at him, he might find him out if he went back to Lincoln and murder him, too." Mark looked at Nicolaa fearfully. "And I'se right, isn't I, lady? Will you be able to save him?"

"I shall do my best, Mark," Nicolaa assured him. She rose from her chair and spoke to Petronille, her expression grave. "If Ernulf and the men-at-arms do not find the boy in the greenwood, we must return to Lincoln at once and organise a search for him."

As BRUET, ERNULF AND THE MEN-AT-ARMS WERE RETURNING to the Riseholme manor house after a fruitless search in the woods, Bascot and Gianni were entering the shop of the barber-surgeon, Gildas. The rotund little barber came forward with a beaming countenance when he saw them and, as before, greeted the Templar warmly.

"Sir Bascot," he said in jovial tones. "I did not expect to see you again so soon. Have you found the murderer yet?"

"No, unfortunately, we have not," Bascot replied. "It is on a different matter that I have come and one that I would like to discuss with you in confidence. Do you have a private room where we can speak without your customers overhearing?"

The little barber's chest swelled out with importance as he replied, "Of course, Sir Bascot. If it please you, there is a room in the back where we may speak privily."

Gildas led Bascot and Gianni to a small chamber lined with shelves laden with pliers, razors and piles of clean cloths. There was only one chair in the room, and Gildas bowed the Templar to it and perched on a small stool nearby. Gianni stood at the door, blocking the passage of any who should inadvertently try to enter.

Bascot phrased his next words carefully. He did not want to alert Gildas to the true nature of his enquiry but, at the same time, it was most important that he extract the information he sought. With a tinge of guilt for deceiving the cheerful little man in front of him, he said, "I wish to speak to you about Simon Adgate, Gildas. Have you ever made his acquaintance?"

"Yes, I have," the barber confirmed. "I have attended him as his barber-surgeon for many years."

The Templar had not expected such good fortune, but had merely hoped that since Adgate and Gildas were near to each other in age, the barber might recall the furrier from the days of their youth, and remember the details of his first marriage. His hope rising, Bascot continued the conversation carefully. "I am sure you are aware that Adgate's young wife was most distressed at being in the castle on the night of the murder."

Gildas gave a nod of agreement, the jowls on his fat face wobbling slightly as he did so. "Yes, we all heard of how upset she was," he said, and then added disapprovingly, "And there were some who claimed she was more friendly with the dead man than she should have been. Such malicious gossip should not be given any credence, and so I have told all those who have repeated it to me."

The Templar believed him. Although Gildas, with his gregarious nature, liked to prattle of the mundane events that occurred from day to day, he was not a spiteful man and Bascot knew he would frown on those who repeated any rumour that cast unfounded aspersions on the reputation of another.

"Just so," Bascot agreed. "And it is because of these tales that I do not wish to go to Master Adgate and ask him my questions directly. This murder has already given him enough upset and I do not wish to discommode him further."

The Templar paused for a moment to ensure Gildas was amenable to respecting the implied confidentiality and, when the barber gave a sympathetic smile, went on. "There is a need to find out some information concerning Adgate's first wife who, I understand, died some years ago. Lady Nicolaa has had the suggestion made to her that the former Mistress Adgate may have been related to Aubrey Tercel. If this is true, then it would be most distressing for the furrier to discover that, in addition to the unkind tales about his present wife, he could also be related, albeit by marriage, to the murdered man. That is why I have come to you. The castellan has asked me to try and find out the truth in a discreet manner, if I can, and I thought that, as a long-standing citizen of Lincoln, and one who meets many of the townsfolk through your trade, you might be able to give me the information we seek. Do you happen to know the name of Adgate's first wife, or the town from whence she came?"

Mention of the possibility that he might be of practical help to the castellan made the barber straighten up in his chair. Nicolaa de la Haye was held in high repute by the townspeople of Lincoln and the Templar had been sure Gildas would be eager to assist her. "Yes, yes, Sir Bascot, indeed I can help you, for not only has Simon been my customer for many years, but has been my friend since our youth. His first wife's name was Martha. Both my own wife and I knew her well. But I do not think the dead man could have been related to her. Tercel was from Stamford, was he not?"

When the Templar confirmed the statement, Gildas went on. "Martha came from Hull; she was the daughter of a tawyer in that town. Simon married her about twenty years ago, soon after he met her when he went to the port to oversee the delivery of some furs from Scandinavia. He had commissioned her father to preserve some of the furs so they could be safely sent to Lincoln before deterioration set in and when Simon went to his shop to inspect the completion of the work, Martha was there and my friend was smitten. It wasn't many months later that they married and they were very happy until, sadly, just two years later, the poor woman was taken ill with an abscess in her breast and died. But while she was alive, she often spoke to my wife and myself of her family and, as far as I can recall, they were all from Yorkshire. I do not think it likely she was related to the murdered man; I am sure she would have mentioned it if she had any relatives in a town so close to Lincoln."

Chagrin surged through Bascot. Adgate's marriage had

taken place too long after the time of Tercel's birth to make it likely that his first wife had been the cofferer's mother and, even had that not been the case, to investigate further and try to discover whether a woman from the distant town of Hull had travelled to Winchester so many years ago would be nigh on impossible.

Nonetheless, Bascot thanked the barber for his time and, as he prepared to leave, said, "It is just as well I spoke to you, Gildas, and not to Master Adgate. To have involved his dead wife's name in such a grisly business may well have brought him further grief, and I know I can trust you to keep the matter in confidence from him."

The barber rose from his stool, his countenance full of gratification as Bascot added, "I shall tell Lady Nicolaa of your cooperation. I know she will be most appreciative."

ONCE THEY WERE OUT ON THE STREET, THE TEMPLAR DECIDED, as a last resort, to go and speak again to Hacher, the barber Tercel had visited just before he was murdered. "I do not expect a further questioning of Hacher will be useful," he said to Gianni, "but there is always the possibility that he may have remembered something pertinent since we last spoke to him. If he does not, I fear this investigation has come to a standstill."

Hacher's shop, when they walked in, was busy. Two customers were waiting on stools near the door, the assistant was trimming the beard of a man seated on a high-backed chair, and Hacher was just finishing the treatment of a man with toothache. As the barber doused the lit candle he had been holding near the customer's aching molar in an effort to draw out the worms believed to cause the pain, he saw the Templar and nodded, saying he would be with his visitor in just a moment. Hacher then handed a small bottle of oil of cloves to the customer, whose face was a picture of misery, telling him to apply the oil to his gums overnight and return the following morning. Bascot winced at the sight. One of his own back teeth ached at times, especially after he had eaten a *candi*. He felt a great degree of empathy for the customer.

"If the ache persists, I will draw the tooth," Hacher said. "And then cup a little blood to balance the humours in your body. If you wish, I have some tincture of poppy to help you sleep."

The customer mumbled that he didn't need it for he had pledged an offering to St. Apollonia, the patron saint of those suffering from toothache, and was sure that she would soon ease his pain. With slumped shoulders he left the shop, his hand held firmly to his jaw.

Hacher came forward to where Bascot and Gianni were standing, attempting to form a smile on his doleful countenance as he asked how he could be of assistance.

"We have come to ask you a few more questions about Aubrey Tercel. I would like you to again recall the conversations you had with him on the two occasions you trimmed his hair. Are you certain he did not mention anyone in the town to you, one of the merchants, perhaps, or some other tradesman?"

Hacher's domed forehead wrinkled in concentration. "He told me he was in the retinue of Lady Nicolaa's sister and held the position of cofferer," the barber said in his slow lugubrious manner, "but I think he only did that to impress on me that he was of some importance for, just after he said that, he warned me to take especial care while attending his hair." Hacher sniffed. "I replied that I always gave the best of my service to every patron, whether of high standing or low."

Bascot gave a nod of seeming sympathy, knowing he would have to be patient if he was going to get any information out of the man. "Did he speak of anything else?"

"We exchanged a few remarks about the quality of wine available in the town," Hacher replied. "I told him I preferred, when I can afford it, a vintage made from the grapes of Portugal and he agreed with my taste and asked where I bought it. I told him there were several merchants in the town who sell the vintage and we left it at that."

Clarice had also mentioned that she and her lover had discussed wine, but it was a common enough subject, and not likely to be of importance. "And you are certain he spoke of nothing else?" Bascot pressed.

"I do not think so," the barber replied and then added ironically, "He did not seem a man much given to conversation."

The Templar and Gianni left the shop, their spirits low. Even though they had achieved the goal of finding out about Simon Adgate's first wife, the information had been of no significance and now Bascot found himself nonplussed as to which direction to take next. So far, they had only discovered what appeared to be two completely disparate motives for the crime—that of a violent reaction from a jealous lover or, alternatively, an attempt by Tercel's mother, or someone close to her, to protect her sullied reputation. Was it possible that the two were linked together in some manner? And, if so, how?

Twenty-one
❦

IT WAS LATE IN THE MORNING BY THE TIME NICOLAA AND PE-
tronille returned to the bail. Bruet and Ernulf had been
thorough in their search for the missing boy, coursing
through the forest all around Riseholme for a good distance, but there had been no trace of him. The castellan had
questioned young Mark exhaustively while the search was
being conducted, but he had not been able to add much to
what he had already told them except that it had been "a
long time before it got light" that Willi crept out from
where they were sleeping. Deciding that the boy must have
gone a good distance, or maybe even reached Lincoln, before they arrived, she gave orders for the party to return to
the castle.

"It is in the town we must search," she said to her sister.
"We must return at once."

Leaving instructions with Stoddard that he was to send
news to her immediately if Willi returned to Riseholme, the

small party went back to Lincoln. Once there, Nicolaa asked Ernulf if he was familiar with the boy's appearance.

"Aye, lady. I saw him when I brought all of the children into the hall on the day of the feast. With that bright red hair of his, it was easy to mark him from the rest."

"Good. Take the groom who drove the children to Rise-holme with you—he also had a good opportunity to note the lad's features—and search for Willi in the vicinity of St. Peter at Arches, where he went for alms. It is unlikely he will show himself at the church, for the priest there would wonder why he is in the town and not at Riseholme, but the streets nearby will be the place that his father left him and it is there that Willi will go to look for him. The other child, Mark, also said that Willi told him his father was over-fond of ale, so visit the alehouses in the area and see if he has been in any of them. And go out to the suburb of Butwerk, too, it is close by and many of the town's poor seek refuge in the hovels there; it may be that he has joined them. Be discreet, do not tell anyone the reason we are searching for the boy; if one of those you speak to is the person he saw in the bail that night, you could place the lad in danger. Simply say you are looking for the boy because he is ill and may be infectious. That should put the fear of God into any that are sheltering him and induce them to reveal his whereabouts."

As the serjeant and groom rode out of the bail, Petronille, who was standing nearby, said, "I pray they find him, and speedily. If the murderer saw Willi looking at him, he will be aware the boy can identify him. If their paths should cross while the child is searching for his father, then . . ."

"He will kill him," Nicolaa finished grimly. "Let us hope Willi is found before that happens."

* * *

$\mathcal{T}$HE SUBJECT OF THEIR SEARCH WAS, AT THAT MOMENT, PEER-
ing out from behind an old ale cask that was being used as a
water barrel. It was behind a house in a street not far from
Pottergate, the town gate which led out into the suburb of
Butwerk. Willi was not aware that anyone was looking for
him, for he had been outside the walls of Lincoln by the time
Bruet and Ernulf had begun their search of the woods. He
had not gone into the town through Newport Arch as he
had intended, but skirted the walls that encircled Lincoln
and slipped into the town through Pottergate on the eastern
side, his first intention to look in the sheltered nook down
one of the backstreets where he and his father had been accustomed to spend their nights. The lane was rarely used by
any of the people that lived nearby; it led only to a high
fence that backed onto a yard where a carter kept his old
horse and there were no doorways in the walls of the houses
on either side. Willi and his father had gathered a pile of old
rags in the corner that abutted the wall to keep them warm
throughout the night and the boy believed that was where
his da, if he had returned, would have looked for him. But
when Willi had gone down into the alley, it was deserted
and the rags lay in an undisturbed heap, crusty with a rime
of unmelted frost.

Willi had then gone into two of the nearby alehouses,
covertly peering at the faces of each customer, hoping to find
the familiar visage of his father. But none of them had been
his da and, when Willi asked the keeper in the second alehouse if he had seen his father recently, the man had shaken
his head and gruffly told the boy to leave.

It had been as he was leaving the alehouse that Willi had

seen two mounted men coming towards him. One of them he recognised as the grizzled serjeant from the castle and the other was the groom that had driven the small party of foundlings to Riseholme. Sheltering in a doorway, he heard the serjeant ask a passerby if he had seen a boy of Willi's description, mentioning that he had a head of carrot-coloured hair. The boy had not waited to hear the man's reply; he scooted as fast as he could down the street away from the alehouse and, seeing the water barrel down a side turning, had hidden behind it. Now he watched anxiously to see if either the serjeant or the groom had spotted him.

They must be looking for him because he had stolen the blanket, he decided, clutching the rolled up swathe of rough wool closer to his chest. He had carried it all the way from Riseholme for use when night fell, but now he cursed the fact that he had taken it. If he had not, they wouldn't be trying to find him. He shivered as he thought of what might happen if they caught him. Thieves were often punished by having their noses slit or one of their fingers cut off. His lip began to tremble as he thought of the pain he would endure. He didn't know what to do. If he left the town, he would never find his da but, if he did not, it was certain the castellan's servants would eventually find him.

Then he saw Ernulf and the groom ride their horses past the end of the turning and continue on down the street. He gave a sigh of relief and, unrolling the blanket, draped a fold of it over the brightness of hair and wrapped the rest around his body, tying the corners at his waist. The food he had brought with him from Riseholme was already gone; the walk into town had made him hungry and he had eaten it on the way but, with good fortune, he would find his da soon and was, for the moment at least, safe from discovery.

* * *

IT WAS ALMOST TIME FOR THE MIDDAY MEAL WHEN BASCOT
and Gianni returned to the ward. When they went into the
hall, tables were being set up and they threaded their way
through the servants engaged in the task, making their way
to the corner tower of the keep where Nicolaa's solar was
located. There they found Petronille, Richard and Alinor
with the castellan, sharing a flagon of wine as they discussed
Willi's disappearance and the dire consequences that could
befall him. At the far end of the chamber, Alinor's maid,
Elise, sat with Margaret, Petronille's sempstress, engaged in
repairing a tear in one of her mistress' kirtles. For once
Elise's merry smile was absent and Margaret's countenance
was even more sober than usual.

Bascot was offered a cup of wine and, while he drank it,
was quickly brought up to date on how Willi had run away
from the foundling home and that one of the other children
said the boy had seen the person who murdered Aubrey Tercel. "Did he recognise him?" the Templar asked.

"Of that we are not certain," Nicolaa replied. "Willi
told the other boy very little beyond claiming he had seen
him, not even whether the villain was a man or a woman—I
wish he had. At least then we would know the gender of
the person. As it is, we can only hope that we find Willi
first, or that the boy did not, in fact, see the murderer but
allowed his childish imagination to manufacture a killer
from a brief glimpse of a servant innocently crossing the
ward."

After Bascot told her of his visit to the two barber-
surgeons and added that, according to Gildas, it did not
seem possible that Simon Adgate's first wife had been Ter-

cel's mother, Alinor's face fell and she reluctantly admitted she might be wrong about the furrier.

"If Ernulf finds the boy, and the child can identify the person that murdered the cofferer, further enquiries will be unnecessary," Nicolaa said.

"Let us hope that turns out to be so, lady," Bascot replied and stood up. After thanking her for the wine, he said he would not return to the preceptory until the morrow. "There is not much more that can be done until Ernulf has completed his search for the boy."

Nicolaa nodded. "We must pray he will be successful," she said.

WHEN BASCOT RETURNED TO THE PRECEPTORY, DUSK WAS closing in and it was almost time for the service at Compline. He went into the office where he was accustomed to do the Order's paperwork and found Everard d'Arderon seated at the desk, poring over an inventory of weapons in the armoury.

When the preceptor saw the disheartened look on Bascot's face, he laid the list aside and asked what was amiss. "A boy we believe can identify the person who murdered Tercel has gone missing," Bascot replied. "If the lad is not found, it is feared he might be the next victim."

D'Arderon listened with grave attention as Bascot explained the details of Willi's flight from Riseholme and how attempts were being made to find him. The preceptor was well aware of Bascot's strong propensity for protecting those less fortunate than himself; it was an admirable trait and one of the prime directives of the Order, but d'Arderon also knew, from his long experience of the evils of mankind, that such an aim could often be unattainable. He cast about in his mind for some way to ease Bascot's apprehension.

"There is nothing more distressing than fearing that a child's life may be in danger," he said finally. "I remember a similar situation once, when I was with a cohort of brothers travelling from Jaffa to Arsuf in the Holy Land, and we stopped to make camp at a native village near an oasis. The little daughter of one of the villagers had gone missing and we offered to help search for her, for it was thought that she might have wandered out into the desert and been taken by a jackal or some other predator. With the men from the village, we combed the area all around, but there was no sign of her. Just as it was coming up to nightfall, and the worst was feared, she was discovered, not by one of those who had been searching for her, but by her older sister. It seems the little girl had stolen some honey from her mother's kitchen and, fearing to be punished, had hidden underneath a pile of wicker baskets. All the time we had been looking for her, she had been only a few feet away from the center of the village. The older sister, who was not much more than a child herself, had remembered how she and her younger sibling had often played a game of hiding and seeking, and that the spot under the baskets was one of the missing child's favourite places to hide."

D'Arderon smiled ruefully. "I can still remember the relief we all felt to find that she was safe. Even though the child and her parents were unknown to us, there is something about the vulnerability of the young that strikes a common chord in all men and women. I hope, de Marins, that there will be a similar success with the missing boy."

It was not often that the preceptor spoke of any of his personal experiences, usually confining conversations to talk of military situations or the daily routine, and Bascot knew that d'Arderon had done so in this instance to hearten him. The preceptor's description of the search for the missing girl had, however, given him a notion of a way in which, if Willi had still not been found by the time he went to the castle in the morning, the boy might be located.

Twenty-two

✦❈✦

W HEN BASCOT ARRIVED AT THE CASTLE THE NEXT MORNING, he saw Ernulf coming towards the gate, the groom who had been aiding him in the search for the boy trailing behind, leading two horses. The serjeant's stocky shoulders were slumped in dejection and, without even needing to ask, the Templar knew Willi had not been found.

With a shake of his grizzled head, Ernulf said, "We searched the town high and low and, except for an alehouse keeper who said the boy had been in earlier in the day asking for his father, there was nary sight nor sound of him. We looked last night until it was almost time for curfew, but wherever the little scamp is, he's found himself a good hiding place."

Ernulf's face was laden with worry. "The more time goes by, the more I fear that when we do find him, it'll be his corpse instead of his living body."

At that moment the Templar saw Gianni running across the bail. After greeting his former servant, Bascot asked the boy if he had seen Willi while the foundling had been in the castle.

Gianni responded by pointing to his eyes and then making a scissor of his first two fingers and moving them to simulate walking and motioned to the keep, meaning he had seen Willi and the other children when they had been brought into the hall on the night of the feast.

"Would you know him if you saw him again?" the Templar asked and the boy responded with a vigorous nod.

Bascot turned to Ernulf. "Take Gianni with you on your search today," he said, his advice prompted by what d'Arderon had told him the night before about how the little girl in the Holy Land had been found by her sister. "If anyone can ferret out the places where Willi is hiding, it will be someone who has been in a similar situation and Gianni, as you know, was living on the streets when I found him."

Ernulf brightened at the notion, and saw the sense in it. "Aye, I reckon you're right," he replied.

After Gianni had clambered up to ride pillion behind the serjeant and they had clattered out of the ward, Bascot remounted his own horse and followed them, guiding his mount along Ermine Street, through Bailgate and down Steep Hill into the town. Last night, after he had lain down on his pallet in the enclave's dormitory, he had reviewed the few facts that had been unearthed about the murdered man. They were scant. No other lover except for Clarice Adgate had been located and it did not seem likely that any of the women who had attended the feast could be his mother. The only tiny clue left was the cofferer's mention of wine to both Clarice Adgate and the barber, Hacher. And it was just possible, if only barely so, that Tercel's love of wine, and the purchase of it, had led him into a liaison with another

woman besides Clarice Adgate, perhaps the wife or daughter
of a wine merchant. Alternatively, there was even a chance
that he may have asked questions about his missing mother
during a visit to a wine shop and alerted her, or her family,
to his search. The Templar knew he was stretching credulity
in posing such possibilities, but he had learned, in the course
of investigations into previous cases of secret murder, that it
is often the trail that seems most obscure that leads to the
quarry. Until the boy was found, he could do no worse that
follow it and, as it happened, Bascot had been closely involved with one of the more influential wine merchants in
Lincoln when a poisoner that had been plaguing the citizens
of the town had attempted to kill the merchant and his
family. If there was any link between Tercel's death and his
penchant for fine wine, Reinbald of Hungate might be able
to help discover it.

IN THE CASTLE KEEP, ELISE WAS HUMMING AN AIR SHE HAD
heard played by the jongleur Lady Nicolaa had hired on the
night of the feast as she placed a *couvre-chef* over her head and
threw a cloak about her shoulders. She had been given permission by Lady Alinor to accompany Margaret into Lincoln
while the sempstress went to purchase a supply of thread.
She would be glad to get away from the castle for, since Margaret had voiced her warning that she might be in danger,
Elise had not been easy inside the walls of the keep. Even
though she had taken the precaution of moving her pallet to
lay across the inside of the door leading into the bedchamber
she shared with her mistress, and slept with her small eating
knife secreted under her pillow, her rest had been disturbed
and filled with nightmares. And, during her waking hours,

she found she had fallen into the habit of avoiding close contact with the women on Lady Nicolaa's staff, lest one of them be the jealous lover Margaret had warned her about. It had all been very unsettling and the thought of a few hours in the town promised to be distracting. Adding to her anticipation was the fact that one of the grooms from the castle stable was to accompany her and the sempstress as an escort. His name was Nicholas and he was a young man about her own age with a handsome ruddy face and a gentle manner. They had spoken once or twice since she had first arrived in the castle and Elise had found him both courteous and attractive. She picked up a small polished silver mirror that Alinor used and regarded her reflection in the surface. She had braided her thick hair and fastened it into two coils over her ears and, even though her head was completely covered by the *couvre-chef*, it was made of a gauze so filmy that the outline of her plaits could be seen through the material. She knew she had lovely hair and was satisfied that the manner in which she had dressed it made her look attractive. She hoped Nicholas would think so, too, and was looking forward to spending the morning in his company.

WHEN GIANNI AND ERNULF REACHED THE LOWER PART OF the town, the serjeant pointed out the alehouse where Willi had been seen the day before. Gianni glanced at it for a moment and then let his sharp young eyes roam over the surrounding shops and cross streets that led off the thoroughfare where they were standing. Slipping down from his seat on the horse, he motioned to the serjeant to leave him and indicated, by pointing at himself and circling his fingers, that he would like to search for Willi on his own.

Ernulf was not sure if this was a wise idea. "With a murderer on the loose, I don't reckon the Templar would be any too pleased if I was to let you roam around unprotected," he said doubtfully. But Gianni forestalled his objections by raising his finger to where a weak winter sun was shining in the sky and then moving it a little to indicate it would only be for a short while. With a shrug he spread his arms out towards all the people that were on the street—women with shopping baskets over their arms, carters driving wagons laden with vegetables and other foodstuffs, and tradesmen walking hurriedly by with bags of tools over their arms—as if to say, "What could happen to me here among so many people?"

After some musing, Ernulf finally gave in, but before he rode away he gave Gianni an admonition. "I don't want to have to search for two missing boys, so you be right careful, do you hear? I'll meet you back here in an hour."

Gianni nodded and gave the serjeant a grin and, as Ernulf and the groom rode off down the street, he strolled along the roadway, seemingly looking at the wares displayed on counters protruding from the bottom stories of the houses he passed but, in reality, searching for any dark corners that were hidden from the general view. He went up one side of the street and then turned and ambled back down the other until he was again standing near the alehouse where Willi had gone to ask after his father, passing the mouth of a narrow alley that he had noticed on his earlier perambulation. It was situated alongside the alehouse premises and its width was no more than the span of a thin man's shoulders. The interior was in a dark shadow with only a small glimmer of light at the far end giving evidence that it debouched into an adjoining street.

In the days before the Templar had found him, and when Gianni had been a waif begging on a dock in the port of Palermo, he and the other urchins had often needed to hide from the *commandante del porto* and his minions. The port reeve and his men made regular excursions to rid the docks of beggars who importuned sailors for money and Gianni and the others had a desperate need to hide from the men, for not only would they chase them away, but might also beat them and take any money they had been given. The best places to conceal oneself were not in the obvious recesses behind bales of goods or among coils of rope, but in narrow apertures that were in plain sight and too small for a man to get into. Gianni could remember countless times when he had taken advantage of this trick, holding his breath as the port officials had passed by within inches of where he was hiding, not realising their quarry was almost under their noses. It was very possible that Willi, having been forced to live on the streets of Lincoln without his father for a time, had learned this ruse. The alley Gianni had seen, too narrow for a grown man to pass down its width with ease, would make an excellent place for a small young boy to hide while he waited to see if his father returned to the alehouse.

Not wishing to make his purpose obvious, Gianni lingered by the shop of a leather merchant, fingering the pairs of shoes and wrist guards on display until it should be time for Ernulf's return. When he saw the serjeant enter the top of the street where it curved to the west, he ran quickly in the opposite direction until he was out of sight of the alley, and waited until Ernulf drew up beside him.

"Did you have any luck, lad?" the serjeant asked.

Gianni, not responding to the question, made a motion

for Ernulf and the groom to ride a little farther down the street. Once they had turned a corner, Gianni began to make gestures with his hands, attempting to tell Ernulf that he wanted to return to the place he had just left, but that he did not want the serjeant or the groom to accompany him, and for them to wait out of sight for a small space of time. It took some minutes for him to make Ernulf understand him—the serjeant was familiar with some of the gestures Gianni used to communicate with the Templar, but not many—and it was the groom, a foxy-faced young man whose hazel eyes had a look of quick intelligence, who finally understood what he was trying to say.

"I think he has a notion where the boy may be hiding, Sarje," the groom said, "but wants to look on his own in case the lad sees us and runs away."

Gianni nodded enthusiastically and pointed to the horses and then to a hitching rail on the street they had just left, making a motion of tying them. Ernulf nodded and Gianni pointed at both of them and then made a walking movement towards a cart laden with bags of flour outside a baker's shop. Shielding the lower part of his face so that only his eyes remained uncovered, he gestured with his other hand back up the street where the alehouse, and the alley, were situated. This time Ernulf understood him.

"You wants us to wait behind that cart and watch," the serjeant said, "while you go and see if you can find the boy."

A broad smile on Gianni's face told Ernulf his understanding was correct and then the boy made a circle with his hand to indicate he could be some time. "Right, lad. We'll stay there until you've either caught the boy or come back here. May you have good fortune."

Waiting until Ernulf and the groom were in position,

Gianni slipped around the corner and made his way back up the street. Casually looking into the shops, he took his time examining the variety of goods on display in each one—iron nails and chisels in the first, an array of combs and ribbons in the next, a pile of besoms and small brushes a little farther along, and then a shop with a shelf on which were laid an array of pots and pans—before buying a couple of hot meat pies from a roving vendor.

Munching on one of the pies he had just bought, Gianni strolled slowly up to the entrance to the alley and sat himself down on one of the empty ale kegs that were stacked there awaiting refilling. He balanced the uneaten pie on a keg sitting beside him and then, as the savoury smell of the meat wafted upwards, took his writing tablet from where it was suspended on his belt and, opening the wooden cover, pretended to be absorbed in reading it.

He hoped his ruse would work. If Willi was, in fact, secreted in the depths of the alley, it all depended on whether or not he had noticed Gianni in company with Ernulf and the groom when they had arrived on the street a little while earlier. If he had, the boy might suspect a trick and not take the bait but, if he did not and was, as Gianni suspected, very hungry, the sight and smell of the pie should prove an irresistible lure.

The moments ticked by. Gianni finished the pie he had been eating and took up his stylus to inscribe some letters on the wax tablet, turning his body so that his back was towards the uneaten pie and he gave the impression of being engrossed in his writing. Still there was no sound of any movement behind him and he began to fear he had been wrong. More minutes passed and it was just as he was about to admit failure that he heard a slight rustle behind him.

Gratified, Gianni smiled inwardly and stood up. Now he must find a way to make it seem safe for the boy to come forward and snatch the pie. Not lifting his head from his study of his wax tablet, he took a couple of steps as though intending to walk away, leaving the pie on the ale keg as though he had forgotten it. Once he was a few paces beyond the alley, he crept back close to the side of the wall and saw the small fingers of a hand creep out towards the succulent pastry. Cautioning himself to patience, he waited until the reaching fingers had almost closed around their objective, then quickly shot out his own hand and grabbed the exposed wrist, dragging the small body attached to it out into the street.

"Let me go," Willi cried, dropping the pie in his struggle to free himself. The blanket in which he had been wrapped fell loose onto the ground, and his bush of red hair was exposed, flaming like a beacon. Although small, he struggled like an eel and it was with difficulty that Gianni kept hold of him. The small bones in Willi's wrist had the fragility of twigs and Gianni, although not much taller, was older and stronger and he feared he might injure the boy if he wrenched his arm too hard. Hoping to get Willi in a grip that would keep him immobile until Ernulf came, Gianni thrust his leg against the back of Willi's knees with a sweeping movement, tumbling the younger boy down hard on his buttocks so he could grasp him fast round the chest with both arms to hold him close. Willi struggled for a moment or two and then, realising he could not escape, went still.

By now a crowd of passersby had gathered, one of them the ale keeper from the nearby alehouse. "Hey, that's the boy the serjeant was lookin' for," he cried as he saw Willi's bright red hair and then, as he reached forward to help Gianni, his expression grew fearful and he stepped back a pace. "Here, you want to be careful, young 'un, he's got some sort of disease that's catchin'."

Gianni shook his head at the man, but his muteness prevented him from explaining the situation or asking for help. It was with a great deal of relief that, as the crowd heard the ale keeper's words and drew back in alarm, he caught sight of Ernulf and the groom hurrying down the street.

"Sorry we took so long, lad," the serjeant said, puffing from the exertion of his run. "A wagon went by and we couldn't see you for a moment or two, but then when we saw the crowd gather, we reckoned somethin' was going on, so we came as quick as we could."

Within moments, the groom brought their horses and Willi was hoisted up onto one of them. "Well done, lad," Ernulf said to Gianni. "Should've brought you with me yesterday, would've saved us a lot of useless traipsin' about."

Gianni nodded his appreciation of the compliment and then, picking up the fallen pie from where it lay on the cobbles, handed it to Willi, who devoured it ravenously.

Twenty-three

✦‑I‑✦

As Ernulf and Gianni were on their way back to the castle with the reluctant Willi, and Elise was strolling down Mikelgate in the company of Margaret and Nicholas, Bascot was knocking on the door of a building in Hungate that housed the shop of Reinbald, the wine merchant. The merchant and his wife had no children, but had taken the two sons of his wife's dead sister's to raise as their own. The eldest, Ivor, had since returned to his native Norway, but his brother, Harald, assisted his uncle in his business and was now his heir.

Bascot had liked both Reinbald and Harald and they, for their part, were grateful to him for unearthing the identity of the man who had tried to kill them. The Templar hoped the pair would be at work in Reinbald's wine store on this morning and, when the door was opened by a servant, was told that they were in a small room at the rear of the building.

The pleasant aroma of wine filled Bascot's nostrils as he followed in the wake of the servant. Kegs were piled high on either side of him, each one branded with the mark of its origin. There were wines from France and Spain, a few barrels of Malmsey from Cyprus and, Bascot was pleased to see, some smaller casks from Portugal.

When the servant admitted the Templar into Reinbald and Harald's presence, they were poring over records of lading but, when they saw the identity of their visitor, quickly rose to their feet and greeted him warmly.

"Sir Bascot," Reinbald exclaimed, "you are well come, well come, indeed. Please, be seated and allow me to pour you a cup of a wine we have just received from Tuscany. Harald and I have both found it to have an outstanding taste and aroma."

Bascot took the chair the wine merchant had indicated and, when the cup was handed to him, took a mouthful of the wine. Reinbald was correct in his estimation. It was smooth and had a lusty bouquet. After Bascot had expressed his approval, Reinbald topped up his cup and both men listened with grave attention as he explained the purpose of his visit, and that he had come to ask if the murdered man had ever visited his shop.

"I am trying to track down any acquaintances Tercel may have made in Lincoln," Bascot added, "in the hope that, by doing so, I may find some trace of the reason for his murder. Since it has been reported that, before his death, he expressed a liking for Portuguese wine, it may be that he visited one of the wine merchants in the town and, while in conversation with them, mentioned something of import. The master of your guild, who was in the castle on the night of the murder, had never met him. That is why I am here—to ask if you might have done so."

Bascot then went on to describe Tercel in detail, his colouring and manner of dress and what he had learned of the dead man's personality. When he had finished, Reinbald shook his head, the jowls on his heavy-featured face waggling slightly as he did so. He then looked interrogatively at Harald, who also gave a negative response, but reached into the open-faced cupboard behind him and extracted a roll of parchment which was, he explained, a record of their customers for the last six months. A quick perusal told him that Tercel's name was not amongst them.

"I am sorry that we are not able to help you," Reinbald said with genuine regret. "There are quite a few wine merchants in Lincoln; you will find it a lengthy task to check all of them."

The Templar decided to try a different tack. Recalling Nicolaa de la Haye's suggestion that if Tercel's mother was not from Winchester, she may have been on a visit there with relatives at the time of her son's conception, he said, "It is thought that the dead man had a connection with the town of Winchester, but the link is an old one, dating back to the time of his birth more than five and twenty years ago. Do you recall, Reinbald, if any of your competitors had occasion to journey to the town about that time?"

Reinbald's face registered his surprise at the question, but he did his best to answer it. "I was a young man then," he said with a rueful expression, "and my father was still alive. Both he and I often travelled to ports on the south coast, either to inspect a shipment that had arrived from across the Narrow Sea or to travel to vineyards in France or Spain to sample a wine before we bought it. But we never went to Winchester—it is not a port, so there would have been no need. The same would be true of other wine merchants. Their business normally only takes them to London or one of the Cinque Ports."

Bascot nodded. It was the answer he had expected, not the one he had hoped for. There was no other place to look for a trace of Tercel's search for his mother except, as Reinbald said, to speak to all of the other wine merchants in Lincoln; a time-consuming exercise that might well prove useless. Disappointed, he finished his wine and was about to take his leave when Reinbald added, "Now that I cast my mind back, I do recall mention of someone making a trip to Winchester about that time, but it was a neighbour of ours who went there, and he was a draper, not a wine merchant."

A flicker of hope rose in Bascot and he settled himself back in his seat as Reinbald, his lips pursed with the effort of searching his memory, continued, "My father died in '79, so it must have been before that. The reason I recall it is that the draper bought a fine new cart to make the journey and had it all gloriously painted in red with bright yellow trim. My father and I were of the opinion that the draper was foolish to travel such a long distance so early in the season—it was about this time of year, February or March, and the weather had been terrible—and that he had wasted his money on the embellishment for it would be ruined by the time he returned. We didn't see the draper for many weeks after that but, when he finally arrived back in Lincoln, our prediction was proved correct. Rainstorms and heavy winds had plagued his southward journey and played havoc with the paintwork. The cart had hardly a scrap of colour left on it that wasn't flaking or scarred."

"Did the draper have a daughter, perhaps, that went with him?" Bascot asked hopefully. Tercel must have been conceived about the time of Eastertide so, if the draper's trip had taken place in the year of 1176, and a daughter had accompanied him, it would have been the right time of year for the girl to have lain with a lover, fallen pregnant, and given birth to the cofferer nine months later in January of 1177. A slim chance, at best, that he had finally found some trace of the woman they were seeking, but worth investigating all the same.

To Bascot's regret, Reinbald shook his leonine head. "He and his wife were a childless couple and getting along in years. They both died not long after my father passed away."

At the words, the Templar began to resign himself to accept yet another failure, but was forestalled from doing so when Reinbald added, "But there were a couple of young girls, relatives of some sort, nieces I think, that used to visit them often. It could be that one of them accompanied the draper."

"Do you remember their names?" the Templar asked.

The wine merchant looked up at Bascot with a smile and shook his head. "Neither of the girls were what I thought of, in those days, as comely, so I never paid them much attention. As I said, I was young, and had not yet learned there is more to a woman than a large bosom and a beguiling smile."

Even if one of these women proved to be the girl he was seeking, the Templar knew that without a name it would be impossible to find them. Once more, Bascot prepared to thank the wine merchant for his time but, as he rose to go, Reinbald said, "But I do recall the draper's family name, if that is of any help."

At about the same time, Margaret and Elise, along with the groom, Nicholas, were walking down Mikelgate. The sudden surge of warmer weather had brought out many of the townspeople and the shops along the main thoroughfare were doing a busy trade. There were also other attractions; on one corner a man with an old and almost toothless brown bear was making the animal dance to the accompaniment of a reed pipe, there was a puppet show set up about halfway along the street and, a little farther on, an enterprising juggler was adroitly tossing balls into the air while a little girl went among the crowd of spectators with her hand held out for tokens of appreciation. Elise was in a merry mood and even staid Margaret had a smile on her face. Nicholas walked beside the young maid, casting appreciative glances in her direction as the trio made their way to the farther end of the street where the shop that stocked the thread Margaret needed was located.

As they neared their destination, their attention was caught by a shabby old man with an exotic bird on his shoulder. The bird's plumage seemed to be comprised of all the colours of the rainbow and glinted red, gold, blue and green in the early spring sunshine. Quite a crowd had gathered around the man, who was telling them that the bird was called a parrot and had been brought back to England from distant lands by a sailor whose ship had taken him almost to the edge of the world. The wonder of the watching crowd increased when, on a prompting from the man, the bird began to squawk short phrases, saying "Give me some dinner" and "You're an ugly fellow," followed by some expletives that made the women in the crowd blush and the men roar with approval.

Margaret and Elise stopped to watch the performance and, as the owner of the parrot threw down his hat with a begging appeal for money, the sempstress gave Nicholas a fourthing—a quarter of a silver penny—to take and add to the collection.

The groom pushed to the front of the press and dropped the coin in a coarse hessian hat that lay on the ground at the parrot owner's feet. Wondrous as the bird was, Nicholas was reluctant to leave the lovely Elise for even a moment, and quickly turned to make his way back to where she stood. He had not gone more than a step or two when he heard a cry of distress and looked towards the spot where he had left the two women he was escorting. The only one he could see was Margaret and she was looking down at the ground with an expression of horror. A similar look was on the faces of the people alongside her as they began to push and shove in a backwards motion, as though something dreadful lay at their feet. A thrill of dread ran through Nicholas and frantically he used his broad shoulders to shove a passage through the crowd to where Margaret stood. When he reached her, he saw that Elise was lying on the ground. She was unconscious, her eyes closed and breathing laboured.

As he fell to his knees beside her, Margaret did the same, pulling back the folds of the girl's cloak as she did so. Blood was welling up from a wound in Elise's side and running onto the cobbles beneath her body.

Quickly, Margaret ripped Elise's kirtle apart and exposed a deep wound in Elise's abdomen. "May heaven help her," the sempstress exclaimed in terror, "she has been stabbed."

AMONG THE CROWD WATCHING THE PARROT WAS MERISEL Wickson. She had been standing near Elise when the maid had fallen and been stunned by what she had witnessed. Normally she would have been in her father's candle manufactory at this time of day, but she had gone to visit her mother's cousin, Simon Adgate, the day before and what he had told her had been so distressing that she was having difficulty keeping her mind on her work. To try and distract her tumbling thoughts, she had begged leave of her father to go and join the crowd watching the outlandish bird and, when he had given his permission, had gone out into the street and spent a few pleasurable moments listening to the parrot's lively speech and watching with fascination the way in which the bird turned its head back and forth as it bobbed up and down on its owner's arm, an expectant look in its beady eyes.

It had only been when she had glanced around her just as Elise had been stabbed that her attention had been torn from the diversion in a horrible manner. She could hardly believe what she had seen. Retreating a few paces, her first instinct had been to scream out an accusation, but her innate good sense had overridden the impulse, for she thought she knew the identity of the person who had committed the crime and, if she was correct, there could be dire repercussions to her family if she made the knowledge public. Trying to set her tumbling thoughts in order, she hurried off down the street. It was imperative that she go to Simon Adgate and tell him what she had seen.

Twenty-four
✛

As Elise's body lay crumpled and bleeding on the cobble-stones of Mikelgate, Willi was standing in front of Lady Nicolaa in the castle solar. Petronille and Alinor were seated alongside her and Richard was by the fireplace, sipping a cup of wine as his mother spoke to the young runaway. A few paces behind the lad Ernulf stood, and Gianni was in his customary place in the corner, seated on a stool and taking notes.

"Do you know why you have been brought here, Willi?" Nicolaa asked the young boy.

"'Cos I stole a blanket," Willi replied disconsolately.

Suppressing a smile, Nicolaa said, "No, that is not so. Neither I nor Bailiff Stoddard would begrudge you the means of keeping yourself warm."

Willi looked up at her in surprise. He knew the woman in front of him was a great lady and had not expected her to be kind.

"You told Mark, the other boy at the foundling home,

that you had seen the person who murdered my sister's servant. If that is so, you are the only one who can identify him, or her, and we were fearful you might be killed because you can do so. That is why we have been looking for you, to bring you back here and keep you safe." Nicolaa leaned forward. "If you told Mark an untruth, you will not be punished, but you must tell us if you really did see the murderer."

Willi's eyes stretched wide as he admitted that he had.

"Was it someone you had seen before—about the town, perhaps, or in the hall when you and the other children were brought before the merchants?"

This time Willi shook his head. "I only saw 'un when they wus comin' out of that old tower across the bail. And later I heard the washerwoman sayin' as how that's where the crossbow what killed that man up on the ramparts was kept."

"And did you see the murderer clearly? Was it a man or a woman?"

Before Willi could answer a servant burst into the solar. "Milady, I am sorry to interrupt, but Lady Alinor's maid, Elise, has just been brought into the hall. She was stabbed while in the town and is like to die. Margaret thinks it was done by the same person that killed the cofferer."

Alinor jumped up from her seat. "I must go to her," she said and ran from the room.

"Richard, attend her!" Nicolaa said to her son abruptly. "Caution must be used until we find the person who is wreaking this havoc. And we cannot be certain that it is not someone within the castle walls."

The castellan's son, his hand going to the dagger at his belt, left the chamber with hurried strides.

Nicolaa looked at her sister, who was on the point of following her daughter, and lifted a hand to forestall her. "You, too, Petra, must be careful. Two of your servants have been attacked and you might be the next target. For now, you must stay here in the solar where Ernulf can keep guard over you."

The serjeant nodded and moved to stand a little closer to the two women, loosening the short sword he wore at his belt as he did so. Willi, frightened by the report of the stabbing, was thankful of Ernulf's presence and now, instead of trying, as he had done in the town, to escape the serjeant's notice, crept closer to his reassuring bulk.

When Petronille would have made a protest, Nicolaa overrode it. "You cannot do anything to help Elise. We must leave her to the care of the castle leech and trust that if she can be saved, he will do it. It is more important, at the moment, to try and find the villain who is perpetrating these crimes."

She beckoned to Willi. "You are safe here, lad. Now, come forward and tell me about the person you saw."

WHEN ALINOR RUSHED INTO THE HALL, RICHARD WAS CLOSE behind her. In the middle of the huge chamber, Elise had been placed on one of the trestle tables used at mealtimes. The castle leech, a man named Hedgset, was bending over her. Closest to the stricken maid was Nicholas; when he had seen Elise lying bleeding on the ground, he had scooped her up in his arms and run from Mikelgate all the way up Steep Hill and into the bail. His exertions had left him gasping for breath but even so, his face, beneath a sheen of heavy perspiration, was ashen.

Margaret rushed forward when she saw her mistress'

daughter. "Oh, lady, the leech says the injury is a grave one."
She, too, was panting, for she had followed Nicholas as
quickly as she could, arriving just after he had taken Elise
into the hall. Her sallow cheeks were tinged bright red and
she was wringing her hands in agitation.

Alinor walked swiftly over to the table and looked at her
maid. Elise was unconscious, her breathing shallow. Her coif
had been removed and the coils of her chestnut braids shone
with a vibrant lustre above her ears, as though belying the
deathly pallor of her face. Hedgset noticed Richard's presence and, without pausing in his examination of the wound,
said succinctly, "A clumsy piercing, lord, with a thick blade,
but it has gone deep and penetrated her abdomen just below
the rib cage. I do not think any of the vital organs have been
damaged, but I cannot be sure."

As he spoke, Elise's eyelids fluttered and she began to
regain consciousness. Her hand, instinctively, flew to the
gash in her side, and Hedgset took hold of her fingers. "I
have to stitch the flesh together, Sir Richard, and quickly.
She must be kept still while I do so."

The castellan's son nodded and, grasping her wrists, held
them tightly at her shoulders. He then gave Nicholas a command to take hold of her ankles. "Hold her fast," Richard
instructed softly as the groom moved reluctantly forward.
"You have brought her thus far, do not fail her now."

With a grimace of fear lest he give further hurt to the girl
he so admired, Nicholas gently took hold of Elise's feet and
held them still. At the touch of his hands on her bare ankles,
and the pressure of Richard's weight on her shoulders, the
injured maid began to stare wildly around, moaning as she
struggled against the double restraint and making an at-

tempt to rise, but she was securely pinioned, and the leech set to work.

Hedgset had not been with the castle household long, having only recently come there after having been recommended for the post by a London friend of Gerard Camville, but it was soon evident that his hands were deft. Although not above five and thirty years of age, he exuded a calm assurance as he ripped Elise's kirtle and gown apart to expose the site of the injury more clearly, and then pulled the edges of her clothing tight across her stomach so that the material screened the more intimate portions of her anatomy. Taking up a bone needle threaded with catgut from his bag of instruments, he began to sew the ragged edges of the wound together. All was done with an economy of movement and speed, despite Elise's agonised screams as the needle pierced her flesh. Richard surmised that the leech, although young, had gained his expertise during the years of his apprenticeship in London, while attending the many victims of assault on the notoriously violent streets of the city.

As Hedgset prepared to make the final suture, the pain became too great for Elise to bear and, her eyes rolling back in her head, she swooned again, her body going limp and offering no resistance as the leech finished his task. Adroitly he wrapped strips of linen over the site of the wound and around her stomach, crisscrossing them at her waist to keep them secure. Then he extracted a small vial from his bag and dribbled some of the liquid it contained into his comatose patient's mouth.

"She should be taken to a chamber where it is quiet," he said as he straightened and replaced the stopper in the vial. "I have given her a small dose of juice of poppy and, if she awakens, it will help keep her drowsy so that she does not tear the stitches I have put in."

"You said *if* she wakes, leech," Richard said. "Is there a danger she may not?"

Hedgset did not answer immediately, first instructing two servants to fetch the top of another trestle table for use as a makeshift stretcher. When they had done so, he bade them hold the litter steady while he eased Elise's prone form onto its surface. Only when that had been done did he make a response to Richard's question, and his reluctance to do so was evident as he glanced at Alinor's white face. Nonetheless, he did not mince his words. "With knife wounds, lord, there is always a chance they may prove fatal," he said bluntly. "I have had strong men die within a few hours from no more than a scratch and others recover completely from what appeared to be a mortal wound. If the humours in the maid's body are not too far out of balance, and if the blade has not pricked her spleen or her liver, she has a chance; that is all I can tell you."

Hedgset stepped back and Alinor, her breath catching in her throat as she tried to keep her composure, told the two servants to take Elise to her own chamber, adding that the girl was to be placed in the large bed that Alinor used. She would nurse the maid herself, she said, but, as she went to follow the servants to their destination, she heard Richard ask Margaret what she had seen of the attack and paused to hear the sempstress' answer.

"It all happened so fast, lord," Margaret replied. "There was quite a large number of people watching a strange bird that spoke words just as though it were human. One minute Elise was exclaiming with the rest of us how clever it was and the next . . . I heard her cry out. Then she fell down onto the ground beside me."

"Did you recognise anyone in the crowd?" Richard asked.

Margaret faltered. "I didn't notice who was there, lord . . . I did not think to look, my attention was on the bird." She turned to Alinor. "Oh, lady, the person that stabbed Elise must be the same one as murdered Aubrey. Who else would have reason to do such a thing? And we do not know where he will strike next. It could even be that he will attack your mother if he gets the chance. We are none of us safe here— please, please, let us go back to Stamford before he kills again."

As she had listened to Margaret, the set of Alinor's mouth had become determined and her response to the plea was firm. "It will do no good to run from this villain. If he is intent on harming another one of us, he will seek us out wherever we are. I do not intend to give him the satisfaction of seeing us flee like a startled hare."

Margaret's face fell in disappointment as her mistress' daughter turned to catch up to the two servants bearing Elise's inert form out of the hall.

Twenty-five

✢

WHEN BASCOT LEFT REINBALD'S HOUSE, HE TURNED HIS horse toward the lower part of town and the shop of Simon Adgate. His route took him away from the top of Mikelgate Street, and so he did not pass the spot where Elise had been stabbed, nor see the little knots of townsfolk standing looking up Steep Hill towards the castle, in the direction that Nicholas had dashed with the unconscious Elise held fast in his arms.

As he rode, Bascot pondered what he had been told by the wine merchant about the neighbour who had travelled to Winchester over twenty years before. "The draper's name was Thomas Adgate and, although I am not absolutely sure, I believe the two young girls were kinfolk of his."

"Do you know if the draper was any relation to Simon Adgate, the furrier?" Bascot had asked.

"I believe so. Thomas was Simon's uncle, I think, or a cousin of some sort." The wine merchant had shaken his head sadly. "Many years ago, the Adgates were a prolific family, all related to an ancestor named Ad who, at one time, owned premises near Stonebow gate, but in my own generation, not many male children were born to the family. All of them were engaged in the cloth trade, fullers, dyers, drapers and a couple of furriers. Now only Simon, to my uncertain knowledge, is left."

"And the girls—are they still here in Lincoln?"

Reinbald had pondered for a moment and then said, "Do you know, I don't believe I ever saw either of them again after the draper returned from his trip. Not that I recall, anyway."

As Bascot reined his horse in at the door to the furrier's premises, he wondered if he had stumbled across yet another connection between Adgate and the murdered Tercel. First it had been discovered his wife was involved in an adulterous affair with the dead man and now it appeared that a relative of Adgate's could be Tercel's mother. Alinor's intuition had been correct when she had insisted that Adgate was hiding something apart from his wife's affair. Was it possible, despite strong evidence to the contrary, that it was the furrier who was responsible for the cofferer's death?

When Bascot entered the shop, Adgate was serving a customer, a man who had brought his wife to select a fur-lined tippet. Clarice was with the furrier, placing various lengths of fur about her shoulders so that the woman could consider which of the scarflike garments she favoured. Adgate's assistant hovered nearby.

When Bascot was shown in by the guard at the door, the furrier immediately came forward, his expression one of watchfulness. The customers looked speculatively towards Bascot as they noticed the Templar badge on the front of his cloak. Clarice looked frightened.

"I would have a few moments of private speech with you, Adgate," Bascot said brusquely.

Signalling to his assistant to take his place, the furrier led Bascot to the hall where they had spoken together before. He offered the Templar a cup of wine which Bascot declined.

"I have come to ask about two relatives of yours, women who were related to a draper named Thomas Adgate. They were, I believe, your cousins."

The furrier said nothing in response, just nodded.

"What were their names?" Bascot asked.

Adgate looked to the side, away from the Templar's gaze. "May I ask why you want to know, Sir Bascot?"

"The information may be pertinent to the investigation into the murder of Lady Petronille's retainer," Bascot replied.

"I do not see how it can be," the furrier replied. "What can either of my cousins have to do with it?"

Irritated by the furrier's avoidance of a direct answer, Bascot decided to be more forceful with his questions and took a bold leap, as though his knowledge was certain rather than nebulous. "I am told that one of your cousins went to Winchester with Thomas Adgate some twenty-five years ago. That is the time, and the place, where Aubrey Tercel—the man your wife was having an affair with—was conceived. Later, the child was given into the care of another and the mother returned to her home in Lincoln. I have reason to believe that Tercel's mother and one of your cousins are the same person."

The vitality seemed to drain out of Adgate. He sank onto the seat of a chair at the table and, with shaking hands,

poured himself a cup of wine before he answered. When his
response came, it was murmured in a voice that was barely
audible.

"Yes, she is," he said quietly.

The Templar experienced a thrill of satisfaction. Although he was still far from obtaining proof of the woman's,
or Adgate's, culpability, he was making progress towards
that end. It was evident in the furrier's submissive attitude
that he was on the verge of revealing that which he had so far
kept concealed. Bascot's voice took on a hard edge as he
pressed his advantage. "Had Tercel discovered that fact?
Was that the matter you discussed with him here, in this
very room, on the day that your wife said you were closeted
with him for a long time? And the reason you were arguing
with him in the street in front of your premises?"

Adgate looked up in startlement at the last statement.

"You were seen, furrier, by a neighbour," the Templar informed him.

The flesh on Adgate's face sagged, and he nodded miserably.

"Then you must tell me your cousin's name."

But instead of responding as Bascot had expected him to
do, and reveal his cousin's identity, the furrier pulled himself
up and squared his shoulders. "I will not do so. She has suffered enough. And I am certain she did not commit the
murder. To know her name will profit you nothing, and will
cause her great distress if it is revealed. I have kept her secret
all of these years and I will not betray her now."

Bascot struggled to keep his temper at the furrier's refusal and consoled himself with the thought that now that
they knew the woman was related to Adgate, it would take

only a little effort to unearth the name of both his cousins. Gildas, the barber, as a good friend of Adgate, would know the identities of the other members of the furrier's family, and so, most probably, would other merchants in the town. It was simply a matter of asking, finding out their names and then questioning both of them to determine which of them had gone to Winchester in the year of Tercel's conception. But even if they found the woman, it did not prove she was linked to the death of her illegitimate son, or that Adgate had been involved in the killing.

The Templar regarded the furrier. Was he a man who would commit murder to protect his cousin's dark secret, or pay another to do so? Adgate had, so far, evidenced a merchant's glib evasiveness, side-stepping all of the questions put to him, never telling an outright lie but confining himself to a partial truth when nothing else would suffice. Despite his irritation at Adgate's continuing subterfuge, Bascot felt that the furrier was an honest man at heart and that if he was involved in the machinations of the murder, would have found it impossible to successfully conceal his guilt. The Templar looked carefully at the man seated before him. For the first time since Bascot had made his acquaintance, Adgate looked his age. The pouches beneath his eyes looked bruised and his skin was sallow. The Templar could not detect any trace of culpability in the furrier's demeanour, instead Adgate exuded an ineffable lassitude, as though the events which had overtaken him—Tercel's haranguing, his wife's betrayal and, last but not least, the admission of his cousin's secret—had wearied him beyond his strength. Although he felt some sympathy for the man who fate had, it appeared, chosen to buffet through the actions of others rather than his own, it remained imperative to discover if the murdered man's mother had a connection with her son's death and, to that end, he must pursue the matter.

"How did Tercel learn that his mother was related to you?" he asked.

Adgate raised haggard eyes to Bascot. "I do not know. Truly I do not. He merely said he had proof of his mother's identity and that she was my cousin. Then he pressed me to tell him who his father was."

"And who was it?"

"I could not tell Tercel and nor can I tell you, Sir Bascot, for I do not know," Adgate replied.

The Templar felt his temper rise. "Come, furrier, surely your cousin's parents, at least, would have known the man's name. Or are you saying they refused to tell you?"

"No, I am not. No one knew who he was."

At Bascot's uncomprehending look, the furrier added, "My cousin was raped, Sir Bascot. The assault took place in the darkness of evening and she was attacked from behind. She never saw the face of her assailant."

The Templar finally began to understand Adgate's reticence. To have borne a child as the result of an illicit liaison would certainly cause damage to a woman's reputation, but it was a sin that, although frowned upon, would have been understood and perhaps forgotten with the passage of time. But to have conceived a child due to a sexual assault would tarnish the mother, and the babe, with a stigma that could never be erased. Any woman defiled in such a fashion would be thought to have attracted her attacker due to her lewd nature, and so it would be she, and not the rapist, who was blamed for her misfortune. She would be considered on a level with a harlot, and her child no better than those born to the women in that profession. It could not be wondered at that she had hid-

den her condition and was willing to give up the babe after
it was born. It was the only means she had of hiding her
shame and, at the same time, protecting the child from a life
filled with the scorn of others.

"Did you tell Tercel the truth of his paternity?" Bascot
asked.

"What would have been the purpose in that?" Adgate
said resignedly. "He seemed to have formed the impression
that his father was of royal blood. Even though he angered
me with the haughtiness of his demand, so much so that I
felt like striking him, I could not bring myself to tell him
what had happened to his mother, for he was, after all, related to me by blood." The furrier looked at Bascot with a
plea for understanding in his eyes. "Surely it was better for
him to believe that a royal prince had been his father than to
be told that his sire was a nameless villain who had violated
a defenceless young girl."

In THE CASTLE SOLAR, NICOLAA AND PETRONILLE SAT WITH
Richard discussing what Willi had told them. The boy was
still in the chamber, standing a little apart from the group,
huddled close to the protective presence of Ernulf at the far
end of the room. Richard had returned to his mother and
aunt after Elise had been removed from the hall and had told
them that the leech and Alinor were watching over the
wounded maid.

Once assured that no more could be done at the moment
for the unfortunate girl, Nicolaa told her son what Willi had
related about his sighting of the person near the old tower.

"The boy says he saw a figure coming through the door of
the armoury while he and the other children were being

taken to the stables. It would have been about the time we
assume that Tercel was killed; just as the meal for the guild
leaders was about to be served and a little while after Clarice
Adgate had left to meet him."

"Could he see the person clearly?" Richard asked.

"Well enough to say it was a woman. Although her head
was covered by the hood of a cloak, the edges of a coif showed
beneath it and there was a trail of skirts below the hem of
her mantle."

Richard considered the information. "There would be
no reason for a woman to be in the armoury, so that fact in
itself is suspicious, and makes me inclined to believe the
boy. Now we have only to find the woman and have him
identify her."

"Yes," Nicolaa said, "but therein lies the difficulty. Willi
is not familiar with any of the guild leaders' wives or, beyond the two or three maidservants he has come into contact
with, any of the females in my household. Neither is he acquainted with many of the women in the town. He says he
believes he would know her if he saw her again, but we can
hardly take him by the hand and traipse him through the
bail and the streets of the town so he can search the faces of
all the women who live here."

"And while she remains undiscovered, the boy is in danger," Petronille interjected. "It will not take long for the real
reason the boy was brought here to become common knowledge. Even though his sighting of the murderer was never
told to anyone directly and is, so far, known only to us few,
such information has an insidious way of being ferreted out
and then travelling from one person to another as though it
was borne on the wind."

"We must contrive a means of keeping him safe and yet,

at the same time, seek an opportunity for him to regard the faces of any of the women who might be deemed culpable," Nicolaa said. "We could start with the wives of the guild leaders. If I ask them all to come here under the pretext of discussing further candidates for the foundling home, Willi could be in the hall when they arrive. . . ."

As the castellan was speaking, Alinor came into the room. Her gown was splattered with bloodstains, but there was a smile of relief on her face. "The leech thinks that, with careful nursing, Elise will recover," she said. "She came to her senses for a few moments and although she is in pain, seemed rational. Hedgset says that her humours are weak, but appear to be in balance, and he has given her more juice of poppy to help her sleep. I have told him to remain with her until I return and that I will personally keep watch over her. I have also asked your steward, Aunt, to arrange for one of your men-at-arms to stand guard at the door."

"Was the girl able to tell you who attacked her?" Richard asked.

Alinor shook her head. "She remembers little; only craning her head to see the talking bird and then a sharp pain in her side."

"Thanks be to God that she was not killed," Petronille exclaimed. "What of Margaret? She, too, must be sore distressed."

"She stayed with me while Hedgset attended Elise and, like myself, is relieved to hear that the leech thinks she is out of danger. I have sent her to the stables to tell the groom, Nicholas, that, as far as Hedgset can determine, Elise is not mortally wounded. I thought it only right that the groom should be reassured, for if it had not been for his valiant effort, Elise could have bled to death in the street."

For a moment, the ghost of a smile appeared on Alinor's face. "I think Nicholas has taken quite a fancy to Elise. If she returns his affection, I may still yet lose her company but, thankfully, it will only be to a husband and not because of her death."

Twenty-six

—✠—

Willi remained standing quietly beside Ernulf at the back of the room as Lady Nicolaa spoke to the young noblewoman who had just come in about the girl that had been stabbed. The young lady had blood spatters on the front of her gown that he supposed must have come from the victim and he stared at them in growing fear until, after she left, Lady Nicolaa began to discuss with her sister and son the ways in which they could manage for him to see the faces of all of the women who had been in the hall on the night of the feast. Then he began to wish he had lied and told the castellan that he hadn't seen the murderer. If he had, they might have let him go. He felt unsafe here in the castle, even with the serjeant standing by his side. What would happen when he went to sleep? Even if they put him in the barracks with all the men-at-arms to keep watch, that murdering woman had managed to slip past everyone in the castle to kill that man up on the ramparts, hadn't she? And it must have been her that stabbed that girl in the town. What was to stop her from creeping past the soldiers and sticking a knife in him in just the same way?

He waited with seeming patience while the lord and the two ladies talked, but his thoughts were whirling. He had felt much safer on the streets of the town and knew he had to get away from the castle. He didn't know where he would go, but his guts had been churning ever since Ernulf had brought him into the ward. He must look for a way to escape. He knew the gates on the eastern side of the bail were left open during the day; if he got a chance, he could dart through them and run across the Minster and out one of the gates in the town wall into the countryside. He didn't know where he would go once he reached there, but he knew he had to get away from here.

As Bascot rode away from Adgate's shop, he pondered on whether or not he should visit Gildas on the way back to the castle and ask the barber if he knew the names of the furrier's cousins. The story of how Tercel had been conceived had saddened him; the dead man's mother must surely have suffered great anguish during that terrible experience, and it would be a calamity if now, after all these years, her secret was exposed for no other purpose than to eliminate her from the suspicion. Although it was commonly believed that women who had been sexually assaulted were the cause of their own misfortune, Bascot had seen the aftermath of many such incidents during the time he had been on crusade in the Holy Land with the Templars, and knew that conviction to be a falsehood. After a battle, there were always a few men in a victorious army, both Christian and infidel, who violated the unprotected women belonging to the foe they had vanquished. And he was well aware that the men who perpetrated such bestiality in war had their counterparts among a peaceful populace, and were entirely capable of inflicting their unnatural lust, by stealth, on an unwary maid. He could not, in all conscience, take the risk of betraying Tercel's mother by openly enquiring about her and decided he would first discuss what he had learned with Lady Nicolaa and Sir Richard. If they felt it necessary to continue the investigation into her identity, perhaps a way could be found to do so discreetly, at least until they could be assured she bore no fault for her son's death.

Perhaps, he reflected, Ernulf and Gianni had found the missing boy and he would be able to tell them the identity of the murderer. The Templar fervently hoped that was so. It would save any more painful delving into the past of the people who had been connected to the dead man and, even if one of them was found to be guilty it would, at least, make the judgement a certain one.

His course settled in his mind, he turned onto the main thoroughfare of Mikelgate and saw, a little way farther along, the figure of Hugh Bruet standing beside his horse with one of the de Humez men-at-arms, engaged in conversation with a small group of townspeople. As the Templar approached, Bruet hailed him and, when Bascot drew near, the knight told him of the attack on Elise.

"This is the spot where she was stabbed, and I hoped I might be able to find someone who saw the person that did it," he said to Bascot, "but, so far, I've not been successful. Everyone had their eyes fixed on the talking bird and saw nothing untoward before Margaret screamed. I've asked all of the shopkeepers along this stretch and a few of the roving vendors that were nearby, as well as some of the goodwives that were on the street, but they all claim they didn't see anyone with a knife approach the girl. If I didn't know better, I'd say Elise's attacker was a wraith."

The Templar commiserated with the knight, and Bruet, deciding he could do no more, mounted his horse and said he would return to the castle as well. "I am reluctant to admit to Lady Petronille that I found nothing that could help us catch the villain who wounded the maid," he said. "And I do not relish having to face de Humez when we go back to Stamford. I was sent to protect his lady and her household; now one of them is dead and another sorely hurt. Margaret was right when she said that Lincoln has changed since the days of her youth. Even with Sheriff Camville's heavy hand upon it, the town abounds with thieves and murderers."

Bascot had forgotten that the sempstress was from Lincoln, but now recalled that Petronille had previously mentioned that Margaret had been in her retinue at the time of her marriage to Richard de Humez and had later accompanied her mistress to Stamford. "There are far more people within the town walls than were here so many years ago," Bascot opined in response to Bruet's statement. "As a population increases, the incidence of crime swells in proportion."

Bruet gave a grunt of agreement. "You are right. And I must admit that it is little better in Stamford. Thankfully, the de Humez manor house is some distance from the town and not so much bothered with the criminal activity that takes place there. I pity the townsmen who have wives and children to protect. Sometimes they must regret ever having been wed."

As they reached the top of Mikelgate, and neared the

turning of Danesgate, Bruet's words echoed in Bascot's mind and, his thoughts still partially on the woman who was Tercel's mother and the ordeal she had undergone, his perspective of her suddenly shifted. Throughout the investigation they had been looking for a married woman or one that had been widowed. They had also considered the possibility that she had died, but never once had they entertained the notion that she may have remained unwed. And therein they might have made an error. The trauma of her experience could well have made her eschew marriage and the only implication that she had not done so was entirely due to Lionel Wharton's letter, and the passage where he stated that such was her intention. But the knight would not have known whether or not she had actually done so, for he had no knowledge of her fate once she left the convent. Suppose she had refused to wed her intended bridegroom and had retained her spinster status? This was a likelihood for which no allowance had been made, mainly because there were few women in society that, unless they entered a convent, remained unmarried—the practise of forming useful alliances through females relative was just as common in the merchant class as in those of noble status—but, nonetheless, there were some females who chose this path in life, and it was entirely possible, nay, even probable when one took into account her devastating experience, that Tercel's mother was one of them.

As he mentally examined the viability of this premise, a number of coincidences occurred to him and he realised there was one woman they had all overlooked. She fit the description admirably—being of the right age, a resident of Lincoln at the time of Tercel's conception and had remained unwed. She had also been in the castle on the night of the feast and present when Elise had been stabbed. And because of her close proximity to the murdered man, it also explained why no evidence of him making a search for her within the town had been found. He had no need to go abroad to seek her, she had been in his company all along, for she was living within the castle walls. Bascot was now certain that he knew her identity, and he was also confident that, despite the furrier's denial, it had been she who had killed her son.

By this time they had passed Danesgate and the street where Gildas' shop was located. He was about to go back and ask the barber for the names of Adgate's cousins as further proof of his theory but instead turned to Bruet.

"The sempstress, Margaret—do you know whether or not she still has family in Lincoln?"

"I am not sure," the knight replied, a little startled by the question. "She said to me once that her parents were dead, but I don't recall her mentioning any other relatives."

"It is important, Bruet," Bascot said tersely, curbing his impatience. "Has she ever said anything about a cousin, or the trade that he followed?"

Recognising that the Templar's peremptory tone was dictated by the importance of his question rather than rudeness, the knight took no offence but pursed his lips and thought back over the years he had spent in Margaret's company while they both served in the de Humez retinue. "About a cousin, no, but she did tell me once that her father was a draper. She said she learned to sew in the shop where he sold his bolts of cloth, helping to stitch vestments for those customers who did not have a wife with sufficient skill to make them." Bruet paused. "Is that what you want to know?"

Bascot made no answer. Reinbald had told him that all of

the Adgate family had been engaged in the clothing trade. He had no doubt now that Margaret was the woman they were seeking and, as the assurance came to him, hard on its heels came the thought that if the missing boy, Willi, had been found and could identify her, she might seek an opportunity to silence his tongue before he could pronounce her guilt. If Ernulf had taken Willi back to the castle, he would not have removed the lad from danger, but placed him directly in its path.

"Bruet," he said urgently, "do you know if Ernulf found the boy that ran away?"

The abrupt change of subject disconcerted the de Humez knight and he looked at Bascot in surprise. "The one from the foundling home? I think he may have. I saw the serjeant return with a red-headed youngster in tow just a short while before Elise was brought into the bail. . . ."

His words were cut off as Bascot dug his spurs deep into the sides of his mount and urged the horse forward up the sharp incline of Steep Hill towards the castle. For a moment, a bewildered Bruet looked after him and then, putting his heels to his own mount, he followed in the Templar's wake.

Twenty-seven
✦✦✦

IN THE CASTLE SOLAR, LADY NICOLAA ROSE FROM HER SEAT. "The midday meal will soon be served below. Let us leave discussing this matter for the moment and take some sustenance. Perhaps food will sharpen our wits."

She called to where Ernulf and Willi were standing. "Take the boy with you, Ernulf, and let him eat at your table. Afterwards, you may bring him back here."

The serjeant did as he was bid, placing his meaty hand on Willi's shoulder in a kindly fashion and motioning with his head for the boy to leave the room. When they entered the hall, Ernulf told the boy to go to the back of the huge chamber where some of the off-duty men-at-arms were already seated while he got them both a mug of ale. "You'll be safe enough in the soldiers' company, lad," he said to Willi. "Go and tell them I said you were to sit in the middle of the bench."

As Ernulf moved towards the ale keg that sat at the rear of the hall, Willi looked around. No one was near him and the door into the keep was ajar, the attendant who manned it distracted by a conversation he was having with another servant. Without giving himself time to ponder the wisdom of his decision, Willi darted between the tables and, weaving his way through the trail of servants bearing platters from the kitchen, slipped through the opening. Once outside, he sped down the steps of the forebuilding and started across the bail. The eastern gate of the castle stood wide open, and no gateward was in sight. Taking a deep breath, he started towards it, rushing past members of the outside household staff making their way to the hall for the midday meal, when suddenly his footsteps faltered and he came to a halt. Just a few paces in front of him was the woman he had seen outside the armoury on the night of the murder and, from her grim smile, he knew that she recognised him. Before he could run around her, she stepped forward and grasped him tightly by the shoulder.

"So, you are the boy that will be my death warrant," she said. "I think it would be best if I forestall that event."

Without another word she dragged him across the ward and into the old tower, pushing him ahead of her up the stairs. "We will hide in here until everyone is in the hall and then, my lad, you and I are going to leave the bail. If you behave yourself, I will let you go once we are outside the castle walls."

Willi struggled to free himself, but her grip was like iron. Behind him he heard a shout and knew the voice was Ernulf's. The boy tried to yell out to the serjeant, but the woman clamped her hand across his mouth and the words died unspoken. "If you don't keep quiet, you will suffer the consequences," she warned and Willi saw light flash on the blades of a pair of scissors she had drawn from the scrip at her belt. "I have killed once already, and will not hesitate to do so again. Do you understand, boy?"

Willi nodded his head mutely as she dragged him into the tower and shut the door behind them.

Bascot and Bruet rode into the bail just as Willi was being dragged into the old tower by his captor. As they rode into the ward, the Templar noted the movement of the door, which was not far from the gate and on his sighted side, but was so intent on reaching the hall that he gave it no more than a fleeting glance. As he slid from his horse, he saw Ernulf standing in the middle of the bail looking frantically around him. Running down the steps of the forebuilding to the keep were two men-at-arms who, once they reached the bottom, ran over to where the serjeant was standing. Ernulf looked shaken and Bascot asked him what was amiss.

"The boy, Willi, we found him this morning and brought him back to the castle, but now he's run away again," Ernulf said, his breath ragged. "Did you see him when you came through the gate?"

The Templar shook his head. "Did he tell you whether or not he saw the murderer?"

"Yes," Ernulf replied. "He says it was a woman and he'd know her if he saw her again, but he doesn't know who she is. Lady Nicolaa told me to keep him safe until he can identify her, and now he's gone. I've got to find him."

Bascot's heart sank as he heard the serjeant proclaim the gender of the murderer. It had to be Margaret that the boy had seen. His thoughts tumbled furiously as Ernulf turned to the men-at-arms and ordered them to search the bail.

"Every shed and storehouse, and look in the kitchen as well. . . ."

Bascot cut the serjeant's words off in mid-flow. "Where is Margaret, Lady Petronille's sempstress?" he asked tersely.

Distracted, and in haste to be off, Ernulf stumbled over his reply. "Margaret? I don't know. She wasn't in the solar, and I didn't see her in the hall. I think I remember Lady Alinor saying she sent her to the stables to speak to the groom that brought the injured girl from the town. Do you think she might know where Willi has gone?"

"I hope not," Bascot replied grimly. He glanced towards the stables but could see no sign of the sempstress, only a few grooms attending to the chore of mucking out the stables and the castle blacksmith inspecting the shoes of one of the horses. Fear gripped his throat. The boy who could identify the person that had killed Tercel was missing and the person he was now certain had committed the crime was not in plain sight. If she had ahold of the boy, where would she have taken him? Scanning the multitude of buildings in the ward, he suddenly recalled how he had glimpsed the door of the old tower closing as he and Bruet had entered the bail. "Sir Hugh and I will search the old tower," he said to Ernulf, "while you and your men look in the other buildings. And if you see Margaret, detain her in the keep until I come."

Anxious to be about his search, Ernulf gave a nod and hurried off after his men.

An unspoken question was etched on Bruet's face as he followed Bascot's hasty steps to the tower and waited while the Templar cautiously pushed open the door. The interior was still and silent, the staircase that led up to the ramparts empty.

"What did you say the lad's name is?" Bruet asked.

"Willi," the Templar replied softly, "but do not call out. We will search the chambers, but quietly."

His curiosity barely restrained, Bruet did as the Templar bid and the two knights ascended the stairs to the second storey. They looked in the rooms that led off the landing at the second level; all were empty. As they came out again onto the stairs, a noise could be heard above, a shuffling sound and the whispering grate of a door being opened.

"Up there," Bascot said and ran up the steps to the third floor. As they reached the top of the staircase, there was a crash as the door out onto the walkway flew back and hit the wall behind it. It was accompanied by the sound of a young boy's voice raised in protest. "No, I'm not going out there . . . let me go. . . ."

The Templar and Bruet charged through the opening. In front of them, at the far end of the catwalk, was Margaret, her arm around Willi's neck and holding a pair of scissors, point downwards, at the boy's throat, her back pressed hard against the stone wall of the parapet.

Bascot's premise was now confirmed. Because of the information contained in Lionel Wharton's letter, they had never considered that Tercel's mother might not have married the Lincoln merchant. And she had not done so. After she had birthed the babe and given him into Lionel Wharton's care, she had returned to Lincoln and obtained a place as a servant in Petronille's retinue, taking the secret of her past safe with her to Stamford in the de Humez retinue. All the time they had been searching for her, she had been in their midst, and had been able to commit the murder without a shadow of suspicion being laid on her. And now she had a young child at her mercy. Bascot had no doubt she would injure, or even kill Willi, if they made an attempt to wrest him from her.

238 MAUREEN ASH

"Margaret, what are you doing up here with the boy . . . ?" The startled exclamation burst from Bruet, then faltered as he remembered the Templar's questions and tried to make sense of what he was witnessing.

Bascot laid a restraining hand on the knight's arm. Margaret saw the motion and gave a small harsh laugh. "You may not know why I am here, Hugh, but I can see that Sir Bascot does." She tightened her grip on Willi. "I am the one this boy saw that night, just after I had killed that misbegotten bastard Tercel. It was right here, on this very spot, that I took his life and I am glad of it. He was the spawn of an incubus and I could not let him blight his mother's life all over again."

As Bruet stiffened with shock beside him, a prickle of unease ran up Bascot's spine. Margaret was speaking of the man she had killed as though he had been born to another woman. Could it be that a resurgence of the terror she had suffered all those long years ago had deranged her mind—and that she was now justifying her crime by denying her motherhood? Whatever the reason, the staid spinster that Margaret had appeared to be was gone and, in her place, it was as though the demon of which she spoke had taken possession of her. Her coif, always so neat, was askew and her plain features twisted with lines of hatred. He must tread carefully, and try to distract her until he was close enough to get Willi free from her grasp. Motioning to Bruet to remain where he was, he took one small step forward.

"Let the boy go, mistress," he said softly. "He is an innocent soul and has done you no harm. Release him and give yourself into Lady Nicolaa's charge."

Margaret gave a short bark of harsh laughter that contained no mirth. "And why should I do that, Templar? So

Richard Camville can hang me from a gibbet? I think not."
She took a jerky step away from the two knights. "Stay
back, both of you. If you do not give me safe passage into
the town, I promise you will see this boy dead, just like
Tercel."

Bruet added his voice to Bascot's in an attempt to persuade the sempstress to release the boy. "Do as Sir Bascot
says, Margaret, I beg of you. I do not know why you killed
Tercel or are threatening this boy's life but I am sure Lady
Petronille will speak up for you. I know she values your service highly."

For a moment, a shadow of remorse crossed Margaret's
face and she looked once again, if only for a moment, sane
and sober. "No, she will not, Hugh, for her conscience is too
tender. And that is my one regret, that I have caused distress
to such a good lady. Tell her . . . tell her that I am sorry, and
Elise also. I never meant to harm the girl badly, only to prick
her, but she moved towards me as I thrust with my scissors.
I thought that if another one of milady's servants was attacked, Lady Petronille would be persuaded to take us all
back to Stamford, a place we should never have left."

Once more Bruet tried to reason with her. "Margaret, I
beg of you, let the child go and give yourself up."

The sempstress shook her head and her face regained its
former malevolence. "It is too late for that, Hugh. Far too
late," she said bitterly.

Dragging Willi with her, she began to move slowly along
the walkway towards the watchtower above the gate while
Bascot and Bruet watched in helpless frustration. At the
door of the watchtower, the gateward was looking in their
direction with a puzzled expression. To the right, along the
expanse of palisade that stretched to the west, the guard who

had been pacing the wall was approaching, his hand hovering uncertainly over the hilt of the short sword at his belt.

"Tell the gateward to let me pass," Margaret directed harshly. "And make that man-at-arms stay back," she added, moving her head in the direction of the approaching guard. "If you don't, the boy dies. I cannot be hung more than once, so another murder will be of no consequence."

Holding up his hand to stop the man-at-arms on the palisade walkway, Bascot called out to the gateward. "The woman and the boy are going down into the ward. Let them by without hindrance."

The gateward nodded and withdrew as Margaret slowly pulled the boy in his direction. Willi's eyes were round with terror.

As they came out from under the shadow of the old tower, they were exposed to the gaze of those in the bail. A servant noticed them up on the walkway and pointed upwards excitedly; soon others were gazing in their direction, trying to make sense of what they were witnessing. A man-at-arms called out to Ernulf, who came running to the front of the crowd that had gathered. After taking a few moments to assess the situation, he sent one of the soldiers towards the entrance that led out onto Ermine Street.

Margaret realised his intention. "Instruct the serjeant to leave the gates open, Templar," she commanded.

As Bascot called down to Ernulf, two figures appeared in the huge portal. It was Simon Adgate and Merisel Wickson. Both looked up aghast at the figures on the parapet and the furrier came farther into the ward, motioning for his companion to stay back.

"Margaret, what are you doing up there?" he called in astonishment. "And why are you threatening that boy?"

"Stay out of this, Simon," the sempstress responded grimly. "It is naught to do with you."

Adgate looked back towards Merisel and spoke to her quietly. When the girl gave a frightened nod, the furrier turned and once again faced the parapet. "I am coming up there, Margaret," he said, a look of determination on his face, "and you will give the child, unharmed, to me."

"This is no concern of yours, Simon," she screamed at him. "I am telling you not to interfere."

"I have heeded your wishes for far too long, Margaret," he replied. "It is time to put an end to this mayhem."

With limping strides he went towards the ladder Ernulf was accustomed to use to go up onto the ramparts and began to ascend. In agitation, Margaret began to shriek at him, telling him to go back. As she did so, her hold on Willi loosened and, with a courage born of desperation, the boy began to struggle, kicking out with the sturdy boots he had been given on the day he came to the castle. One of the thick heels caught the sempstress with a sharp rap on the shin and she recoiled in pain.

It was all the advantage Bascot needed. Leaping forward, he took hold of her arm and the hand that held the scissors. With an outraged cry, the sempstress tried to shake herself loose from his grip, but he held her fast as Willi sprang away from her and into the safety of Bruet's waiting arms.

Twenty-eight

＊✚＊

As two men-at-arms escorted Margaret across the bail
to a holding cell in the castle gaol, Bascot walked over to
where Simon Adgate stood with a trembling Merisel Wickson. As he saw the Templar approach, the furrier laid a hand
gently on the girl's shoulder and whispered something in
her ear. With a nod, she turned around and, with but one
fleeting glance over her shoulder, ran quickly out onto Ermine Street and disappeared.

"Your intervention was timely, furrier, and you have my
thanks for making it," Bascot said when he came up to
Adgate. "But I am afraid I must still ask if you were complicit in the murder."

"No, I was not, lord," the furrier responded quietly.

"Nonetheless, you could have saved today's anguish if
you had told me Margaret was Tercel's mother."

"But she is not," Adgate replied. "It is true she is my
cousin, but . . ."

Bascot did not let him finish. "She has just confessed to the killing, you have no need to protect her anymore."

"You do not understand, lord," Adgate protested. "Margaret was not his mother. It was her sister who bore him."

The statement took Bascot aback until he remembered his puzzlement at the way the sempstress had spoken up on the ramparts, her words implying that the man she had killed had not been her own son.

"And this sister, she is the one who went to Winchester with your uncle?" he asked Adgate, trying to make sense of what the furrier was saying.

"They both did, lord," Adgate replied, "but although Margaret also made the journey, it was her sister who was violated."

It had not occurred to Bascot that both of Adgate's cousins had travelled to Winchester. He had thought of only one but now, with the furrier's revelation, the insinuation behind Margaret's words became clear.

"I did have a suspicion at first, terrible though it seemed, that Margaret might be responsible for Tercel's death," Adgate said, "and sent her a message to meet me so that I could ask if she was involved. But when she came, she assured me most fervently that she was not the one who had murdered him, and that the culprit must be the husband of one of his paramours." He took a deep, and shaky, breath. "May God forgive me, after discovering that my own wife had lain with the man, I was only too ready to be convinced that what she said was the truth. And, until this morning, I kept to that conviction."

"What changed your mind?" Bascot asked.

"I was told, by a witness, that it was possible Margaret

had stabbed a young woman. The witness had never met my cousin and came to me for verification of her appearance. When I was given the description and, even though, in my heart, I realised there could be no mistake, I came here with the person who saw the act, intending to bring my cousin before her so she could personally identify Margaret as the woman she had seen. If it was confirmed that it was she who carried out this morning's assault, I knew it must have some connection with the murder—that perhaps the girl she attacked had, like Tercel, learned our family secret and threatened to expose it—and I intended to implore my cousin to give herself up to Sir Richard's justice."

The witness Adgate was referring to must be Merisel Wickson, the Templar surmised, for the chandler's daughter had been with Adgate when he came into the bail. And the candle-maker's manufactory was very near to the spot where Elise had been attacked. Recalling the hesitancy which Merisel had shown in answering the questions he had put to her on the day he had gone to the chandlery, the Templar now saw the connection and also why, if it had been she who saw Margaret stab Elise, she had gone to Adgate instead of reporting what she saw to Bruet, who only minutes later was at the spot where the stabbing had taken place, attempting to find a witness.

"I vowed, along with Margaret, that I would never reveal her sister's shame," Adgate said with abject resignation. "But now, I have no choice."

"Let your conscience be easy, furrier," Bascot said. "You do not have to tell me, for the truth is plain to see. The woman you and Margaret have been protecting is the chandler's wife, Edith Wickson, is it not?"

"Yes, lord, it is," Adgate confirmed miserably.

* * *

An hour later, Nicolaa and Richard, along with Petronille and Alinor, were in the solar, listening as Bascot related the details of his conversation with Adgate. Hugh Bruet was there as well and so was Gianni, the latter taking down notes of what his former master was recounting. The furrier had been left outside the chamber in the company of a man-at-arms.

When Bascot had finished, Nicolaa asked, "Do you think Adgate is telling the truth when he says that he and Mistress Wickson were not involved in the murder?"

"I cannot be certain, lady, but I think so. He is a very shaken man but also, I believe, an honest one. If you will recall, he has never told us an outright untruth, but has simply avoided revealing what he knows. As for Mistress Wickson, the furrier tells me that after he told her that her illegitimate son was searching for her, she feigned illness on the night of the feast out of fear that, if she came to the castle, Tercel might, because of some passing resemblance between them, recognise her as his mother. After he was killed, so Adgate says, the news of his death made her truly ill and she has not risen from her sickbed since. These facts bear out what we were told by her husband—who, apparently, is not privy to her secret—and led to the conclusion that she could not have been, at least actively, involved in the crime."

"Did Adgate tell you how Tercel discovered that Edith Wickson was his mother?" Richard asked.

"He was not aware that she was," Bascot said, surprising them all. "Adgate says that when he came and asked to speak to him privily, he seemed to believe that Margaret was his dam. He told the furrier that he had challenged the sempstress with his accusation, but that she would not admit to it, nor tell him who his father was. Adgate, of course, told him that Margaret was telling the truth, but his protestations fell on deaf ears. What happened next is only conjecture on the furrier's part, but he thinks that Margaret killed Tercel because she feared he was getting too close to his objective, and would soon discover that it was her sister, not she, who had birthed him. She murdered him to prevent that from happening."

"But what gave Tercel cause to think that Margaret, out of all the women in Lincoln, was his mother?" Nicolaa said.

Bascot shook his head. "Adgate spoke to Margaret only once before she committed the murder. That was shortly after she first arrived in Lincoln when he attended the second service of Christ's Mass in the cathedral and saw her among the congregation. He was delighted to see her after all the years she had been away, and went over to her and asked why she had not contacted him when she arrived. He says she seemed distant and told him that she was very busy with her duties, but would try to visit his shop soon. When he asked if she intended to call on Edith, Margaret said that she would do so in her own time and asked him to convey her love to her sister, but asked that neither Adgate nor Edith try to contact her for the present. Even then she must have had some intimation of Tercel's interest in her, but she never mentioned it to Adgate, nor did she do so when the furrier, alarmed by Tercel's visit and his subsequent murder, defied Margaret's request and sent a message to the castle asking her to meet him. How Tercel came to discover that Margaret was in Winchester at the time of his conception must, I fear, remain a mystery."

"I think that perhaps I may be able to explain it," Bruet said quietly and they all turned towards him.

"How so?" Nicolaa asked.

"It is something that puzzled me at the time but, since I did not know you were searching for a woman who had travelled to that town all those years ago, I dismissed it." The taciturn knight seemed uneasy at being the focus of attention, but continued without hesitation. "It happened the day after we arrived in Lincoln, just before Christ's Mass. As Margaret and I were walking into the hall to break our fast, she mentioned how tired the journey had made her, saying it had fatigued her far more than a much longer trip she had made to Winchester when she had been a young girl. She laughed, saying it must be because her bones had grown old and were not so resilient. Tercel was just behind us when she made the remark and the next day I heard him ask her in what year she had made the journey of which she had spoken. I did not hear her reply, but just a few days before Tercel was killed, I saw him and Margaret in conversation with each other. She was angry and I heard her castigate him for eavesdropping and making a ridiculous deduction from a chance statement."

Bruet looked solemnly around the company. "With hindsight, the exchanges between them now reveal their significance, but it was one that I was not aware of at the time. I did, I confess, ponder on their conversation later but, as I said, came to the conclusion that the matter was of no importance."

"Nonetheless, Tercel must have somehow discovered that Adgate was related to Margaret, for even though she took the precaution of trying to hide their relationship as best she could, he still went to question the furrier about her," Nicolaa said to Bascot. "Does Adgate know how that came about?"

As Bascot began to shake his head, Petronille spoke up. Still in shock from learning that the woman she had held in such close company had committed murder, her voice was slightly tremulous as she explained, "I fear I am to blame for that. I knew that Margaret still had some family in Lincoln and that one of them was a furrier although, in all the years she has served me, she never mentioned a sister. When I instructed Tercel to obtain some fur samples for me to examine, Margaret was there, and I asked her if her relative still had his furrier shop in the town and that, if he did, I would be pleased to give him my patronage. I recall now that she was somewhat noncommittal in her reply, saying that she had lost touch with him many years ago and did not know if he still lived here, but I did press her for his name and told Tercel to ask among the fur merchants he visited for Adgate's shop and, if he found it, to select some of his wares for my approval. I am afraid it must have been that conversation that led him to the furrier."

"I wonder if that is why he paid his attentions to Clarice Adgate?" Richard suggested. "Perhaps he hoped to find out more about Margaret through the furrier's wife."

"I asked Adgate that same question," Bascot replied. "But he said that while that may have been Tercel's initial intention, he would soon have discovered it to be a fruitless quest, for Clarice did not know that Margaret, or Edith Wickson, were related to him."

"I find that hard to believe," Alinor said. "When you marry a man, it is natural to meet his relatives, or at least be told their names."

"I agree it would be commonplace for most brides," Bascot replied, "but apparently, according to Adgate, he is not on friendly terms with Edith's husband and visits her only rarely, so she was not present when he and Clarice took their vows. He also told me that, very soon after their marriage, his new wife made it evident that her sole reason for agreeing to marry him had been for the material advantage she would gain and that she showed no interest in meeting the wives of the other members of his guild, let alone enquiring about any family he might have. Because of her attitude, he never mentioned any details of his relationship with either Edith or Margaret to her. If that is so—and I cannot see any reason to doubt Adgate's words—then Tercel must have soon realised he would gain no useful information from Clarice. Since he appears to have had continued his affair with her for several weeks, it is more than likely that he continued the association purely out of lust."

"There still remains one last piece of the puzzle that has yet to be explained," Nicolaa said, "and it is at the crux of the matter, for it is the one that prompted Tercel to begin his ill-fated quest. How did Lionel Wharton come to be involved with Edith and her illegitimate child and why did he leave Tercel a ring inscribed with an emblem used by Lionheart? Can the furrier shed any light on that aspect of this misadventure?"

"I believe that he can, lady," the Templar replied, "but I did not question him in detail about it, for I thought that you and Sir Richard might prefer to do so yourselves."

Twenty-nine

+-I-+

WHEN SIMON ADGATE WAS BROUGHT INTO THE SOLAR, THE
man-at-arms who had been guarding him brought him
across the room to stand before the group of nobles. The furrier's limp was more pronounced than formerly and his
shoulders were slumped in dejection. With a bowed head he
listened as Richard, in stern tones, admonished him for not
revealing his kinship with Margaret earlier. It was not until
Richard added that, for the moment, they were prepared to
accept his statement that neither he nor Edith Wickson had
been involved in the murder, that Adgate raised his head
and his expression lightened.

"The sempstress will be questioned shortly," Richard
told him. "If she confirms what you claim, then charges will
not be laid against either of you."

Adgate's relief was palpable and he humbly thanked the
castellan's son, on behalf of himself and his Mistress Wickson, for accepting, albeit with reservations, his protestation
of their innocence.

"But there are still some aspects about Tercel's birth that need to be explained," Richard said. "How is it that Lionel Wharton came to be involved in the matter?"

"It was because of Queen Eleanor," Adgate replied. "Even though she was being treated most cruelly at the time by her husband, King Henry, she still found it within her heart to concern herself in the plight of my poor cousin. She is a great lady."

At mention of the queen's name, the nobles looked at one another in confusion and Nicolaa leaned forward and said to Adgate, "I think you had better explain what happened from the beginning, furrier, and tell us, to the best of your knowledge, what you know of the events that took place so many years ago."

"I did not learn the details until after the happenings, lady, for I was not in Winchester when they occurred," Adgate replied. "I, and the girls' parents, learned of them some weeks later, when my uncle and Margaret returned to Lincoln. But although I received the accounting at second hand, I believe it is accurate."

"Then continue," Nicolaa directed, and Adgate, taking a deep breath, began the tale.

"The purpose for which my uncle, Thomas Adgate, went to Winchester was to take some Lincoln *greyne*—the red cloth for which our town is so famous—to show to Queen Eleanor. He had been urged to do so by a longtime acquaintance of his, a draper of Winchester, who had learned of the queen's interest in the material. Margaret and Eleanor begged to be taken along on the trip and my uncle, a widower with no children of his own, indulged the girls and acceded to their request. Not long after they all arrived, an interview with the queen was arranged and my uncle took samples of *greyne* to the fortress where Queen Eleanor was incarcerated. The girls went with him and were allowed to wait in an antechamber while he kept the appointment. They were both overjoyed to be so near to the presence of such a noble lady and even more so when, while they were sitting there, the queen's young daughter, Princess Joanna, passed through the chamber and stopped to talk to them. The princess was most kind and must have been lonely for the company of girls her own age for, a few nights later, she invited both Margaret and Edith to come to the castle and listen to a troubadour that was to play for the queen and her ladies. It was on that evening, as Edith was making her way back to the rooms my uncle had hired for their stay in Winchester, that the attack took place."

Adgate regarded the nobles with a look that begged understanding. "Margaret has always blamed herself for the fact that she sent Edith, who was younger than she, out alone onto the streets of Winchester that night. The reason Margaret did so was because she had caught the eye of one of Princess Joanna's young menservants on their earlier visit and, after they left the hall where the troubadour had been entertaining the company, she stopped to talk to him for a while, telling Edith to go on ahead of her so that she could speak to him privily. Margaret never thought for a moment that Edith would be in any danger, for the rooms my uncle had taken for their stay were not far from the castle gate. As it turned out, Margaret's assumption was a grave error. Edith had gone only a few steps outside the castle walls when she was attacked. She never saw her assailant's face. He approached her from behind, dealt her a heavy blow to the head and then dragged her into a dark passageway where he violated her."

The women drew their breath in sharply at Adgate's bald statement and Richard cursed under his breath. The furrier paused and then, at a nod from the castellan's son, continued.

"Edith, rendered unconscious by the attack, lay in the passageway for some time, her absence unnoticed until Margaret returned to the hired rooms and found that her sister had not returned. Alarmed, she and my uncle immediately set out back along the path to the castle to try and find her, but to no avail. It wasn't until the guard on the castle gate heard them calling out Edith's name and sent some of the castle's men-at-arms to join them in the search that she was found. She was in a dreadful state; her clothes were torn asunder and blood was gushing from the wound in her head. The gateward, seeing the severity of her condition, decided that the queen must be informed and despatched one of the soldiers to tell her."

The furrier's voice, choked with emotion, was barely audible as he went on. "The men-at-arms carried Edith to the castle bail and Queen Eleanor herself came out to meet them. Margaret told me that when the queen saw Edith's pitiful condition, she directed that my cousin be taken to her own private rooms and the royal physician called to attend her. The queen even draped her own cloak over Edith's prostrate form, not caring that it would be stained with blood, and walked by my cousin's side as the soldiers carried her into the keep."

Visibly shaken by the strain of his recounting, Nicolaa gave Adgate a moment to compose himself, and then gently urged him to continue. "The queen's physician was unable to rouse Edith from her stupor," he told them haltingly, "but he confirmed what everyone feared, that the object of the attack had been to defile her. He thought it best that my cousin was given over to the care of women for, he said, when she regained her senses, the presence of a male so near to her person might cause her great distress. The queen ordered Edith taken to a nearby nunnery and the good nuns, only too willing to oblige a request from the royal lady, readily took my cousin into their care."

"It must have been a terrible ordeal for such a young girl to suffer," Nicolaa said. "And, from what you say, she was never able to identify the man who attacked her."

"No, she was not, lady," Adgate confirmed. "In fact, she hardly remembered anything of it at all, for which we all gave thanks to God. But, notwithstanding that, she lay unconscious for some days and, when she finally came to her senses, could not stand erect without losing her balance. The infirmarian in the convent thought that the blow to her head was the cause of her unsteadiness but, whatever it was, it took some weeks for her to recover from it."

"And she remained in the convent during that time?" Petronille asked.

"Yes, Queen Eleanor had asked the nuns not to remove her from their care until her health was restored," Adgate replied. "But by the time she finally managed to keep upright, the infirmarian in the convent noticed that she was beginning to show signs of gravidity and my uncle and Margaret—who had remained in the town awaiting the time that Edith should be well enough to travel back to Lincoln—were devastated by this further disaster. They had told their acquaintances in Winchester that Edith had tripped and fallen, hurting her head badly, and had been taken to the nunnery to be cared for. The queen, too, had concealed the truth about Edith's injury, instructing her guards to tell no one what they had seen on that night. But now that Edith was with child, my uncle and Margaret knew it would be impossible to hide what had truly happened from the prying eyes of the world, and my cousin's reputation would be ruined. There was also the problem of Edith's impending marriage to Thomas Wickson. While the fact that my cousin had been assaulted could be hidden from him, it would be impossible to hide the babe swelling in her womb and they knew he would never countenance taking her as a bride when he learned of her condition. They did not know what to do until the queen, having heard from the nuns that Edith was with child as a result of the attack, sent for them to attend her."

The furrier's eyes were shining with admiration as he told of his uncle and Margaret's visit to the queen. "She received them with great sympathy and, learning of their dilemma over Edith's impending marriage, suggested that it might be best if my cousin was removed to a nunnery nearer to Lincoln—one not far from Stamford where the abbess was a personal friend of the queen's—and kept there until her confinement was over. That way, the queen said, the approaching birth could be kept privy from any who knew Edith or her family and, once the child was born, my cousin could return to Lincoln without her future husband, or any of their neighbours, having knowledge of what had befallen her. My uncle, grateful for the queen's support, readily agreed to the plan, and she sent for Lionel Wharton, who had lately arrived in Winchester carrying despatches from Lionheart. When he arrived, the queen told him of Edith's predicament and said that since he lived near Stamford, she wished him to covertly escort my cousin to her destination and once there, and with her authority, to make whatever arrangements were necessary for the duration of Edith's confinement and also for the child's welfare after it was born. And so it was done."

"And how was Edith's absence explained to those who knew her?" Nicolaa asked.

"My uncle and Margaret returned home after Edith was gone from Winchester and they told Thomas Wickson, and all their friends and neighbours, a tale that was as near to the truth as they dared. They said that Edith had been taken with a falling sickness and that a physician in Winchester had kindly arranged for her to be incarcerated in a nunnery on the outskirts of the town with every hope that, if she was kept in quietness and solitude for a few months, she would recover. No mention was made that she had been removed to a place much closer to Lincoln in case Wickson, or one of his family, should wish to visit her."

His recounting nearly finished, Adgate took another deep breath and finished his story in a concise fashion. "After the birth of the babe, Edith's father, pretending to have journeyed to Winchester, went to the convent and brought her home, telling everyone, including the chandler, that she was now restored to her former health. A few weeks later, she and Wickson were married. And that is how the matter has stood for all of these years."

"And would have stayed so had not Stephen Wharton revealed the contents of his brother's letter," Nicolaa observed.

At Adgate's look of non-comprehension, Nicolaa told the furrier how Stephen Wharton had come to Lincoln shortly after the murder with the letter he had discovered after Lionel's death. After explaining the contents to Adgate, she told him that a ring had been enclosed with the missive. "It must have been given to Sir Lionel by the queen," she said, "as a token of her authority in his dealings with the abbess at the nunnery near Stamford."

"And explains his use of the phrase that he 'owed a debt of loyalty' to the person who bid him see to the welfare of Edith and the child. Queen Eleanor was fiercely devoted to Lionheart and it would not be untoward for Lionel, who was carrying out a commission for his lord's mother, to have referred to the matter in such a manner. Tercel completely misconstrued the meaning of the letter and the ring."

"I agree, Richard," Nicolaa said to her son. "And it is appalling that the queen's, and Lionel Wharton's, innocent acts of charity should have been twisted in such a fashion."

They were all silent for a moment as they contemplated how the dead man's egotistical desire to be raised above his station had been the cause of his demise.

Aware that he had aroused their compassion, Adgate began to plead that clemency be shown to Margaret. He knew, he said, that she could not be exonerated of guilt, but maintained that she would never have committed such a crime if it had not been for her desire to protect her sister. "Margaret was beside herself with guilt for letting Edith go out alone that night. For many a day, after she returned home, Margaret came to me and cried piteously, saying that if she had not been so selfish as to indulge in dalliance with the manservant, she and Edith would have walked home together and the villain would not have had the opportunity to carry out the attack. I tried to dissuade her, but she would not be swayed. She spent hours on her knees repeating acts of contrition, trying to find some way she could make reparation for her laxity. I ask you to be merciful to her."

"I can understand her feelings of guilt and desire for

atonement," Nicolaa said, "but surely she cannot have believed that such a deadly penance would be pleasing to God. Killing Tercel was an act inspired by the Devil, not heaven."

Adgate looked at Petronille, his eyes directing one last unspoken plea to the mistress that had earned Margaret's long-standing devotion. But, although she was moved by his earnestness, Petronille shook her head regretfully. "I cannot help her, Master Adgate. Murder is an evil act, no matter how well-intentioned."

The furrier's face fell at her words, and she added gently, "You must remember that Margaret's crimes were not limited to the taking of her nephew's life. She maliciously wounded my daughter's maidservant and held a young boy hostage. I am sorry for your misery, but her crimes were cold and calculating and, much as it pains me to say of someone I previously held in high regard, I do not find her worthy of clemency."

Adgate nodded dumbly, his face a mask of hopelessness, and Nicolaa, taking pity on the man, said reflectively, "I do think, however, that Edith Wickson deserves to be shown some charity. Throughout all of this matter, she has been the innocent party. Through no fault of her own she was viciously assaulted and now, after all of these years, the consequences of that terrible act have returned to cause further misery in her life."

The castellan turned to her son. "As your father's deputy, Richard, the final decision rests with you but I think, with circumspection, Edith's name could be kept out of the proceedings at Margaret's trial. Since it was the sempstress' aim to shield her sister, I am sure she will agree if it is charged that she killed Tercel because of an unstated affront he had given her. If the judges wish to know more of the matter, it can be told to them in confidence."

Richard considered the proposition for a moment, and then nodded his head. "Yes, Mother, I agree. Justice will still be served whether Mistress Wickson is mentioned or not. Father will have returned by the time the itinerant justices arrive in Lincoln for the next session of the assizes, but I do not believe he will have any objection to making it so once he has heard the details."

Adgate was fulsome in his thanks and conveyed his gratitude both on his own behalf and that of Edith. "Nothing can alleviate the grief she feels for her son's death and her sister's part in it, but she has also been fearful that if her husband should discover her shameful secret, he will renounce her and thereby make their daughter, Merisel, suffer the pain of public ignominy. I am sure, when I tell her of your understanding, it will bring her some comfort."

Thirty

✢ I ✢

LATE THE NEXT MORNING, NICOLAA DE LA HAYE WAS SITTING
in the solar with Petronille and Alinor when a servant entered the chamber bearing a letter from her husband, Gerard
Camville. It had just arrived by messenger from London and
said that the sheriff expected to return to Lincoln within a
week.

"Gerard sent this before he received the despatch I wrote
telling him about the murder," she said to her sister. "But,
nonetheless, it contains news that makes me relieved we discovered that your servant was not Lionheart's bastard."

Petronille and Alinor listened as she read out the portion
of the letter to which she was referring. It had been written,
at Gerard's dictation, by a cleric, and explained in detail how
reports had lately come to the capital from Falaise in Normandy, where the king had imprisoned Arthur, his legiti-
mately born nephew, after capturing him when his young
relative had made an attempt to seize Queen Eleanor. It was
said that the king had ordered Arthur to be castrated and

blinded, and so make it impossible for him to become a figurehead for those who would remove the crown of England from John's head.

As her two companions listened in horrified silence, Nicolaa went on to say that the king's instruction had been circumvented by the intervention of Hubert de Burgh, the noble into whose care John had given Arthur, but it was rumoured that the king now intended to remove his nephew from the baron's custody and incarcerate his nephew at Rouen instead.

"Surely John does not still intend to carry out his threat," Petronille exclaimed. "Arthur is his own blood kin; such cruelty would be unthinkable."

The news saddened Nicolaa. She had always given John her support and, despite his mercurial temperament, knew that his motives were often misconstrued. Had the king, with his impetuous tongue, made the threat, but with no intention of carrying it out? She could imagine him, in anger, saying such a thing for, like his father before him, he was given to excessive displays of temper, and it was unlikely the remark had been more than a venting of his frustration with his nephew's rebellious actions. If this was so, it was unfortunate he had not taken more care of those who heard him say it. John had many enemies, ones who would be only too pleased to repeat anything that would prove detrimental to his cause. She could only hope that the details of the incident had been exaggerated as they had passed from one to another but, even so, the king may have done himself more harm by voicing the threat than he would ever have gained if it had been carried out.

"Perhaps it is a blessing that Tercel died before he could make public his claim of royal kinship," Alinor opined. "If

262
MAUREEN ASH

it had remained unproven, the king might well have un-
leashed his anger on him in a similar manner to that with
which he is threatening Arthur."

Not wishing to dwell on the subject, Nicolaa did not
reply and instead asked her niece how the injured maid,
Elise, was faring. "She is still slightly feverish," Alinor told
her, "but the leech says she is out of danger, for which I am
truly thankful."

"If only I had remembered earlier who Tercel reminded me
of when he first came into our service, I might have prevented
some of this misery," Petronille mused. "But it wasn't until
Simon Adgate was standing before us yesterday that I realised
there was a family resemblance between Margaret and my cofferer, for it was also there in Adgate's face. A certain cast of the
cheekbones and the way the eyes are set—a subtle similarity,
but there nonetheless. But I never connected it with Margaret's feminine features; it was only when I saw the same
expression on a man's face that it came to me. If I had realised
from the beginning that Margaret could be related to Tercel,
especially when you were looking for his mother . . ."

Nicolaa reached over and patted her sister's hand. "It was
not discernment you were lacking, Petra, but knowledge;
facts that were not evident until long past the time of which
you are speaking. Please, do not judge yourself so harshly,
but instead join me in giving thanks that Elise was not mortally wounded, and that the boy, Willi, suffered no hurt."

Petronille was comforted by her sister's words and asked,
"What will you do with the lad now? He cannot be considered a candidate for the foundling home if he has a living
parent."

"I have sent Willi back to Riseholme with the assurance
that instructions will be given to the keeper at the alehouse

his father frequents that if the boy's sire returns, he is to be given a message directing him to come to the castle to claim his son."

She paused for a moment, recalling the boy's white face when Bruet brought him back to the keep after the Templar had rescued him from Margaret's clutches. He was so pale that the freckles on the bridge of his nose stood out like drops of blood. "The boy was content with my promise. I think he realises that his father has been gone too long to expect his safe return. The weather, until lately, has been so frigid that many of those who lack shelter out in the country-side have died of exposure and it could well be that his father has suffered a similar fate. But Willi was very brave and continues to hope, even though he knows his optimism is likely to prove unwarranted."

She paused and smiled, remembering her interview with the young boy. "Four more orphaned children were taken to Riseholme earlier this morning and I sent Willi with them. The newcomers were all a little apprehensive, but he took charge of them in a most natural fashion and allayed their fears. I think that if his father does not return he will, in the years to come, prove a valuable addition to my household staff, just like young Gianni."

"And Margaret?" Alinor said. "Has Richard spoken to her and asked if she agrees to keep Edith Wickson's name out of the charges that will be brought at her trial?"

"Yes, Richard said she seemed thankful for the offer and was more than willing to comply. And she did confirm that neither Simon Adgate nor her sister was involved in her mach-inations. She said that she never told Agate of her intention to kill Tercel and that she has not, since she arrived in Lin-coln, had occasion to speak to her sister."

Nicolaa frowned as she continued. "She is, Richard told me, still unrepentant of her crime. Apparently, on the day of the feast, and after Adgate had refused to reveal his father's name, Tercel threatened Margaret, saying that if she did not tell him what he wanted to know, he would go to you, Petra, and disclose the fact that she was his mother and had borne him illegitimately. She was fearful that if he carried out his threat, not only would she lose her position, but that Edith's involvement would be discovered. Tercel gave her twenty-four hours to comply with his demand and she was desperate to find a way to silence him. That night, when he left the hall, she followed him and watched as he went into the old tower. Nonplussed as to why he should go there, she was waiting in the shelter of one of the buildings for him to come out, considering whether or not she could successfully despatch him by a stealthy attack with her scissors, when Mistress Adgate appeared and followed Tercel into the building. Realising what they were about, it did not take Margaret long to decide she could use the situation to her advantage."

Nicolaa paused. "It was at this point in her tale that Richard says he became certain Margaret has lost her sanity. She looked at him with wildness in her eyes and said that she knew she had not committed any sin in killing Tercel for, from that point on, God showed her the way. All of a sudden, she said, Our Lord put into her mind the tale she had been told of how I had fired the crossbow in my youth and told her that the weapon would suit her purpose admirably. She hurriedly returned to the hall, retrieved a tinderbox and candle from the supply kept in the buttery, went back out into the bail and crossed the ward to the armoury. Once inside she lit the candle and by its light found the crossbow

and armed it—after living so many years in a baron's household, she had often watched the de Humez squires being
instructed in the use of an arbalest, so had no trouble doing
so. She then went into the old tower and, by listening, determined which chamber Tercel and Mistress Adgate were
using and, with the crossbow, waited outside the door."

Nicolaa shrugged. "The rest we know. When Clarice
Adgate left the chamber and went downstairs, Margaret
lured Tercel up onto the ramparts and killed him. It was a
daring move and filled with danger—the crossbow could
have misfired or the guards have been alerted—but while I
decry her actions, I have to admire her courage."

"I wish she had come to me when Tercel first made his
demands," Petronille said. "I would have kept her confidence and sent him back to Stamford for Dickon to deal
with."

"I do not think it ever occurred to her to do so," Nicolaa
replied. "Richard says he is certain that the guilt she feels for
being the cause of her sister's fate has turned her brain. He
said she kept repeating that Tercel had been spawned by an
incubus, and that by killing him she had not broken either
the laws of God or those of man. When Richard pointed out
that if she wished to keep her sister's name out of the legal
proceedings during her trial, it would be unwise to use that
premise as her defence, she said it did not trouble her
whether the true reason was given in evidence or not, for
Our Lord would know that she was innocent. It was in God's
name, she said, that she had taken her vow of secrecy all
those years ago and He would know that she had kept faith."

The three women pondered for a moment on Margaret's
misguided devotion and then Petronille said musingly, "It is
strange how old sins can resurface, and that so often, when

they do, the repercussions do not fall on the perpetrators, but on those who have been victimised. Edith was completely innocent of any crime, as was her son, yet it is they and, by association, Margaret, who have paid for the crime. The villain who was responsible has entirely escaped justice."

"It may be that the rapist has already been dealt vengeance, Mother," Alinor said. "Such a rogue is certain to have attempted similar offences in the intervening years and may have been caught. If so, he will have long ago paid the ultimate penalty for his crime."

"I hope you are right, Daughter," Petronille said sadly. "But even if that has not happened, it comforts me to know that he will suffer the flames of eternal damnation when he dies."

IN THOMAS WICKSON'S CHANDLERY IN LINCOLN TOWN, EDITH Wickson sat alone in the bedchamber she shared with her husband. From the bottom of a coffer she took a square of satin that had been wrapped around some wisps of fine blonde hair and tied with a length of narrow yellow ribbon. Rubbing her thumb over the silky softness she remembered the kind young nun who had clipped the strands from her newly born baby's head and given them to her. How often over the years since Aubrey's birth had she taken them out and held them close to her breast, wondering what had become of the child she had only glimpsed once, and then so fleetingly, as he had slipped from her womb.

She knew herself to be timid in nature; had she not been so she would have gone to the feast and gazed on the man Aubrey had become. Now she would never have the chance.

And she would never see Margaret again. Dear Margaret, who had always been so protective of her younger sister and had suffered such pangs of guilt for letting Edith go out alone onto the dark streets of Winchester on that fateful night. Simon had told her that Margaret was sure to hang for her crimes, even if the reason for the murder was not made public. Not only had her sister killed Aubrey, who was, in truth, her own nephew, she had also attacked a maid-servant and wounded the girl most grievously. There was nothing to be gained, and all to be lost, by revealing the truth now.

A tear fell down Edith's cheek and she replaced the tress of hair in its soft covering and put it back into the bottom of the chest. She wondered if all the lies had been worth such a heavy cost. Would it have been better to have admitted the truth at the time and borne the shame? But then she would never have married Thomas Wickson and Merisel, her be-loved daughter, would not have come into existence.

She stood up and straightened her coif, then patted her tear-stained face dry with the hem of her kirtle. She had lost her son many years ago, but she still had her daughter, and in that precious gift she would rejoice.

IN SIMON ADGATE'S HOUSE IN THE LOWER PART OF TOWN, THE furrier, as proscribed by law, meted out the punishment a husband was allowed to inflict on an adulterous wife. On his return from the castle, he ordered Clarice to their bedroom and once there, brusquely commanded her to remove her coif. Turning a deaf ear to her tearful pleas for clemency, he cut off her luxurious auburn plaits with a sharp pair of scis-sors and removed the expensive fur trimmings from the cuffs and neck of her gown. Then, taking his sobbing wife firmly by the arm, he marched her downstairs, past the astonished eyes of his shop assistant and guard, and through the front door of the premises.

As they emerged into the street, Simon's determination to persist with the chastisement began to falter. With her shorn head, tattered garments and tear-streaked face, Clarice was a pitiful sight. But remembrance of her deceitful behaviour quickly extinguished his incipient feelings of sympathy and, taking a deep breath, he pulled her alongside him through the streets of Lincoln towards Stonebow gate and her father's house on the banks of the river.

Alerted by the sounds of Clarice's outcry, it took only moments for a crowd to gather. The news of what had happened in the castle bail had spread throughout the town like wildfire and although the details of Adgate's involvement were not known, speculation ran rife. All of the neighbours had been surreptitiously watching the furrier's house and, when he returned home with set face and clenched jaw, had been waiting for the next scene in the drama to unfold.

As Clarice stumbled along beside her husband, the spectators followed in their wake. Although there were a few amongst them, such as Imogene Sealsmith, who were mean-spirited enough to derive pleasure from her disgrace, most of them were neighbours who wished to show their support for the action Adgate was taking. They had lived alongside the furrier for many years, and knew him to be, for all his wealth, a man of tender conscience, always ready to exchange a friendly word or give assistance to those in need and were unanimous in their condemnation of his young wife's betrayal.

By the time Adgate reached his destination, the tanner

had been alerted by the hubbub and was waiting at the door of his humble wooden cot. He had already heard the rumours that were circulating about his errant daughter and how she had brought shame to his good name. His face set in harsh lines of anger, he watched in grim silence as Adgate led Clarice to his door.

When the furrier reached his father-by-marriage, he spoke not a word, just released his grip on Clarice's arm and strode away. The crowd parted before him as though cleaved by a gale force wind. Once the furrier was out of sight, they turned back to where the tanner stood, and regarded his daughter with silent disapproval.

Clarice's father surveyed them all for a moment until, with a sudden movement, he pulled his daughter inside the house and slammed the door shut. It was not long before they heard the sound of a leather belt slapping against tender flesh, accompanied by a wave of wailing. Only then did the crowd disperse, confident that, in accordance with the law, the furrier's unfaithful wife was receiving the beating her husband had failed to administer.

Thirty-one

✛

In the Templar preceptory, Bascot de Marins was attending to the neglected paperwork. It was already into the month of March and there was much to be done before Eastertide arrived in the first week of April. Outside, the weather had become even warmer and a few spatters of rain had fallen, signalling the end of the cold spell. Soon, the winter season over, Templar brothers from all over the kingdom would be on their way to London and thence to active duty in Outremer and Portugal, and it was Bascot's duty to ensure that all those who passed through Lincoln were well equipped with arms and clothing. The list he was compiling was necessary to that task, being drawn from inventories he had taken and was now comparing to the expected requirement. He must ensure there were enough supplies on hand to outfit the newly arrived knights and men-at-arms before they were sent to their various posts.

But try as he might, his mind would not focus on the columns of figures, and kept returning to the murder of

Aubrey Tercel, and the violent assault that had, all those years ago, set in motion a train of events that had eventually led to the young man's death. In one way, the solution to this most recent murder investigation had been the least satisfying of all those he had undertaken. And although he did not condone Margaret's actions, he felt some sympathy for the woman; she had not committed the murder for self-ish reasons, but to protect a sister who was dear to her, and her desperation, although misguided, was understandable. It was not Edith Wickson and her family who should have suffered so much pain, but the miscreant who had attacked and raped Edith all those years ago. The injustice left a vile aftertaste of bitterness.

Knowing he would not be able to complete the task in front of him while his thoughts were so distracted, Bascot threw down the quill pen he had been using, laid his papers aside and went out into the compound.

In the middle of the enclave was an area used as a training ground where the brothers practised the military skills that were a prerequisite of the Order. On the edge of the bare circle of beaten earth, Preceptor d'Arderon was examining a shipment of blunted swords that had been sent by the Order's armoury in London. They were of the longer, heavier type that were wielded by those of knight's rank in mock combat, as opposed to the short swords used by the men-at-arms. D'Arderon was hefting one of them to test the balance. The preceptor looked up as Bascot came into the compound and, seeing the black look on the younger knight's face, recalled the conversation they had had the evening before and made an accurate guess as to the cause of his gloom.

Although Bascot, in keeping with his reticent nature,

had spoken little of his dissatisfaction with the outcome of this latest enquiry, D'Arderon was aware of it. The younger knight was adept at concealing his emotions, but the preceptor knew they ran deep. Even though, after so many years, it would be impossible to apprehend the villain who had attacked and violated a young and innocent girl, the failure to mete out retribution for the crime offended Bascot's strong sense of probity. D'Arderon's younger confrere needed an outlet on which to vent his frustration and as the preceptor's glance fell on the wooden case that held the recently arrived weapons, a notion came to him of a way in he which he could provide one.

Picking up one of the swords, d'Arderon tossed it, haft forward, to Bascot. With an automatic reaction, Bascot caught the weapon and looked at the older knight in surprise.

"What think you of the weight?" the preceptor asked, reaching down and extracting another blade. "They seem to me to be lighter than usual." Grasping the hilt in his two broad hands, he arced the sword experimentally through the air, then shook his head uncertainly. "I think perhaps they should be tested before they are put to use by any new initiate to the Order."

Since there were only d'Arderon and Bascot of knight's status in the commandery at the moment, Bascot realised that the only way the swords could be tried was for the preceptor and himself to face each other in mock battle. It was not often that d'Arderon engaged in such an exercise, although he kept himself fit by spending at least two hours each day raining blows with a heavy metal bar on one of the wooden blocks set up at the far end of the compound. Now past his sixtieth year, the preceptor's wide, stocky body was, nonetheless, still heavily muscled and Bascot knew that despite being a score of years younger, he would be hard put to keep pace with the older knight. Still, he welcomed the challenge and appreciated the preceptor's purpose in offering it. To put his skills to such a hard use would divert his mind from the darkness that was engulfing it.

D'Arderon sent one of the men-at-arms for two of the kite-shaped shields kept in the armoury, and told him to also bring a pair of helms, solid steel caps fitted with nasal bars. Both the preceptor and Bascot were wearing the heavy boiled leather tunics that were commonly donned in wintertime and, since the swords were blunted, there would not be any need for chain mail. When the soldier returned with the equipment, the rest of the brothers in the enclave stood back, expectant grins on their faces, to watch the two senior officers engage in combat.

As he and d'Arderon circled each other, Bascot knew he had to be wary of the preceptor's larger bulk. The older knight, he was certain, would not be as quick on his feet as in the days of his youth, but the strength of the preceptor's arm would more than make up for his lack of speed. They traded a few tentative blows and then Bascot was taken by surprise as d'Arderon surged forward and rained blows on his helm. He had not expected the preceptor to move with such alacrity, a mistake he would not make again. Turning so that his sighted left side gave him more clarity of vision, Bascot locked his shield into that of his opponent, and pushed d'Arderon back, then aimed a blow at the preceptor's momentarily exposed sword arm. D'Arderon barely had time to ward off the attack and retaliated with eagerness, his blunted sword whirling.

The battle went on for some minutes, both knights enjoying the fray, with first one gaining the advantage and then the other. The watching men-at-arms could not contain their admiration for the skill they were watching, and above the clang of metal, their whoops of approval could be plainly heard. When the small bell in the chapel tower rang out a warning that it was almost time for the service of Vespers, it was to the disappointment of all that the contest was called to a halt. Reluctantly, both combatants lowered their shields, and then grinned at one another.

D'Arderon slung his buckler across his shoulder and, coming over to where Bascot stood, clapped him on the shoulder. "Are you tired enough now to let your anger rest?" he said.

"I am, Preceptor, and thank you for your instruction," Bascot replied gratefully.

"Then come, and we will go and worship Our Blessed Lord together."

As they and the other Templars filed into the church, Bascot felt the warmth of camaraderie engulf him. The strenuous exercise had lifted the cloud of his despondency and it was with a joyous heart that he went forward to join his brothers in prayer.

Author's Note

The setting for *A Deadly Penance* is an authentic one. Nicolaa de la Haye was hereditary castellan of Lincoln castle during this period, and her husband, Gerard Camville, was sheriff. The personalities they have been given in the story have been formed by conclusions the author has drawn from events during the reigns of King Richard I and King John.

For details of medieval Lincoln and the Order of the Knights Templar, I am much indebted to the following:

Medieval Lincoln by J.W.F. Hill (Cambridge University Press)

Dungeon, Fire and Sword—The Knights Templar in the Crusades by John J. Robinson (M. Evans & Company, Inc.)

MAUREEN ASH was born in London, England, and has had a lifelong interest in British medieval history. Visits to castle ruins and old churches have provided the inspiration for her novels. She enjoys Celtic music, browsing in bookstores and Belgian chocolate. Maureen now lives on Vancouver Island in British Columbia, Canada.